PRAISE FOR LISA GRAY

"Lisa Gray explodes onto the literary stage with this taut, edge-of-the-seat thriller, and her headstrong protagonist, Jessica Shaw, reminiscent of Lee Child's Jack Reacher, delivers a serious punch."
—Robert Dugoni, *New York Times* bestselling author

"*Thin Air* is an exciting whodunit that kept me guessing until the end. PI Jessica Shaw is so capable and strong I couldn't get enough of her!"
—T. R. Ragan, bestselling author of the Lizzy Gardner series

"*Thin Air* is an assured and fast-paced debut with a compelling central character and plenty of twists to keep you guessing until the very end."
—Victoria Selman, author of *Blood for Blood*

"Opening with a killer premise and dragging me along for a thrilling ride, this is a cracking read and a brilliant start to a new series with a kick-ass female protagonist."
—S. J. I. Holliday, author of *The Lingering*

"An assured and explosive debut with a premise that grabs you by the throat and refuses to let go. The pace never drops as it hurtles to a stunning conclusion."
—Craig Robertson, author of *The Photographer*

"Smart, sassy, and adrenaline fueled, this kick-ass debut is a must read for thriller fans."
—Steph Broadribb, author of *Deep Down Dead*

"Lisa Gray's thriller is so assured it's hard to believe it's a debut. It's so fast paced it should be pulled over for speeding!"
—Douglas Skelton, author of *The Janus Run*

BAD
MEMORY

ALSO BY LISA GRAY

Thin Air

BAD
MEMORY

A JESSICA SHAW THRILLER

LISA GRAY

THOMAS & MERCER

Published by Thomas & Mercer, Seattle

www.apub.com

Amazon, the Amazon logo, and Thomas & Mercer are trademarks of Amazon.com, Inc., or its affiliates.

ISBN-13: 9781542092326
ISBN-10: 1542092329

Cover design by Ghost Design

Printed in the United States of America

In loving memory of my dad

PROLOGUE

The dream is always the same.

High summer, and the night is heavy with heat so thick you could stick a knife in it. She's grateful for the cool air that blasts from the car vents, drying the sweat on her tanned skin. A key chain shaped like a four-leaf clover hangs from the rearview mirror and bobs and sways in the artificial breeze whipped up by the AC. Her dress is hitched up around her thighs, her bare feet on the dash, toenails painted bubblegum pink to match her fingernails.

Her feet tap in time to the song on the radio. Some British band. A power ballad. Number one a couple months back and still getting plenty of airplay. Something about dying in your arms tonight. She likes it. She throws her head back and sings along.

They both laugh at her tuneless singing, and she takes another hit from the joint and blows out smoke rings. The sweet smell of weed fills the car. She drains what's left of her beer and tosses the empty bottle onto the passenger seat floorboard, and it lands with a thunk next to her sandals. She wipes the back of her hand across wet lips and joins in with the chorus again.

She's drunk and high and happy and excited about what the rest of the evening holds. Fourth of July. Independence Day. Party time. Somewhere in the distance, she hears a whistle and a crash and a bang.

Fireworks.

The car makes a sharp turn and bounces and lurches beneath her, and she feels the road change as smooth blacktop is replaced by dirt. She rocks from side to side in the seat as the wheels clamber over the rough terrain. It's darker now. The lit end of the joint glows faintly in the gloom. The lights from the highway get smaller and smaller behind them before being swallowed completely by the night. The car's headlights switch to high beam suddenly, and she blinks. Her eyes adjust after a second or two, but she sees nothing on either side of the dirt road other than the shadowy outline of Joshua trees, their thick branches reaching out to the charcoal sky like the arms of grotesque monsters.

The song is still playing.

The mood changes.

The dream becomes a nightmare.

She hears them before she sees them.

Moaning and whimpering. Panting and groaning. She doesn't want to see what they're doing. Doesn't want to face the reality. But she knows she has to.

She reaches out a trembling hand and opens the door.

The smell hits her first.

Sweat and beer and . . . something else.

Then she sees them.

He's on top of her. His shirt is stretched tight across his back. Black-and-white plaid. Moist circles spreading under the armpits. Blue jeans are bunched around his knees. The milky skin on his ass is shockingly exposed. A pale, slender hand snakes out from beneath him and grips the sweat-matted hair on the back of his head.

She doesn't understand what she's seeing at first.

And then she does.

It's wrong, and she's angry, and she knows she has to make it stop.

She doesn't remember picking up the knife.

Or moving toward them.

Or plunging the blade into soft flesh over and over again.

But she remembers the blood.

And she remembers the screaming.

Rue Hunter opened her eyes.

Damp strands of hair were stuck to her forehead, and sweat pooled beneath her breasts under the cotton nightgown. Her jaw and teeth ached from being clenched too tight together. She was breathing hard, and her heart pounded too fast against her rib cage.

She sucked in a lungful of air. Let it out slowly. In and out, in and out. The dream began to fade, her breathing returned to normal, and her heart slowed to a regular beat again.

But the screaming didn't stop.

It never did.

Screaming and wailing and shouting and cussing echoed all around her, the sounds bouncing off the walls of the empty corridors. The soundtrack of the condemned. Twenty-one women, like Rue Hunter, waiting to die.

Dawn light bled through the tiny window facing her and softly illuminated the small space around her: the single cot she lay on; the industrial stainless steel toilet and wash basin unit in the corner; the desk housing a couple of well-thumbed paperback books; the white tiled walls, unadorned with posters or family photos.

She threw back the thin bedsheet and slowly swung her legs over the side of the cot. Placed bare feet on cold concrete. Three strides took her to the far side of the six-by-eleven-foot cell.

She held her hands up to the light from the window. There was no maroon residue caked beneath the fingernails. No carmine red stained the creases and folds of the knuckles or the webbing between the fingers. No thick burgundy liquid flowed past the wrists like hot, bloody tears. She lowered her hands and clenched them into fists, curled her fingers tight until the short fingernails dug into the palms.

She stared out of the barred window as the sun continued to rise over the horizon. She knew there wouldn't be many more sunrises or sunsets to witness from this spot.

She would be dead in ten days.

Strapped to a gurney the color of pistachio ice cream. Arms outstretched like she was flying. Facing a ghoulish audience behind windows on three sides. An institutional clock above her head ticking away the minutes and seconds until the drugs flowed through her veins. First inducing unconsciousness, then muscle paralysis and respiratory arrest, before her heart finally stopped beating.

She wasn't scared of dying.

It was much harder trying to live in a place like this.

But she was scared of never knowing the truth.

Never knowing what really happened that summer night a long time ago.

Rue Hunter needed to know if she really did have blood on her hands.

And she had less than ten days to find out.

1

JESSICA

Jessica Shaw had been in town for only six months. Not long, but long enough to know the car didn't belong there.

It had been parked on the other side of the highway, about eighty yards east of the small detective agency where she worked, when she'd taken a stroll to Randy's for lunch with her boss, Ed Crozier. The car hadn't budged an inch by the time they'd returned a half hour later, and it was still there in late afternoon when she had stepped outside the front door for a smoke.

Metallic blue. Five doors. Some sort of family sedan. Sun glinting off the windshield, the driver's side sun visor pulled down so that whoever was behind the wheel was shielded from view. Not a particularly ostentatious vehicle but too fancy for Hundred Acres, that was for sure.

Then there was the license plate screwed to the front fender. Too far away to make out any individual digits, but Jessica could see the plate had dark lettering embossed on a turquoise, orange, and white gradient backdrop. Not the kind of car to have specialty plates, and definitely not the blue on white of regular California plates, so Jessica figured the driver was from out of state.

In any case, she knew most of the cars in town by now. Maybe not who drove each and every one of them, but she definitely recognized the majority by sight. One of the bonuses of working out of a shop front set back just off the main highway. The agency's big picture window faced north, framing a view of flat yellow scrub that stretched for miles on the other side of the two-lane highway, the scrubland empty save for the occasional electrical pylon, some mountains far off in the distance.

Not much to look at other than the traffic.

The unfamiliar vehicles were almost always just passing through. Short- and long-haul freight trucks. Pickups, station wagons, two-seaters. All using the Hundred Acres Highway as a bypass of the Los Angeles metropolitan area on their way to and from Sin City.

Unlike them, Jessica was going nowhere. At least for the time being.

She had spent most of her life—and the first five years of her career as a private investigator—in New York. Following the sudden and unexpected death of her father, Jessica had sold their home and taken to the road, leaving the Big Apple behind for good. She'd moved from town to town, case to case, happy to go wherever the work took her. Then, last year, an investigation in Eagle Rock, a neighborhood in Northeast Los Angeles, had gotten way too personal, and Jessica had been lucky to come out of it alive.

She had been working a missing persons case in Josephine County, just over the state line in Oregon, when the New York State Division of Licensing Services finally caught up with her. Her PI license was up for renewal, and they weren't going to rubber-stamp another two years while she was out of state. Her old boss, Larry Lutz, had covered for her as best he could while she was on the road, but even he could do nothing about the headlines that had followed the events in Eagle Rock and that had alerted the DLS to the fact she had been operating outside of her jurisdiction.

Returning to New York simply wasn't an option for Jessica, and so her days as an investigator appeared to be numbered. Then Jason Pryce, an LAPD detective who had known her father, suggested an alternative to waiting tables or finding bar work. A friend of a friend owned a small detective agency in Hundred Acres, a desert community in the Antelope Valley, sixty miles north of LA. She could help out veteran gumshoe Ed

Crozier while her application for a California PI license was pending. Then the state, if not the world, would be her oyster.

"California's a big place," Pryce had pointed out. "Plenty of room to roam."

Jessica powered down her laptop now and began to gather her stuff. Ed had left an hour earlier to "take care of some business" in the next town. She knew the only business he was taking care of was a quick shower and shave before catching the end of happy hour at Ruben's over in Shady Bluff. In his sixties and a widower for the last five years, Ed was determined to grow old disgracefully and had no intention of slowing down anytime soon.

Jessica consulted her watch. Just after six p.m. A later finish than usual for a Friday evening, but she'd wanted to complete the paperwork on her latest case. A thirty-year-old Hundred Acres lifer, Michelle Foster, was about to be fired from her job at the local liquor store, just as soon as Jessica delivered confirmation to Jed Lockerman, the store's owner, that his assistant manager was tampering with stock orders and invoice slips and selling the booze she stole to teenagers from the back of her daddy's truck.

Just to complicate matters, Michelle was also the pissed ex-girlfriend of the guy Jessica was dating, so an angry visit from her was definitely in the cards. But not yet. It was too soon. Which meant the mystery blue car had nothing to do with Michelle Foster.

Jessica slipped Lockerman's copy of the Foster file into a manila envelope and stuffed it in her bag. She would drop it off in his mailbox on the way home. She turned off the office lights and stepped outside into the warm desert evening. The sun had yet to begin its lazy descent, and Jessica still had a clear view along the highway. She turned to lock up behind her. The sedan was still there, by the roadside, a few yards in front of a giant sun-bleached billboard for a gentlemen's club in Victorville forty miles away.

Jessica was just about to make her way to her Chevy Silverado when the sedan's door opened and the driver emerged. It was a woman. She just stood there for a moment or two—the evening breeze blowing a small cloud of dust around her—as though debating what to do next. Then she took advantage of a break in the traffic and strode purposefully across the two lanes in the direction of the detective agency.

The woman was in her midfifties. Tan slacks, white linen blouse, strappy sandals with a modest heel. White-blonde hair stylishly bobbed and huge sunglasses like Jackie Kennedy used to wear. She held a white leather purse tight against her body as though expecting an opportunist thief to snatch it from her grasp. Jessica watched her approach. Up close, the woman looked like an aging soccer mom. The type who would have been an active member of the PTA and made the best cookies at the bake sale when her kids were still at school.

"Is there something I can help you with?" Jessica asked.

"I wanted to discuss hiring you for a case."

Jessica detected the hint of a southern accent. Arizona or Texas maybe. Not quite strong enough to be a native but probably someone who had lived there for a long time.

"Sorry, we're closed now." Jessica nodded to the CLOSED sign hanging behind the glass on the door to emphasize the point. "Drop by Monday morning after ten. We can talk then."

"Monday will be too late. I need to speak to you tonight."

"So why not just stop by the office earlier? You've been parked along the highway for most of the afternoon."

"I wanted to talk to you alone."

Jessica frowned. "My boss left the office over an hour ago. You've had plenty of opportunity for a private chat."

"I wanted to make sure he wasn't coming back."

"Okay. What do you want to talk about?"

The woman took a deep, shuddering breath, as though psyching herself up for what she was about to say next. Then the words all tumbled out in a rush, like she had to get rid of them fast.

"My sister confessed to killing two people more than thirty years ago. Right here in Hundred Acres. She's been on death row ever since. Her execution is scheduled to take place in a week's time."

Jessica arched her eyebrows. She'd always thought of the town as a sleepy place, where nothing interesting ever happened, so she was surprised to learn about its dark past. "Wow," she said. "Not what I was expecting to hear. I'm sorry about your sister. But I don't see where I fit in."

The woman regarded her for a long moment from behind the Jackie Kennedy sunglasses. Jessica could see her own distorted reflection staring back at her in the black lenses. The barely concealed impatience on her face as Jessica wondered how soon she'd be able to kick off her own happy hour.

Then the stranger said, "I want you to prove my sister is innocent before they kill her."

2

JESSICA

The woman glanced around again. "Can we talk inside? I don't want anyone from town seeing me here."

"Um, sure."

Jessica fished in her bag for the office keys and unlocked the door. She pushed it open and stepped inside, flipping the light switch. The overhead fluorescent beam hummed loudly and then blinked to life, bathing the room in a dull yellow glow. The woman followed Jessica into the small office space.

She said, "You know, I must've passed by this place hundreds of times, but this is the first time I've actually been inside."

"You used to live in Hundred Acres?" Jessica asked.

"I grew up here. My name is Rose Dalton, although I was Rose Hunter back then. My sister is Rue Hunter. We lived with our mom over on Perry Street."

Rue Hunter.

The name was vaguely familiar, but Jessica's brain wasn't offering up the details.

She watched Rose Dalton as her eyes took in every inch of the room, like a house hunter sizing up real estate. Jessica wouldn't blame her if she walked out now and offered the gig to a fancy Los Angeles detective agency instead. Plumped for a penthouse rather than a basement studio.

The office was nothing special and probably hadn't changed much since the Hunters had lived in town. Five four-drawer metal file cabinets took up most of one wall. A long shelving unit housing stationery supplies, an office fan that no longer worked, and a fax machine that still spewed out cheap, shiny paper filled another wall. There were two big old wooden desks that had long since lost their luster, each with a battered leather chair on either side, a green-and-gold banker's lamp on top, and in-boxes with not enough current case files for Ed's liking.

His desk was in the rear of the room so his clients had a good view of the framed certificates hanging on the wall behind him. Jessica's was next to the picture window so she had a good view of the highway that would take her the hell out of this town one day.

She took a seat behind her desk and gestured to the visitor's chair on the other side.

"Please, sit down."

Rose Dalton perched on the edge of the seat, one hand gripping the leather purse tightly on her lap. She used the other to slide the sunglasses on top of her head, pushing back thick bangs and revealing the deep frown lines of someone who spent a lot of time confused or worried. Her eyes were puffy and had dark circles underneath, like she hadn't been getting much sleep lately.

"I couldn't believe it when I found out Ed Crozier still worked here," she said. "He must be almost seventy."

"Yep," Jessica said. "And still rooting around in folks' garbage and exposing shocking infidelities in Hundred Acres, Shady Bluff, and Silverdale. In fact, anyplace where he can make a buck. What's your problem with Ed, anyway? Why did you want to make sure he wasn't here?"

"Oh, it's nothing personal," Rose said quickly. "I'm sure he's very good at his job. But he knew me, and he knew my sister. Not very well but well enough to say hello whenever he saw us around, you know? And, like everyone else in town, old enough to remember what happened back then—I've no doubt his mind would have been made up a long time ago about Rue's guilt. I want someone who's a familiar face in Hundred Acres, with some local knowledge, but who can look at the case with an objective viewpoint. I saw your photo on the agency's website and figured you fit the bill."

"Oh yeah? How so?"

"You're too young to know my sister, for a start. Remember, we're talking more than thirty years ago. Plus, you don't look like someone who's spent their whole life in Hundred Acres. Now that I've spoken to you, you don't sound like you're from around here either."

"I'm from New York. What does someone from Hundred Acres look like?"

She watched as Rose sat back in the chair and appraised her. Jessica was slim, five-five, with peroxide blonde hair. Right arm covered in brightly colored tattoos, tiny diamond stud in her nose sparkling under the fluorescent lighting. Sweating in a pair of tight leather pants and a vintage CBGB tee.

"Not you."

Jessica smiled. She wasn't sure if the comment was meant as a compliment, but she decided to take it as one anyway.

"Why don't you give me the highlights, and we'll see if we can do business?"

Rose Dalton hugged the purse tightly against her body again, in the same way a toddler might cling to a blankie, and then she began to tell her story.

The murders had taken place during the sweltering hot summer of 1987. Fourth of July, to be exact. It had been a Saturday night, and most of the young folks were exactly where they always were on a Saturday night—at Cooper's bar on the edge of town.

Jessica knew the bar Rose was referring to. The cinder block structure had been abandoned for years now, paint scabbing off the red-and-white exterior, weeds sprouting from what was left of the flat roof. A faded ghost sign was the only clue to the good times that had once taken place inside its now crumbling walls. It was situated on the city limits like an afterthought and had long since been forgotten. Jessica had been horrified when she'd first discovered the only watering hole in Hundred Acres was now a rotting carcass on a patch of sun-scorched land, where the only sign of life was a cluster of Joshua trees.

She opened the top drawer of the desk and pulled out a yellow legal pad and pen so she could make some notes while Rose Dalton spoke.

Rose had been at Cooper's with a bunch of friends, spending the tips she'd earned during the week while waitressing at Randy's. It had been a sultry night, and the place had been packed. Condensation steamed the bar's windows and rolled in rivulets down ice-cold bottles of beer. Hot bodies were pressed close together. The place smelled faintly of sweat and cheap perfume and spilled liquor. A mix of blues and rock 'n' roll pounded from the speakers. Everyone was having a good time. Some were getting a little buzzed, others totally wasted.

Rose Hunter was in the first category; Rue Hunter was in the latter.

Rose remembered spotting her younger sister among the crowd, over on the other side of the room, and thinking she was really going for it. Throwing back tequila shots and bottles of Coors like there was another Prohibition looming. Rue was underage, only eighteen, but the owners didn't care as long as they were making money. And the cash registers were ringing all night long. Not with Rue's cash—she never had any—but she always seemed to find someone willing to buy her a drink.

The sisters didn't hang out together at Cooper's, Rose said. Didn't speak to each other at all in the bar that night. The four-year age gap between the two seemed like a lot back then, and they moved in completely different circles. Rose and her friends had been in a couple booths in the back corner, away from the younger high school crowd. Far too cool to mix with the underagers. When Rose had looked over again a while later, Rue was gone.

Jessica looked up from her notes.

"Did she leave with someone?"

"I have no idea," Rose said. "That part of the evening remains unclear. Most of her crowd were still in Cooper's. I remembered thinking I hadn't seen Lucas or Megan, so I assumed she'd gone off to meet them."

"Lucas and Megan?"

"Lucas James and Megan Meeks. Rue's boyfriend and her best friend. The three of them had been inseparable since they were kids. In the last year or so, Rue and Lucas's friendship had turned into something more, but the three of them still hung out together all the time. Lucas and Megan were the kids who died that night."

Jessica noted the older woman's use of the word *died*, rather than *killed* or *murdered*, as though their deaths had simply been some terrible accident.

"What happened?"

Rose's eyes dropped to the desk. Her knuckles were as white as the purse she held. Jessica wondered how many times she had replayed the events of that Fourth of July in her head in the three decades since.

"It was early the next morning before I even knew anything was wrong," Rose said. "I mean really early, before dawn. I was awakened by a loud banging on the door, which is never good news at that time in the morning. My first thought was that something was wrong with Rue. I jumped out of bed and ran down the hall to her room and opened the door. She was in bed, asleep. I noticed the room stank like a nauseating mix of vomit and bleach. I assumed she'd thrown up in the middle of the night and had tried to clean up the mess. There was another bang on the door. Much louder this time, more urgent. It was Sheriff Holten and one of his deputies. I could tell from the looks on their faces that something terrible had happened. They both wore these really serious expressions and looked badly shaken. They asked if Rue was at home and if she was okay. Said they needed to speak to her right away."

"And was she okay?"

Rose paused for a beat or two and then nodded.

"Sheriff Holten's deputy found the dress Rue had been wearing dumped in the laundry basket. It was soaked in blood, but it wasn't Rue's blood. She didn't have a mark on her, except for some minor cuts and scratches on the soles of her feet and the red patches on her skin where she had scrubbed too hard with a nailbrush. The bleach was still in the bathtub. Then Sheriff Holten said Lucas and Megan were dead, that their bodies had been found at Devil's Drop."

"Devil's Drop?"

Again, the name was familiar, but the tiny spark of recognition at the back of Jessica's brain fizzled out before she could grab hold of it.

"It was the local make-out spot," Rose said. "They were in the back seat of Lucas's car. They'd both been stabbed. Rue just sat there, shivering in a nightshirt despite the heat, not reacting, not saying anything. Kind of dazed looking, I guess. I was worried I was going to throw up or faint or something, but I knew I had to be strong for Rue. Our mom wasn't at home—she was spending the night with whatever guy she was seeing at the time—so it was left to me to take care of Rue. I sat next to her on the couch and put my arm around her and stroked her hair, and I told her everything was going to be okay."

Rose's voice broke slightly, and she looked at Jessica, her puffy eyes now wet with unshed tears. She swallowed hard a couple times, tried to compose herself before speaking again.

15

"I was wrong," she said finally. "Things were about to get a whole lot worse. Holten's deputy found something else in the laundry basket, along with the dress."

"What did he find?" Jessica asked.

A pause.

Then Rose said, "The murder weapon."

3

MEGAN

1987

Megan Meeks chewed the top of the pen while mulling over what to write.

The next couple entries in her journal would be more important—more *significant*—than anything else she had ever committed to the scented pages. That's how big a deal it was, so she had to get the words just right. Maybe one day, when she was old and married with kids, she would pull the diary from a box in the attic, carefully wipe the dust off the pink leatherette cover, reread these words, and reflect on one of the biggest nights of her life.

The night when she stopped being a kid and finally became a woman.

That's it, she thought.

Became a woman.

It was perfect.

She scribbled the words quickly, before she forgot them.

> *July 3, 1987*
> *L is "The One"—I'm sure of it. We may only have been together properly for a matter of weeks, but, when you know, you know. I always wanted it to be just like*

the movies when it happened. And that's exactly what it's like. Butterflies explode in my stomach every time I see him, and I actually feel weak at the knees when he smiles at me. I just never thought in a million years that L would feel the same way about me. But he does! I'm surprised I'm not covered in bruises from pinching myself so often.

Now I'm so glad I decided to wait for someone special, until the time was right. And tomorrow night will be the right time, with the right person. It won't be L's first time, of course, but that doesn't matter. What matters is how we feel about each other.

The only bit that sucks is all the lies—they're tearing me apart inside—but I know he's worth it. Anyway, the course of true love never runs smoothly in the movies, right? Boy meets girl, and boy and girl both have to overcome a bunch of obstacles before they can finally be together. For me and L, the waiting is almost over. Tonight, I'm still a girl. Tomorrow, I'll be a woman.

PS: I wonder if I'll look any different afterward? Will people be able to tell just by looking at me?

Megan read the diary entry again and felt a hot flush creep from her neck all the way up to the roots of her hair. Thank God for the tiny lock and key. She would absolutely die if anyone else ever read her journal.

She opened the top drawer of the dresser and hid the little book under her underwear. Her face flushed hard again as she spotted the fancy black lace set she'd purchased a couple weeks ago in Silverdale, where she knew she wouldn't be recognized. The price tag was still attached, a reminder of how much more expensive the lingerie was than her usual sensible underwear purchases. Most of her savings had been blown on the flimsy bra and panties, but, *What the hell,* she thought— occasions didn't really get any more special than this one.

Megan closed the drawer and dropped the tiny brass diary key into the jewelry box on top of the dresser, in among the cheap costume stuff and the diamond-and-emerald bracelet that had once belonged to her mother. It had been a gift from Megan's father, and she decided she'd wear it tomorrow night too. She lay back on the queen bed and opened the latest copy of *Seventeen* magazine to where she'd folded down the corner of one of the pages earlier.

Ten Ways to Make the First Time the Best Time.

She'd gotten only as far as number four when she heard a soft knock on the door. Megan quickly shoved the magazine under the pillow, before her mom peeked her head into the room. Patty Meeks was wearing a ratty old bathrobe and big rollers under a hairnet, but Megan was struck once again by how pretty her mother was. She didn't look anywhere near old enough to have a seventeen-year-old daughter. Megan just hoped she'd look half as good when she was her mom's age.

"I'm off to bed now, sweetheart. Don't stay up too late."

"Just another half hour, Mom."

"Okay, but turn the music down."

"Sure thing."

Megan rolled off the bed with a groan and twisted the dial on the stereo, reducing the volume by a couple of notches.

"Much better. Good night, sweetie."

"Night, Mom."

Patty pulled the door shut behind her, leaving her daughter with Jon Bon Jovi for company. Megan had spent ages making a mixtape, meticulously writing out each song listing on the glossy cassette cover, carefully choosing the music they would listen to in the car afterward.

Now she was worried her selection was too schmaltzy. She wanted the mood to be romantic but not *too* romantic. She was considering whether to tape over "Open Your Heart" by Madonna with something else when the baby-blue Princess phone on her dressing table began to ring. She snatched up the receiver quickly before her mom heard it.

"Hello?" she whispered.

"Hey, it's me."

"Lucas!" she hissed. "It's past midnight. My mom will go nuts if she knows you've called at this hour."

"Yeah, yeah. What's the worst that could happen?"

"Uh, she could ground me for, like, the next month?"

Lucas chuckled. "Relax, Megs. You're practically a grown-up now. Speaking of which, you, uh, all set for tomorrow night?"

"Um, I guess."

Megan suddenly felt shy and embarrassed, which was ridiculous because she'd known Lucas forever.

"Hey, you know you don't have to do anything you don't want to do?" His tone was softer now. "No one's going to judge you. I'm not going to judge—"

She cut him off. "I want to, Lucas. I really do. I just hate all the sneaking around. All the lies."

"Yeah, I know. It sucks big time."

They were both silent for a moment, and Megan could hear the faint burbling of a TV in the background on Lucas's end of the line. It sounded like commentary on a ball game.

"What about Rue?" he asked eventually.

"All taken care of."

"Where will she be?"

"Cooper's. Where else?"

"Yeah, I figured as much."

"I'm worried about her."

"Me too."

There was more silence on the line. Megan could hear the commentator picking apart the Dodgers' loss to the Pittsburgh Pirates earlier in the evening on the late-night rerun.

Lucas finally spoke again. "It'll be fine, Megs. Don't worry about it. It's gonna be a blast. A night you'll never forget. Let's not allow anything to ruin it, huh?"

"I know. You're right. It's just . . . not how I thought it would be."

"You'll have fun. I promise. Pick you up around eight thirty?"

"Yeah, sounds good. See you tomorrow."

"Night, Megs."

"Good night, Lucas."

"Oh, and Megan?"

"Yeah?"

"Are you seriously listening to Bon Jovi?"

"Asshole!"

She laughed and replaced the handset in the cradle. She stripped off her jeans and T-shirt and pulled on her summer pajamas. Decided to leave the window open a crack to let the cool night air into the room. Megan turned off the stereo just as "Livin' on a Prayer" was replaced by Glenn Medeiros. She'd definitely tape over that one, she decided; it was way too schmaltzy.

As she climbed into bed, Megan glanced over at the *Top Gun* poster scotch-taped to the back of the bedroom door. A smug-looking Kelly McGillis was draped over Tom Cruise's shoulder as he smoldered for the camera. Megan and Rue had gone to the movie theater at least ten times after its release last year.

"Sorry, Maverick," she said. "You're only my second-favorite guy now."

Megan switched off the bedside lamp and lay there in the dark, wondering how long it would take to drift off to sleep. She felt like a kid on Christmas Eve, hoping Santa Claus would deliver everything she'd asked for.

Only this time, as well as excitement, there were nerves and that niggling feeling that what she was doing was wrong. Megan shook her head in the darkness. How could it be wrong to be in love? Lucas was right, she told herself firmly. Everything was going to be just fine.

Better than fine.

This weekend was going to be one she would never forget.

4

JESSICA

It was easy for Jessica to see why things had gotten so bad so quickly for Rue Hunter.

It had begun with an anonymous phone call to the sheriff's department, Rose told her. The caller had spotted a teenage girl walking along the side of the highway sometime after ten p.m. She was barefoot and covered in blood and appeared to be disorientated. The guy pulled up alongside her, rolled down his car window, and asked if she was okay. She gave him a weird kind of empty stare before telling him, "They're both dead."

The guy was so spooked that he immediately drove off. A half mile down the road, he started regretting his actions, figured the girl probably needed help. So he made the call from the next pay phone he came to. Told the cops it was like a scene from a horror movie, right at the end when the main character is the last one left standing.

Hundred Acres was the seat of the county that shared its name, and the Hundred Acres Sheriff's Department was located not far from where the girl had been seen. The sheriff's deputy, who was working the overnight shift and picked up the call, headed straight out in his cruiser to try to track down the "horror movie girl," but there was no sign of anyone near the main highway. He would later testify at the trial how he had returned to the station after a short while, writing off the anonymous caller as a crank, unaware that the town had already been changed forever. *A horror movie, indeed,* he'd remembered thinking to himself with a smile. It might not be Halloween, but it was a holiday weekend, and that meant the crazies were still out in force.

A little over three hours later, the sheriff's deputy's phone rang again. This time, a local resident, Patty Meeks, was on the line. She wasn't one of the crazies. She was worried about her daughter, Megan, who had missed her midnight curfew. Patty had already tried phoning around to Megan's friends. She had gotten the Hunters' machine, while the Jameses weren't overly concerned that their son Lucas hadn't come home yet either. After all, he was eighteen, lots of parties were happening, and it was only one thirty a.m. They'd just returned home from a get-together with friends themselves. It was perfectly understandable for kids at that age to lose track of time, they'd pointed out. No need to worry.

But Patty Meeks *was* worried. Megan never broke a curfew. Patty knew she was probably a little too strict with her daughter, but Megan was a good girl. By far the most sensible one out of the three friends. If she had planned to stay out later than agreed, she definitely would have phoned home to ask her mom's permission.

The sheriff's deputy knew Patty Meeks, and he knew Megan, so he immediately picked up his car keys again, climbed into the cruiser, and followed the same route along the highway he had driven earlier in the evening.

Only this time, he also decided to swing by Devil's Drop, a well-known make-out spot popular with the town's young folks.

Just in case.

Later, once the shock began to wear off and the crime scene was processed, the sheriff's deputy remembered the phone call about the barefoot "horror movie girl." A pair of sandals had been found at the crime scene that didn't belong to Megan Meeks. The caller had said the girl on the highway was tall and slim and had long blonde hair.

The description sounded a lot like Rue Hunter, a close friend of both of the deceased.

The cops initially thought Rue might be a third victim, who had somehow managed to survive the attack. They hoped she might be an important eyewitness.

Instead, Rue Hunter quickly became their prime suspect.

The evidence stacked up against her pretty fast: her dress soaked in blood that tests later confirmed belonged to Lucas James and Megan Meeks; entries from Megan's journal revealing she had been secretly dating Lucas behind her best friend's back; the murder weapon covered in Rue Hunter's bloody fingerprints found at the bottom of the laundry basket under an old bath towel that stank of bleach; the teenager's unwillingness to tell the cops what the hell had happened at Devil's Drop.

Plus, the girl had been trouble for a long time, and everyone in town knew she had begun to go off the rails big time in the last year or two. Like mother, like daughter, they whispered behind cupped hands. Only Barb Hunter was nothing worse than a drunk who would open her legs to whoever was willing to buy her the most liquor, while her daughter wound up being a murderer on top of the booze and drugs.

As far as local law enforcement was concerned, Rue Hunter checked all the boxes.

Means. Motive. Opportunity.

Bang. Bang. Bang.

Like shots fired from a gun.

Only instead of a smoking gun, Sheriff Charlie Holten had had a five-inch switchblade stored in a clear plastic bag that would be their key piece of evidence when charging the teenager with double homicide.

That was until Rue Hunter's confession had sealed her own fate.

Jessica was silent for a moment after Rose had finished speaking.

The story reminded her of the crime scene photos she'd seen of her own mother's murder. A woman Jessica had never gotten the chance to know. Like Megan Meeks and Lucas James, Eleanor Lavelle had had her life cut short in a violent and horrific way by a killer's knife.

"I'm not going to sugarcoat it," Jessica told Rose. "I can see exactly why the cops liked Rue for the murders almost from the get-go. I can also see why she was convicted. What does surprise me, though, is that it was a death penalty case. I mean, it was a terrible crime and all, but she was only eighteen. There was no rape or torture of the victims, no murder of a child or death of a police officer involved."

Rose nodded. "You're right, but the prosecution put forward a case for murder along with several other special circumstances." She held up a finger for each one. "Multiple murders. Lying in wait. Murder during the course of a robbery."

Jessica paused midway through the sentence she was writing and looked up.

"A robbery? I thought the motive was revenge because Lucas and Megan were getting it on?"

"It was," Rose said. "But there was also some jewelry and cash stolen from the victims. The prosecution argued that Rue went to Devil's Drop and killed them in a jealous rage. Classic crime of passion. Then, the prosecution said, she decided to rob their dead bodies in order to fund her drink and drugs problem. The jury at the sentencing trial bought it."

"Did the cops find the stolen jewelry and cash?"

"No, they were never recovered." Rose laughed bitterly. "Apparently, Rue was smart enough to stash stolen goods somewhere no one would ever find them but dumb enough to hide the murder weapon covered in her fingerprints at home."

"Uh-huh. Tell me about the confession."

Rose sighed and gazed out the picture window. There was still a steady flow of traffic on the highway. Folks who had clocked out for the weekend and who were heading to Vegas to try their luck on the roulette wheel or in the poker rooms or with the opposite sex or with the same sex. Whatever floated their fake Venetian gondolas. Nine-to-fivers who wanted to immerse themselves in the seductive neon desert and forget about the real world for a couple of days.

Rose turned back to Jessica and gave a tiny shrug of her shoulders.

"I've thought about it a lot over the years," she said. "In a way, I can't imagine why she would confess to something so terrible. Something, I'm absolutely sure, she didn't do. Then I think about how scared she must have been. She wasn't much older than a kid. She was hungover, in shock, traumatized. Her best friends were dead. The people she was closest to in the world. Even closer than she was to me. She was interrogated for hours in a small, stuffy room, first by the cops and then by the police psychologist. Asking her the same questions over and over and over again. In the end, I think she just told them what they wanted to hear so they would let her go home. Of course, that never happened. She never set foot in our house again."

"What about appeals?" Jessica asked. "I take it they all failed?"

Rose hesitated. "Rue never appealed her conviction. The defense attorney at her sentencing trial was woefully out of his depth. Later, plenty of so-called top lawyers came crawling out of the woodwork, all offering to take on an appeal on a pro bono basis, knowing full well it was a high-profile case that would guarantee plenty of free publicity in return. Rue turned them all down."

"Why would she do that?"

Rose looked at Jessica, a challenge in her eyes.

"Why don't you ask her yourself?"

"Huh? How?"

Rose Dalton unzipped the white leather purse and pulled out a small clear plastic folder. She snapped open the fastener and withdrew several sheets of paper and unfolded them. Passed them across the desk to Jessica and tapped the sheet on top.

"A visitation order to meet with Rue at the prison tomorrow," she said. "The visit is already approved. All you have to do is call the number at the top of the page to confirm you'll be there."

"That was quick. Don't prison visits usually take a while to arrange?"

"Processing times vary. I guess it's a little faster when someone's about to be executed."

Jessica didn't know how to respond to that comment, so she scanned the document instead. Rue Hunter was being held at the Central California Women's Facility in Chowchilla. Jessica had no idea where that was, other than it was clearly somewhere in California. And California was a big place, as Pryce had reminded her. She flipped over to the next two pages, which were stapled together. It was Jessica's copy of a contract.

"Holy shit." Her eyes widened. "Twenty-five grand?"

Rose Dalton was offering $25,000 for Jessica's services, and the fee would rise to a cool $150,000 if Rue Hunter was cleared of the murders and compensated by the state. Ed would be doing cartwheels across the office when he found out how much dough was involved. It would keep him in Cuba libres at Ruben's for months.

"Is it enough for you to take on the case?" Rose asked.

For a week's work? Hell, yes.

The agency needed the money, but Jessica had to be straight with the woman.

"It's too much," she said. "A lot more than our usual fee would be."

"But I'd need you to prioritize this case over all your other clients," Rose said. "Start your investigation immediately. Work the case morning, noon, and night if need be. Is what I'm offering enough?"

Jessica nodded. "It's enough."

"I hoped that's what you'd say."

Rose produced a thick brown envelope from her purse and laid it on the desk between them.

"It's all there. You can count it if you like."

Jessica was incredulous. "You brought twenty-five grand in cash?"

No wonder the woman had been holding onto the purse tighter than a kid clutching a candy bar.

"I withdrew the money from a couple of different savings accounts. I didn't want to write a check. This way you know I'm good for the money."

Jessica jutted her chin toward the gold band on the ring finger of Rose Dalton's left hand.

"What's your husband saying about you splashing out thousands of dollars on a private investigator?"

"He doesn't know."

Jessica had suspected as much.

"And he doesn't know you're here in Hundred Acres either?"

Rose shook her head. "Bob's back home in Tucson. I hate airplanes, so he thinks I'm spending a couple of days driving up to Chowchilla. Which isn't really a lie, to be fair. He just doesn't know about the diversion to Hundred Acres. Bob and the boys will fly up for the, um, you know, the funeral. Rue has never met my sons, didn't ever want them to see her in that place, and she's adamant that she doesn't want Bob or the boys at the execution. If there is an execution, that is."

The hope in her voice squeezed at Jessica's heart.

"Look, Rose," she said. "I've got to be honest with you. What you've told me so far, it sounds to me like Rue did it. Even if she didn't, it's going to be a hell of a job trying to prove her innocence in such a short space of time."

"Yes, I know. But Rue didn't want me looking into all this stuff before now. All I'm asking is for you to do some digging, ask some questions, get me some answers. There's so much that we still don't know about what happened that night."

"I don't know," Jessica said. "It's a lot of money for a long shot."

"I owe her."

"You owe her? What does that mean?"

"Do you have any brothers or sisters?"

Jessica shook her head. Her own family history was almost as fucked up as Rose Dalton's, but she wasn't about to start comparing notes with a complete stranger.

"Only child."

"So you couldn't possibly understand. The money means nothing to me compared to my sister's life. Our mom drank herself to death soon after Rue was sent to the row, so she's the only blood relative I have left, other than my kids. I owe it to Rue, and I owe it to myself, to give it one last shot to save her. Especially now that she's finally asked for my help."

Jessica glanced at the envelope stuffed full of Rose Dalton's life savings. She felt a thrill of adrenaline course through her veins and realized she was excited. Six months of preemployee background checks and adultery cases and asset investigations had left her desperate for something that would get the blood pumping, spark her imagination, challenge her.

But still, she didn't pick up the cash.

Rose said, "Meet with Rue tomorrow and then decide. I'm driving up to Chowchilla tonight. This is where I'll be staying, and I can be contacted on this number anytime, night or day." She handed Jessica a sheet of lined paper torn from a notepad with the name and address of a motel and a cell phone number scribbled on it. "The money is yours once you sign the contract. Hopefully I'll see you tomorrow, Miss Shaw."

Rose Dalton slipped the brown envelope back into the white leather purse, stood, and headed for the door. Then she stepped out into the desert dusk without a backward glance, leaving Jessica alone with her thoughts.

She sat there for a while, the sky outside the window growing darker and the traffic becoming lighter. Then she opened the bottom drawer of the desk where she kept a glass tumbler and a bottle of Talisker. Jessica poured two fingers of Scotch into the glass. Then she added another finger.

It had been a hell of a night.

She fired up the laptop, sipped the whiskey, and realized she had already made up her mind about taking on the case. She pulled up Google and typed Rue Hunter's name into the search bar. Figured she might as well get a head start on the investigation. She hit "Enter" and read the first result at the top of the page, and her fingers froze above the keyboard.

Jessica stared at the screen.

The Rue Hunter case had just gotten more interesting.

5

JESSICA

The Central California Women's Facility was one of the largest female correctional institutions in the United States. Even so, whoever had drawn up the plans hadn't reckoned on quite so many West Coast women being unable to stay on the right side of the law. As such, its sprawling 640 acres weren't enough to cope with the demand, and the current inmate population stood at around a thousand more than its intended capacity.

The prison also housed all twenty-two of the state's female condemned, including Rue Hunter, who had the dubious distinction of being the row's longest-serving resident. Chowchilla, where the facility was located, was around 250 miles north of downtown Los Angeles and a four-hour drive from Hundred Acres, meaning an early start after a late night at the office.

What had started out as a quick Google search had rapidly led to Jessica falling down an internet rabbit hole for several hours. There were the usual historical articles and sensationalist "killer women" documentaries on YouTube. Dozens of threads on true crime forums discussing whether Rue Hunter was guilty, if her confession had been forced or coerced, if she had deserved to be handed the death penalty.

Right at the top of the search results were the breaking news stories about Rue Hunter's impending execution—and why it was such a big deal.

Jessica discovered California had not executed a prisoner since 2006. Even more striking was the revelation that a woman had not met her end in the death chamber in the Golden State since 1962. Which meant Rue Hunter would be the first female to be executed by the state of California in almost sixty years—and that made her big news as far as the media was concerned.

For the first time since the late eighties, the notorious teen murderer was back in the headlines. Only this time, #DevilsDropMurders was trending on Twitter, and her old mug shot was being shared all over Facebook. Reporters from online news sites regurgitated details from old newspaper cuttings and tried to pass their clickbait stories off as real reporting.

As she cruised north along State Route 99, Jessica glanced at her cell phone, charging in the holder on the dashboard, and sighed. She hadn't heard from Dylan since she'd blown off their date the night before. She knew he'd be pissed that she'd put work ahead of him yet again. She also knew he wouldn't stay mad at her for long.

A roadside sign for the state prisons appeared up ahead. Jessica flipped on the blinker, eased into the lane for the off-ramp, and turned her thoughts back to the visit with Rue Hunter. She'd never been inside a prison before, and she was surprised to discover she was a little nervous about the whole experience. Jessica reached over, fumbled in her bag on the passenger seat, and found a pack of Marlboro Lights. She shook one out, lit it with the truck's cigarette lighter, and rolled the window down halfway. She took a long satisfying drag and promised herself for the millionth time she would quit soon, even though she knew she wouldn't.

The gray clouds that had kept her company through Selma and Fowler and Calwa had finally given way to a clear blue sky, and the blast of cool, fresh air through the open window instantly made Jessica feel more awake and alert. The deafening roar of the wind drowned out a dull radio phone-in show broadcasting out of Fresno that, Jessica realized, had been contributing to her state of drowsiness.

A huge mill with giant cylindrical drums as big as houses appeared on the horizon, and Jessica hooked a right after the concrete-and-metal monstrosity onto Avenue 20 1/2 and then onto Road 22. She stubbed out the cigarette in the truck's ashtray.

After she'd driven awhile on the narrow two-lane highway, which was flanked on either side by unexpectedly lush almond trees, the GPS announced loudly that she was almost at her destination.

The Administrative Segregation block housed some of the most dangerous women in the country.

Confined to single cells for twenty-three hours a day, most of the inmates who found themselves in solitary confinement, usually for disruptive behavior or violence against a guard or fellow inmate, returned to the general prison population after several weeks.

Those on Condemned Row, a group of cells behind a special caged-off section of the building, never left.

The death row mesh cage and the cell doors were painted salmon pink, the metal walkways a clashing mint green. But, despite the unlikely pastel color scheme, the place was clearly no summer camp. Guards wore bullet- and stab-proof vests strapped to their chests, nightsticks swinging lazily from bulky utility belts slung around their waists. Bunches of keys as big as baseballs jangled with each step they took.

Two things struck Jessica as she was escorted to the visiting room—the smell and the noise.

The sweet scent of the almond blossom was now a distant memory, replaced by the eye-watering stench of industrial-strength disinfectant and body odor. Maybe just a hint of fear, too, although Jessica was pretty sure that aroma was oozing from her own pores. A dizzying cacophony of noise—yelling and crying and whistling and cell doors slamming shut—was only just louder than the thunderous pounding of her heart.

Everything Jessica knew about prisons she'd learned from watching TV shows like *Orange Is the New Black*. She'd expected the meeting with Rue Hunter to take place behind a thick sheet of bulletproof glass in a cramped space where conversations were whispered into sweat-slick telephone receivers and plastic chairs were nailed to the floor. Where damp palms pressed against the partition was the closest prisoners and their visitors ever came to physical contact.

She was wrong.

Jessica was escorted to a cinder block room with indiscreet cameras fixed in the highest corners. Cracked leatherette seats oozing foam were scattered around a scarred wooden table. As a "Condemned Grade A" prisoner, Rue Hunter was permitted contact visits, which meant no bulletproof glass. Jessica's heart beat faster, her stomach flip-flopped, and she wiped her hands on her pants as she awaited the prisoner's arrival.

That was her first surprise.

The second was Rue Hunter herself.

The mug shot Jessica had seen plastered all over social media showed a skinny young woman with sharp features and empty brown eyes sunk deep into a pale face framed by unwashed blonde hair that hung limp to her elbows. Rue Hunter might have been pretty under better circumstances.

Once again drawing on her vast experience of bingeing on Netflix Originals, Jessica had fully expected to meet someone with jail-hardened features and a bright orange jumpsuit fitted snugly against a thick body, maybe some prison ink less skillfully applied than her own tattoos, definitely an air of menace or defiance.

Wrong again.

Rue Hunter was tall and willowy. Her long blonde hair was steaked with silver and styled in a loose braid draped over one shoulder. Her skin was so pale it was almost see-through, the ghostly pallor of someone who didn't get to spend much time in natural daylight. However, lack of exposure to the sun's harmful rays for thirty years also meant a face free of the lines and wrinkles that had been noticeable on her sister. Clearly, a long stretch inside was a cheaper way to a youthful complexion than $200 jars of face cream and regular Botox injections.

Rue was dressed in loose-fitting blue denim pants and a blue-and-white long-sleeved tee and wore white no-brand sneakers on her feet. Were it not for the shackles connecting the handcuffs on her wrists to her ankles, she could almost pass for a friendly neighborhood power walker, albeit one with slightly dubious taste in leisure wear.

Despite the metal restraints, Rue moved gracefully as she was escorted into the room. She offered Jessica a small smile.

"Thanks for visiting, Miss Shaw. I wasn't sure that you would."

"Please, call me Jessica."

"Jessica it is, then. I'm Rue. It's good to meet you. My sister says a lot of good things about you."

Rue sat on the other side of the table, across from Jessica, the restraints clinking tunelessly as she lowered herself into the chair. A male prison guard stood close behind her, while a female officer faced the inmate over Jessica's shoulder.

Jessica said, "As you know, I met with your sister yesterday evening. And I have to admit, I'm intrigued by what she told me."

"Rose is great, isn't she?" Rue said. "You know she comes to visit me every other month? Regular as clockwork, all the way from Arizona. And she doesn't do airplanes, so it's a hell of a drive. It's what keeps me sane in here, knowing I'll get to hug my big sister again soon."

"Do you get many other visitors?"

"I used to." Rue shrugged. "Not so much these days. Folks would write me a lot in the early days and ask if they could meet me. Then they'd just sit there, gaping. Not offering much in the way of conversation. I think they just wanted to boast to friends they'd sat face to face with a killer. So I stopped sending them visiting orders. I guess I got tired of being a freak show."

Jessica nodded and tried not to gape herself.

Rue went on. "I still like receiving letters, though. There can be as many as a hundred different people writing me at any one time. Some send photos and books; others send marriage proposals." She laughed. "Can you believe that? None of them are even close to being cute enough to get hitched to."

Jessica smiled and felt herself begin to relax a little.

"Is that what you do to pass the time?" she asked. "Write letters?"

Rue nodded. "I write, exercise, meditate, read, study. I never graduated high school, so I earned my GED diploma in here. I never bothered with books at school either, but I read two or three paperbacks a week now. My body has never left California, but my mind has traveled all over the world through those pages."

Jessica had been granted only sixty minutes with Rue because Rose had also been to visit her sister earlier in the day. She was just about to move the conversation on to the delicate topic of the murders, when Rue's mood, and the subject matter, changed.

"Do you know what my name means, Jessica? The meaning of the word *rue*?"

"I think it means street in French?"

"Yes, so it does. It also means regret. As in, 'Lucas James and Megan Meeks must rue the day they met Rue Hunter.'"

Jessica didn't know what to say, so she said nothing. Waited for Rue to continue.

"I think about them every single day," Rue said eventually. "Sometimes I talk to them too. Does that sound crazy? I bet it sounds crazy, but there's a hell of a lot of crazy to go around in a place like this. Don't tell Rose, but I loved them even more than I loved my own family. Megan was just the sweetest girl. The opposite of what I was like back then, I guess. I really couldn't have asked for a better best friend. We never argued, never had a bad word spoken between us. And Lucas? He was just so goddamn handsome that my heart actually ached every time I looked at him."

Jessica stared at her. She was looking at a middle-aged woman, but it felt like she was listening to the gushing nonsense of a teenage girl. She realized she was gaping again and averted her eyes.

"Did you see his picture in the papers?" Rue asked suddenly. "Don't you think Lucas was handsome, Jessica?"

The old newspaper cuttings had carried a few different photos of Lucas James. A smiling senior class photo lifted from the high school yearbook. A family snap with his parents and two older brothers while on vacation in Florida. A posed shot standing between Megan and Rue on junior prom night, an arm slung casually over each girl's shoulders, taken a year before the murders.

That one had made Jessica's blood run cold.

"Yeah, he was a good-looking guy."

"He was the only person I ever had sex with," Rue said matter-of-factly. "Ask anyone in Hundred Acres, and they'd say that's a lie. They'd tell you I was a whore like my mother. But it's not true. Lucas was the only one. Thankfully, I didn't make him wait. Could you imagine if I had? At least I have those memories, the *good* memories, to turn to when I'm lying in my bunk at night. I mean, it's not like there were ever going to be any serious contenders in here." Rue turned in her seat slightly and glanced up at the guard behind her. "No offense, Pedro."

The man, a stocky Latino in his early forties, smirked but didn't say anything. The female guard huffed out a noise someplace between a snort and a laugh, her warm breath ruffling Jessica's hair. She estimated at least twenty minutes of her allotted hour had been used up already. Time to get to the point of the visit.

"It, uh, must have been hard when you found out Lucas and Megan had hooked up," she said.

Rue's demeanor changed so fast Jessica almost got whiplash. Her eyes darkened, and her lips pursed in an ugly thin line, and Jessica caught a glimpse of the hardened criminal she'd been expecting to see when she'd first walked into the visitors' room.

"Yeah, whatever," Rue snapped.

Then, just as quickly, the moment passed, and the scowl was replaced by a broad grin.

"Hey, you got a boyfriend, Jessica?" Rue leaned forward, as though they were enjoying a gossip over lunch and a bottle of wine. "Pretty little thing like you, I bet you've got plenty of guys after you."

Jessica shifted uncomfortably. The leatherette seat felt damp under her butt, and a sharp edge where the material had split open jabbed her skin through her pants. She wanted to get the hell out of there. She'd thought the woman was smart, funny, articulate at the start of the visit.

Now she realized Rue Hunter was crazier than a shithouse rat.

"Yeah, I'm seeing someone."

"Someone from Hundred Acres? What's his name?"

"Dylan."

"Dylan . . ."

Rue scrunched up her sallow, unlined face in concentration, trying to place the name from thirty years ago; then her eyes widened under raised eyebrows.

"Not little Dylan McDonagh?" she asked. "The cop's son? He sure was cute as a button as a baby. I bet he's still cute now that he's all grown up, right?"

"Right." Jessica decided she'd had enough. "Time's marching on, Rue. Why did you confess to murdering Lucas and Megan? Why did you never appeal your conviction?"

Rue Hunter held Jessica's gaze for what felt like forever, and then she shrugged in a casual sort of way, as though she was discussing the weather or what to have for dinner, instead of her best friends' murders.

"Same answer to both questions," she said. "I guess I thought I deserved to be punished for killing them."

6

MEGAN

1986

Megan squeezed into the stall next to Rue before slamming the door shut behind them and sliding the lock into place.

Rue leaned a hand on her friend's shoulder for support and hoisted a foot onto the toilet seat lid, the spiky stiletto adding another deep score to the already scarred plastic. She pulled back folds of pale-pink taffeta and satin until a small silver flask strapped to her thigh was exposed. She slipped the flask from the garter strap, twisted off the top, and grinned at Megan.

"Time to liven things up a bit."

Rue threw back her head and sucked down a healthy gulp and winced.

"Neat vodka," she said. "Stolen from my mom's not-so-secret stash under the kitchen sink. I swear, one of these days, she's gonna down a bottle of bleach by mistake."

"Rue!" Megan giggled from behind her hand. It was a habit she still had even though her braces had been off for a month now. "What if your mom finds out?"

"She won't. I topped the bottle off with water. The silly old bitch will never know. She'll be too wasted to even notice next time she goes looking for it." Rue passed the flask to Megan. "Here you go."

Megan hesitated, just for a second, then took a quick swallow to keep Rue happy. It tasted revolting.

"Hey, can you believe Darcy Kendrick was voted prom queen?" Rue said, shaking her head. "And what the fuck is she wearing? The only way you'd set foot outside the door in that meringue monstrosity is if you'd lost a bet."

"Rue, you're terrible." Megan laughed, pretending to be shocked.

"I'm being serious. They might even withhold the tiara when they see that ugly dress."

"Yeah, I suppose it's not the best."

"Not the best? It's fucking hideous. Jeez, Megan, you're too nice—do you know that? Now, take a proper slug of that vodka and say something bitchy!"

Megan did as she was told and took a long swallow of booze. It didn't taste so bad this time. She handed the flask back.

Rue stared at her expectantly.

Megan said, "Um, well, I guess her dress does kind of remind me of the toilet paper cover in the bathroom at home. You know, the creepy little doll with the knitted dress that my mom made?"

"Exactly!" Rue laughed, screwing the top onto the flask. She slid it back into the garter strap and smoothed down her dress. "We'd better get back before Lucas sends out a search party."

She opened the stall door, and they both froze when they saw Darcy Kendrick standing in front of the sink applying lipstick the same color as the bright pink spots of anger on each cheek. She dropped the tube into her purse and eyeballed Rue and Megan in the mirror. Then she turned and headed for the restroom door, satin lemon-yellow ruffles swooshing with each step. Just as the door swung shut, Darcy Kendrick spoke without looking back.

"Fucking bitches."

Megan and Rue just stood there for a stunned moment, not moving or saying anything. Then they looked at each other and collapsed into a fit of giggles.

"Shit." Rue wiped away a tear. "Do you think she heard us?"

"Um, yes!"

Rue pulled a paper towel from the wall dispenser and dabbed at a smudge of mascara under her eye. She balled the paper towel, trashed it, and appraised them both in the mirror.

Rue had opted for a strapless pink satin-and-taffeta dress with a sweetheart neckline and a full skirt that fell just above the knee. She wore matching fingerless fishnet gloves, and her hair was curled and swept to one side, just like Madonna used to wear hers before the singer cut it short and dyed it peroxide blonde.

Megan's choice was a full-length gown with a side slit and chiffon-capped sleeves. It was the same shade of blue as her eyes, and, her mom said, complemented her long, dark, permed hair. She was curvier than Rue and about five inches shorter, and she felt like a frump in comparison.

Rue said, "I know I'm biased, but, damn, we look hot."

"Well, you do anyway," Megan said glumly.

Rue surprised her then by grabbing her in a tight hug and kissing her cheek. Megan could smell the booze on her breath as she said, "You're beautiful on the inside and out, Megan. Don't you dare let anyone ever tell you any different." Then she pulled back, gave Megan a woozy smile, and took her hand and led her to the door. "Let's go. Lucas is waiting."

The events committee had been tasked with transforming the gym from a sweaty jock haven into a fancy party space, and Megan had to admit they'd done a pretty good job. The color theme was blue, white, and silver, and the room was filled with balloons and streamers and a dozen round tables topped with real linen tablecloths. A huge glitter ball had been strung up on the ceiling, dappling dancing couples with tiny rectangles of light on the makeshift dance floor. A four-piece band was performing recent chart hits on a small stage that had been erected at the front of the gym, while the long folding tables that took up much of the back wall held bowls of fruit punch and soft drinks.

Lucas strolled toward them, a cup filled with punch in each hand.

Megan thought he looked handsome in his smart white tuxedo and pink bow tie that matched the wrist corsages he'd presented them both when he'd picked them up. When they'd first arrived at the school, the three of them had had their picture taken at the photo area under a balloon archway and a banner declaring "Hundred Acres High School Junior Prom 1986." Lucas had stood in the middle, an arm slung casually over each girl's shoulders, and Megan had noticed he smelled good too. Probably his daddy's expensive cologne, but still.

"Finally," he said. "I was beginning to think my dates had ditched me. I was just about to send out a search party."

Megan and Rue were just friends with Lucas, but he'd taken to calling them both his dates this evening, and Megan felt like giggling every time he said it.

"What did I tell you?" Rue said, rolling her eyes at Megan. "We can't even pee in peace."

Lucas grinned and handed them both a drink.

"Here you go," he said. "Rumor has it, Rudy Turner emptied a fifth of JD into one of the punch bowls when Mr. Jackson was distracted. It's got a hell of a kick to it."

"Excellent," Rue said. She tossed back the drink in one go, while Megan sipped hers. It tasted almost as bad as the restroom vodka.

As she went to dump the empty cup on the nearest table, one of Rue's spiky stilettos skidded on the polished gym floor, and she grabbed hold of Lucas's tux sleeve to steady herself. Megan guessed Rue had drunk a fair amount of her mom's booze before she'd filled the flask at home earlier.

The band launched into a cover of "Alive and Kicking" by Simple Minds, and Rue squealed something about it being her favorite song and dragged Lucas onto the dance floor. Megan noticed she hadn't let go of his arm after her near fall. She slumped into a seat, drank some more of the revolting punch, and felt a bit weird as she watched her two best friends wrap their arms around each other.

As the song played, Lucas and Rue got even closer. Rue's hips jutted suggestively from side to side, pink taffeta and satin swishing in time with the music, her eyes never leaving Lucas's, and his eyes never leaving hers. By the time their bodies were pressed tight together, the heat was practically radiating off them.

Megan could only look on in horror, already knowing what was coming even before it happened, and then the band's singer reached the *Ooh oh oh oh* part of the song, and Lucas and Rue were kissing, and it was so much more than just a kiss. It was a kiss filled with the kind of passion and longing that said they'd been waiting for the moment to happen forever. The kind of kiss where you forgot the rest of the world existed. The kind of kiss where you forgot that other people were watching.

But plenty of folks were watching.

Two girls from Megan's chemistry class sat across the table, eyes bulging, and mouthed the word *wow* to each other. Mrs. DePalma stood at the edge of the dance floor with her lips pursed and her arms crossed and threw a worried glance in the direction of Mr. Jackson, who just smiled and shrugged like it was no big deal.

But it was a big deal. At least, it was to Megan.

She looked at her hand, still holding the punch, and noticed for the first time how the pink wrist corsage gifted to her by Lucas clashed with her own dress but was a perfect match for the one Rue wore, and Megan knew his choice of color had been no accident.

What else had she missed? Had there been stolen glances or light touches that lingered a little too long? Crackling electricity flowing between Lucas and Rue that she had been too stupidly oblivious to notice? Tears pricked Megan's eyes as she realized, yes, the signs had been there for months, and she had just been too dumb to see them.

She ripped off the corsage and threw it on the table. Fled the gym and kept running until she burst through the exit doors and was out in the school's parking lot. Megan gulped down cool air and wiped hot tears from her cheeks. Doubled over and retched. Bile tasting of vodka and whiskey burned the back of her throat.

She clutched her stomach and felt like she was actually going to throw up, and it dawned on her that there was something else, other than nausea, making her gut churn.

Then she realized what it was.

Jealousy.

7

JESSICA

As she sat in the prison visiting room, Jessica pictured herself emptying all the dollar bills out of Rose Dalton's brown envelope and watching helplessly as they swirled around in the breeze before being carried away, one by one, out of her reach.

She knew now that she wouldn't be getting her hands on a single cent of that money.

Rue Hunter had as good as confessed to double murder once again, more than thirty years later, so there was no case here for Jessica. She was just glad she hadn't yet told Ed about the unexpected windfall before it was snatched away from him. Hadn't gotten the old guy's hopes up for nothing.

"So, what you're saying is, you did kill Megan and Lucas? Okay, I think we're done here."

Jessica began to rise from the chair.

"What I'm saying is, it's what I believed for a long time. Now? Now, I'm not so sure."

Jessica lowered herself slowly back into the seat, sat back with her arms crossed, and regarded Rue from across the table.

"You're not sure?" she asked. "How does that work exactly? Surely, you're guilty or innocent. Which one is it?"

Rue showed Jessica the upturned palms of her hands. "Honestly? I don't know. Maybe I did do it. Maybe I didn't. I don't remember what happened."

"Why did you think you were guilty?"

Rue laughed bitterly. "I guess that cop psychologist was pretty convincing. A daddy who split town and abandoned us before I was even born. A drunk for a mother who cared more about getting laid than her own kids. An older sister who was smart and conscientious and hardworking, whereas I was a hot mess. According to that head doc, I had a lot of rage inside of me just waiting to come out. It wasn't my fault, he said, just a really shit set of circumstances that led to something bad happening. He also told me I'd feel much better once I confessed."

"And did you feel better?"

Rue gazed around the stark cinder block room, at the paint flaking off the walls and the ripped chairs, and tried to make a sweeping gesture that was hampered by the metal restraints.

"Oh sure," she said. "Best thing I ever did. This place is just like Canyon Ranch."

"You confessed because a police psychologist convinced you that you were guilty?"

Rue stared down at her hands, picked at a jagged fingernail. She shook her head.

"It wasn't just down to the things he said to me. There's the flashbacks and the nightmares too."

"Tell me about those."

Rue nodded and looked up at Jessica. "Did you ever have one of those View-Master toys as a kid?"

Jessica shook her head. "I don't think so."

"The one I had was this red plastic thing," Rue said. "I think my mom bought it for, like, fifty cents from a yard sale. It had a reel of seven or eight photos. You looked through it like a set of binoculars and clicked to see each image. That's what it's like whenever I close my eyes and think of that night. It's like clicking through a bunch of images on a View-Master, only, instead of pictures of the Taj Mahal or the Eiffel Tower, I see snapshots of terrible things. Sex and violence. Blood and death. It's the same when I go to sleep every night. I've had the same goddamn nightmare for more than thirty years."

Unbidden, terrible images flashed in front of Jessica's own eyes. Her mom, Eleanor, lying on a cream carpet, surrounded by blood and red wine. Her dad, Tony, lifeless on the kitchen floor, his lips already blue. Both her parents taken from her more than two decades apart.

"These images you see?" Jessica asked. "Are you talking about memories?"

Rue frowned. "I think so. That's what I always thought they were anyway. I mean, what else could they be?"

"What do you see exactly?"

Rue squeezed her eyes shut now, as though calling up the pictures on that imaginary View-Master. The one that held a gruesome gallery only she could see.

"He's wearing a black-and-white plaid shirt and blue jeans," she said. "The jeans are down, around his knees, and his ass is exposed. He's sweating. He's on top of her, and her hand is in his hair."

Rue opened her eyes and stared at her. The woman's eyes were dry, but Jessica thought they had a haunted look about them.

"What else?" she asked.

Rue paused a beat or two. Outside the visitors' room, Jessica could hear cell doors slamming. Lots of yelling. A male voice told someone called Jenkins to settle down. Jenkins told the guard to go fuck himself. Jessica didn't know how anyone could sleep long enough in a place like this to have nightmares.

Rue said, "I see the knife in my hand. The blade tearing through the material of the shirt. There's so much blood. Lots of screaming." She swallowed hard. "Then I see Lucas and Megan's faces. Eyes wide

49

open and staring at me. Accusing. Like they're saying, 'Why did you do this to us, Rue?'"

Jessica glanced up at Pedro. His eyes were fixed straight ahead at the wall above her head. He showed no reaction to Rue's words. There was no shock or horror or disgust. She figured the guards in this place must hear, and see, a hell of a lot worse all the time.

"What about the nightmares?"

"The same kind of thing," Rue said. "Except it's like watching a movie instead of looking at pictures. It always starts in the car. It's a hot night, but it's cool inside the car because of the AC. I'm drinking beer and smoking weed and having a good time. I'm singing along to a song on the radio, a big hit that year. I found out later the song is called 'I Just Died in Your Arms Tonight' by Cutting Crew."

"How apt," Jessica said. "You're not driving?"

"No, I never got my license. Didn't have a car."

"Whose car is it? Who's driving?"

Rue smiled sadly and shrugged. "I don't remember. I think it was a guy. In the dream, I can hear him laughing."

"What about the cops? Did they try to find the driver?"

"They seemed real interested at first," she said. "Asked lots of questions. I told them what I told you. I couldn't remember anything about the guy or the car. Except for a key chain, shaped like a four-leaf clover, hanging from the rearview mirror. Then, all of a sudden, the cops dropped their interest in the car and the driver. Later, they told the jury at the sentencing trial the driver didn't exist, that I'd made him up in an attempt to have someone else to share the blame with."

Jessica frowned. "Seems pretty weird to me that the cops never properly followed up on this guy. That they wrote off the possibility of someone else being involved so readily."

Rue just shrugged.

"Rose told me you'd been drinking in Cooper's bar," Jessica said. "Did you leave with anyone?"

"I don't remember."

"Did the guy in the car take you all the way to Devil's Drop? Or did he drop you off someplace nearby?"

"I don't remember."

"What about the stolen jewelry and cash? What happened to them?"

"I don't remember."

"Five more minutes," said the female guard.

Jessica sighed. "I think we're pretty much done here."

Rue said, "I'm sorry, Jessica. My memory of that night is just so fucked up. That's why Rose wanted to hire you. I guess she thought you might be able to find out the answers to some of those questions."

Jessica said, "What I don't understand is how you can remember a key chain and a specific song and what Lucas was wearing, but you don't remember who you were with? If you killed two people?"

"Do you drink alcohol or get high, Jessica?"

Jessica narrowed her eyes, wondering where this was going.

"I like a decent Scotch. Drugs? No."

"I used to get drunk all the time," Rue said. "I'd steal from my mother's liquor stash, persuade guys in bars to buy me drinks. I suppose I was following in my mother's footsteps in that respect. Plenty of drugs too. Weed, speed, even coke if I could get my hands on it. The path I was on back then, if I hadn't been sent to prison, I'm sure I'd be dead by now." Rue laughed. It was a sad, hollow sound. "I guess it's ironic that being sentenced to death is what's kept me alive for so long."

"Uh-huh."

"I guess what I'm trying to say is, have you ever been so blackout drunk that you don't remember how you got home or who the guy lying in bed next to you is? Then, while your head's down a toilet bowl, and you're throwing up the contents of your belly, flashes of the night before come back to you? Maybe you got in a fight or thrown out of a bar and you don't even remember until someone reminds you what happened."

Jessica had been in that movie more times than she'd care to admit, especially in the weeks right after her father's death. Her eyes stung suddenly, and she told herself it was because of the strong disinfectant used to mop the room. The smell reminded her of public swimming pools she'd visited as a kid with her dad.

"Sure, I've had the odd blowout," she said. "Maybe once or twice when I was younger. Who hasn't? But I think I'd remember if I killed someone."

Rue held her eye, a small smile playing on her lips.

"But would you, Jessica? Would you really?"

"Time's up," said the female guard. "Let's go, Hunter."

Rue nodded and stood, shackles jangling, as Pedro opened the door behind her. As she turned to leave, she glanced back at Jessica.

"What you do next is up to you," Rue said. "But just ask yourself one thing."

"What's that?"

"If I didn't do it, who did? Maybe the guy's dead or in prison or living in another state. Or maybe he's still walking the streets of Hundred Acres among folks just like you, and you don't even know it."

8
JESSICA

A home-cooked dinner and a glass of red wine at Pryce's apartment were just what Jessica needed after a long drive back from the prison.

Once the lasagna was eaten and the salad bowl was cleared, the detective popped open a second bottle of Barolo.

"No more for me." Jessica covered the rim of the glass with her hand. "Don't forget—I have to drive back to Hundred Acres tonight."

"Why not spend the night here?" Pryce's wife, Angie, said. "The sofa bed in the living room is pretty comfortable. Isn't that right, Jase?"

Pryce said, "Oh, sure. Like sleeping on a cloud."

Jessica laughed, wondering how many nights Pryce had spent on the couch when he'd been foolish enough to fight with his wife.

"Yeah, stay over, Jessica," said Pryce's teenage daughter, Dionne. "It'll be so much fun."

Jessica thought about the offer. She'd never spent the night at Pryce's place before, but the wine was going down nicely, she was enjoying the conversation, and the thought of at least an hour's drive ahead of her later in the evening didn't really appeal.

"Only if you're sure?"

"We're sure," Pryce said. "It's decided. Top up?"

"Sounds good to me."

Pryce filled the glass, while Angie looked at Jessica with a mischievous smile.

"What?" Jessica asked.

Angie said, "We thought you might have brought Dylan along with you tonight. We're dying to meet him."

"Another time, maybe. It just feels a bit too soon to be introducing him to folk."

"Too soon?" Angie laughed. "Honey, it's been six months."

Jessica smiled and shrugged. "I guess."

"Well, if things don't work out with Dylan, there's always Vic," Angie said lightly. "He's still single."

Vic Medina was Pryce's partner at Hollywood Division. The two cops had worked together for more than a decade.

Dionne scrunched up her face. "Vic? Oh, gross."

Pryce said, "He's forty-three. He's far too old for her."

Jessica said, "I'm almost thirty. I'm probably too old for him."

Dionne turned to Jessica. "What about Dylan? Is he gross too? Is that why you don't want us to meet him?"

"Dionne!" Angie said. "Don't be so rude."

"It's fine," Jessica said. "And no, he's not gross." She winked at Dionne. "He's actually pretty cute."

"Is he an asshole, then?"

"Language, young lady," Pryce chided.

Dionne rolled her eyes. "Whatever, Daddy. I'm almost seventeen."

Jessica laughed. "He's not an asshole either. He's a nice guy."

It was true. Dylan McDonagh was good people, as everyone in Hundred Acres kept telling her. Thirty-three, definitely cute like she'd just told Dionne, no kids or previous marriages (just one crazy ex-girlfriend). Best of all, he owned Randy's Diner, which meant free coffee and cheeseburgers whenever Jessica wanted them. Great on paper. Pretty good in the bedroom too. There was no doubt he checked a lot of boxes.

But something was holding Jessica back—and she knew Dylan could sense it too. He was aware of her past, of how she'd been through a particularly tough time right before she'd arrived in Hundred Acres, how she still had problems trusting people. So he didn't push her too hard on why it felt like there was such a distance between them even when their bodies were wrapped tightly together. About why she rarely spent the night. Why she never referred to him as her boyfriend. Why she didn't invite him over to friends' places for dinner.

Then, about a month ago, he'd come right out and asked her if there was someone else. She'd told him no, absolutely not. Then she'd kissed him hard to stop him asking any more questions. But, even as he was pushing up her dress and sliding down her panties, and she was climbing on top of him, Jessica's thoughts had turned to a different pair of hands on her body, a different mouth pressed against her own. A late summer's night in Hollywood not so long ago. A smile as dirty as a slow striptease that she couldn't stop thinking about.

Afterward, Jessica and Dylan had clung to each other, both of them slick with sweat and trying to catch their breath and shaking a little because of the sheer intensity of what had just happened. Later, when she'd drifted off to sleep, one of the few occasions she'd agreed to spend the night, Jessica had wondered who she was trying to convince—Dylan or herself?

Her face flamed as red as the Barolo at the memory, and she took a long drink of wine. Angie noticed her discomfort and mistook it for embarrassment at Dionne's questions.

"Stop teasing Jessica," she said to her daughter. "How would you like it if we quizzed you about your boyfriend?"

Dionne shrugged. "Wouldn't bother me."

Pryce said, "What boyfriend?"

Dionne ignored him, nudged Jessica, and grinned. "I haven't told you yet, have I? His name is Jayden, and he's superhot. Not as hot as Justin Bieber, obviously, but still hot. I'll show you his Instagram photos later."

"How long has this been going on?" Pryce asked.

"About a week," Angie said.

"Why am I only hearing about it now?"

Dionne said, "Because you're always at work."

Pryce frowned. "You're too young for a boyfriend."

"Seriously, Daddy? I'm almost seventeen."

"So you keep saying. And you'll be grounded until you're twenty-one if you keep up the attitude."

Angie said, "Okay, let's save the boyfriend talk for another time. I'm sure Jessica doesn't want to spend her Saturday evening listening to you two arguing over Jayden Schultz. This is supposed to be a fun evening."

Pryce said, "Jayden Schultz? How're you spelling that?"

"*Daddy!* Don't even think about running a check on Jayden at work."

Jessica laughed. Despite Angie's concerns, it was one of the most enjoyable evenings she'd had in a long time. She realized just how much she missed being part of a normal family. How much she missed her own father and all the silly quarrels they used to have over inappropriate boyfriends and bad language at the dinner table.

Angie cleared the table and then retreated to the kitchen with Dionne to wash the dishes, leaving Pryce and Jessica to talk shop. Pryce scraped back his chair and picked up the bottle of red.

"Let's finish this out on the deck. It's a beautiful night."

Jessica collected her half-filled glass and sipped the wine as she followed him through the living room. She felt a little woozy from the booze and remembered she hadn't slept much before making the early-morning trip to Chowchilla. Pryce pulled back the slider, and they stepped out into a balmy evening.

Los Feliz Towers was a condo community northwest of downtown and practically on the doorstep of Griffith Park, nestled in the Santa Monica Mountains. Jessica was struck, as always, by how spectacular the view was this high up. But it was a view she was willing to enjoy only from the safe distance of the rear of the deck. She wasn't good with heights. On her first visit to Pryce's place, she'd looked over the ledge to the sidewalk below, and her stomach had dropped faster than the condo's elevator.

The sky blazed shades of coral and peach now as the sun set over the City of Angels. Shadows crawled across the sprawling chaparral terrain of the park, and the Griffith Observatory glistened like a pearl brooch pinned to thick dusky velvet. A warm wind whipped Jessica's hair around her face. She drained what was left of the wine. As Pryce provided a generous refill and topped off his own drink, Jessica stifled a yawn.

"Sorry," she said. "Late night at work and an early start this morning."

"Oh yeah? How come?"

"Long drive north to Chowchilla for this case I'm working."

Pryce frowned. "Chowchilla? Not much there other than a prison."

"Exactly. I was visiting an inmate."

"I assumed it was a Hundred Acres investigation."

"It is," she said. "A woman by the name of Rose Dalton wants me to look into her sister's case. Thinks she might be innocent, even though the sister confessed to a double murder years ago. Took place in Hundred Acres back in '87. Pretty exciting, huh?"

Pryce said nothing, and Jessica glanced at him. His jaw was clenched, and his eyes were as dark as Griffith Park in the distance. He walked over to the ledge and stood there, his back to her. She could tell from the rise and fall of his shoulders that he was breathing hard.

"Pryce? You okay?"

"Please tell me Rue Hunter isn't your client."

"Well, technically, her sister is my client. I take it you know the case?"

Pryce finished what was left of his wine. Turned to face her.

"Oh yeah, I know it all right." His voice was low and furious. "And I want you to stay the fuck away from the case—and from Rue Hunter. You hear me, Jessica?"

Jessica was stunned. She'd never heard Pryce use such profanity before. Never seen him this angry.

"I appreciate the concern, but I'm a big girl, okay? I can handle it. Whether she's guilty or not, it's something interesting to get my teeth into."

"She's guilty as hell."

"Maybe she is, but Rose Dalton is offering a lot of cash to find out for sure. You know money's been tight at the agency for a while. I'm not going to turn it down."

"I'm not asking, Jessica. I'm telling you. Drop the case."

Jessica's own temper flared.

"Why the hell should I?" she demanded. "I'm not Dionne. You don't get to tell me what to do. What's it to you if I work the case or not anyway? Why's it such a big deal?"

"The guy who put Rue Hunter away was my old partner. That's why it's a big deal."

"What? Charlie Holten was your partner?"

Pryce nodded. "Before I partnered with Medina, and after Charlie left Hundred Acres. I was a rookie at the time, not long out of the academy. Charlie taught me a lot, what it meant to be a good cop. And he was one of the best, Jessica. Digging up the past, trying to throw doubt on his investigation? It's like questioning a cop's integrity. Questioning his entire career."

"Shit, Pryce. I had no idea."

"So you'll drop the case?"

"I can't. I already signed the contract."

Pryce closed his eyes and massaged his temples with his thumb and forefinger.

"Fuck," he whispered. He looked at Jessica. "What's Crozier saying about all this? I can't believe he's happy to let you shit all over Charlie's reputation."

Realization dawned on Jessica.

"That's the Hundred Acres connection," she said. "Holten is the reason you know Ed. He's the friend of a friend."

"That's right," Pryce said. "Crozier and I met at the funeral. We've kept in touch ever since."

"The funeral?"

Ten stories below, Jessica could hear the hiss of the evening traffic cruising along Hillhurst. An engine idling, a car door slamming, a burst of laughter from somewhere down on the sidewalk. Folks enjoying their Saturday night.

"Charlie Holten is dead," Pryce said. "My partner was murdered."

9

HOLTEN

1987

Charlie Holten whacked the plastic ice tray hard against the tiny kitch-enette counter and emptied the cubes onto the dish towel he'd spread out on top. He bunched the towel together, the ice snapping and crack-ing inside, and twisted the top tight. Held the makeshift ice pack gin-gerly against his right cheek with a wince as he made his way back to his desk.

The desk's surface was covered with wobbly stacks of case files; a couple photos of his wife, Maggie, in decorative pewter frames; and a large blotter filled with notes and doodles and ink splotches. There was also an open bottle of Jim Beam and a chubby tumbler with a tiny pool of amber in the bottom, the remnants of the double he'd insisted his deputy, Pat McDonagh, drink before sending him home.

Holten removed a couple ice cubes from the towel and dropped them in the tumbler. Poured himself a generous measure. More gener-ous than the one he'd thrust into McDonagh's hands. Two-thirds of the bottle was gone, the bourbon purchased around four months ago and kept in his drawer to toast making arrests and closing cases or to take the edge off a particularly tough day. Today, or yesterday as it was now, had been the toughest day he had experienced in his career. Holten knew there would be more to come before this was all over.

He swallowed back some of the liquor and felt the burn in his throat and the fire in his belly, the warmth spreading through bones that had been chilled since he had first received the call from McDonagh. The bourbon would either kill him or cure him, and, the way he was feeling right now, he wasn't sure which option he preferred most.

He took another drink and held the towel against his cheek again. Some of the ice had begun to melt, and it felt wet against his skin. There was a mustiness, too, like the towel hadn't been washed properly in a while, but he was willing to tolerate the smell to savor the damp coolness. The ice pack wasn't because of the heat. At this hour, the temperature outside had dropped by at least ten degrees, the dry humidity of the day replaced by cold desert night. The ice was because he'd noticed his cheekbone was now purple and blue and swollen when he'd looked at himself in the restroom mirror.

Barb Hunter had shown up at the sheriff's station midafternoon. Drunk and outraged, having just been told about her youngest daughter's arrest by her eldest daughter when she'd finally returned home from her latest lover's place in last night's clothes. The clothes might even have been from the night before that, Holten thought.

Barb had been ripe with stale body odor and old perfume. Her breath sour from vodka and God knows what else when she had gotten right in his face and screamed at him. The woman had been like a wild animal, snarling and scratching and biting and spitting. Holten was a big guy, and Barb Hunter was a small woman, but she'd managed to land a surprisingly hard punch with her left hand that any amateur southpaw this side of the Vegas rings would've been proud of before McDonagh had dragged her off him.

Right now, the quiet stillness of the office was being disturbed by the sound of Barb Hunter's snoring drifting along the hallway from the detox cell, which was just a fancy way of saying the drunk tank. Holten reckoned she must've spent as many nights sleeping it off in that cell as she had getting it on in the beds of strangers she picked up in bars in neighboring towns.

The snoring was really pissing him off. It was loud and wet, with a rhythmic rattle that set his teeth on edge. The deep sleep of the intoxicated. Holten wasn't even close to being drunk enough for slumber to claim him tonight, even though he had been awake for—he glanced at his watch—twenty-one hours now. At least the snoring meant Barb Hunter hadn't choked on her own vomit. She'd thrown up in the tank's toilet bowl twice before passing out.

Holten refilled his glass and considered whether he was drinking only because of a particularly tough day or partly because he was also celebrating making an arrest. He thought of the scene up at Devil's Drop and shook his head. Definitely not a celebration. There would be no winners in this case.

He thought back to when he'd first been told about the murders—a matter of hours ago, but it felt like a lifetime now. Holten had been asleep in bed when McDonagh radioed in the news; he hadn't heard the static hiss and crackle of the police scanner he kept at home.

After his shift had finished at ten, he'd joined Maggie at the Donaldsons' place two doors down. They'd hosted a barbecue earlier in the evening for a bunch of couples in the neighborhood, and by the time Holten had arrived, the charcoal had been smoldering for hours, thin wisps of smoke drifting through the grill. Leftover chicken thighs and corn dogs and potato salad were congealing on paper plates; a faint aroma of grease and charred meat hung in the air. But there were still plenty of beers in the coolers, and chilled chardonnay for the ladies, and then the whiskey came out, and it was after one a.m. before Holten and Maggie, and Steve and Heather James, called it a night.

Holten had hit the sack straightaway, out for the count as soon as his head was on the pillow. The deep sleep of the intoxicated. Unaware that he would soon be breaking the news to Steve and Heather James that their youngest boy was dead.

Maggie had gently roused him, a soft hand on his shoulder, a worried expression on her face, as she'd handed over the police scanner.

"It's Pat," she'd said. "It's almost three. Something must have happened, Charlie."

He'd listened in disbelief as McDonagh described the scene at Devil's Drop. Then the numbness had subsided, and Holten had jumped out of bed, pulling on clothes and shoes as he'd headed for the front door and the car parked in the driveway.

He was undoubtedly well over the legal limit for driving, but it was the middle of the night in Hundred Acres, and the streets were dark, empty ribbons. So still and quiet that he could have been the only person on earth. Who was going to pull him over anyway? The only cop in town on duty was at Devil's Drop protecting a murder scene. And what he saw there sobered up Holten pretty damn fast in any case.

Both kids were in the back seat of Lucas James's burgundy Toyota Cressida.

Lucas was sitting upright, head back against the padded headrest, eyes wide open and unseeing. One stab wound in the groin area and three to the back between the shoulder blades. Megan Meeks, whose mother, Patty, had made the initial call to the station house, was hanging halfway out the rear door on the passenger side. Head upside down, her long, dark hair tickling the dirt, blood smeared around her mouth like a child who had badly applied her mom's lipstick. One fatal stab wound to the heart.

The medical examiner, the police photographer, and the rest of the crime scene unit would take at least an hour to reach Hundred Acres. Holiday weekend. Holten had waited in McDonagh's cruiser with his deputy. They both sat up front, McDonagh behind the wheel, Holten in the passenger seat, engine off, not talking. The black-and-white Crown Vic pointing in the direction of the hundred-foot drop that provided the make-out spot with its alliterative name. Like a couple on a date at a drive-in movie, only there was no big screen, and no popcorn and soda, and no box office picture. Only inky blackness straight ahead and the grisly horror show thirty yards to their right that neither of them wanted a repeat viewing of.

Now, sitting in his office, Holten swallowed what was left of the bourbon, eased himself wearily out of the chair, and followed the sound of the snoring down the hallway. There were three cells, each with a white plastic sign screwed above the welded steel doors: DETOX, FEMALE, MALE.

He stopped in front of the detox cell, pulled down the hatch cover, and peered inside. Barb Hunter was on the cot, on her back, one arm thrown carelessly behind her head, sharp collarbones vibrating with each almighty snore. She was skinny, with loose, wrinkled flesh hanging off the bones of her upper arms. Her short dress had ridden up above dimpled thighs; one of her legs flopped over the side of the cot. Holten noticed the woman wasn't wearing any underwear. He quickly closed the hatch cover and latched it. Moved along to the next cell door, this one marked FEMALE.

He looked inside. Rue Hunter was awake, sitting on the cot, back against the wall, pressed tight into the corner. Hands clasped tightly around bony knees pulled up to her chin. Watching him, watching her. She didn't move or say anything or show any emotion on that pale face framed with stringy, dirty blonde hair. Just looked at him with those brown eyes in a way that gave Holten the unnerving feeling that she could see right inside him, knew exactly what he was thinking.

And what he was thinking of was a late summer's day about seven or eight years ago. Not long after he'd moved to Hundred Acres from Hollywood, swapping seedy, neon-soaked nights with LAPD Vice, and its whores and dealers and meth addicts, for the sheriff's gig in a sleepy town where nothing bad was ever supposed to happen.

Holten and Maggie were both almost forty when they'd met, and they had married quickly. Back then, they were still hopeful of conceiving, and Hundred Acres seemed like a better place to raise a child than the city. A year into their marriage, just the sight of babies and kids could turn Holten's insides to mush, fantasizing that would be him and Maggie one day—pushing a stroller down Main Street while grocery shopping, family days in the park, Little League games and school shows. So when he'd spotted the girl on her own by the side of the road, he'd parked the cruiser, wanting to make sure she was okay.

She was about ten years old, maybe a shade older. Sitting cross-legged on the dry, baked mud, around fifty yards from her front porch, gazing down at something cradled in slim arms burned pink by the blazing sun. The position of her body meant Holten's view of what she was hugging to her chest was blocked, and he'd assumed it was a baby doll, even though she was a little old for such toys.

He'd gotten out of the cruiser and walked toward her, and she'd tilted up her face enough to show him empty brown eyes and sharp features framed by sun-bleached blonde hair. He'd glanced down and saw that she wasn't holding a baby doll, and he'd almost thrown up, right there, onto the packed-dirt sidewalk.

In her arms was some kind of roadkill. A raccoon or a squirrel maybe. It was hard to tell for sure. All he could see was a mangled crush of light fur and dark flesh and pale bone and wet blood. She was caressing the carcass tenderly, like a new mom trying to soothe an irate infant. Then she'd put a bloodied hand to her forehead to block out the sun, a carmine smear scarring an eyebrow, and she'd looked up at Holten and said, "Why is there always so much blood?"

Later, Holten had found out all about the Hunters. How the daddy split town years ago and the mother was a lush, and the youngest kid had been sweet once but was now just plain odd. And he'd felt sorry for the oldest girl, a teenager who, by all accounts, was the only normal one in the family.

The same dead brown eyes stared back at him now. Holten fixed the hatch cover back in place and stood with his back against the cell door, breathing heavily. He was still waiting for an out-of-town latents unit to match the prints on the knife with the ones they'd taken earlier from Rue Hunter when she'd been arrested.

But Charlie Holten knew in his heart the girl was a killer. Didn't need tests to prove it to him. He could see it in her eyes, feel it in his gut. He didn't doubt it for a minute.

He also didn't doubt that she knew that he knew what she was.

And, for some reason, it was a thought that terrified him.

10

JESSICA

Jessica had slept in her truck in the Los Feliz Towers underground parking lot after the heated exchange with Pryce. A sleepover at the detective's apartment was out of the question following their argument, and she'd not felt sober enough to get behind the wheel.

After a rough night, she faced the drive back to the Antelope Valley with a takeout coffee and a cigarette, the light Sunday-morning traffic at least making the journey more bearable. The smog gradually burned off to reveal a gorgeous, cloudless day, but not even the free-moving freeways and California sunshine could brighten her dark mood as she thought about the pain in Pryce's eyes when he'd spoken about Charlie Holten's murder.

A bullet to the head.

No witnesses.

Still unsolved.

Upsetting the Hundred Acres locals by digging up the past was one thing, but she was pissed at herself for ripping open painful old wounds for Pryce.

As she drove, she felt the patch of bare skin on the inside of her right wrist pulse and throb. After her father had died, Jessica had found a strange sort of comfort in the tattoo artist's needle. The sharp sting had pierced through the numbness that had followed Tony's death. The physical pain, a pain that she was in control of, had been an almost addictive distraction from the hollow feeling of loss that still hadn't faded almost three years later.

She was glad the tattoo parlors she cruised past were still shuttered this early on a weekend. No way to give in to temptation and quiet the small square of flesh that screamed for the sweet relief of the electric needle.

Jessica pulled into the parking lot in front of Randy's and parked next to Dylan's beat-up old station wagon. The diner had been a part of the town since the fifties and had been snapped up at a good price by Dylan, with the help of a loan from his father, following the death of the original owner, Randy Brooks, eight years ago.

It was just past nine, and Randy's was still quiet ahead of the brunch crowd. The only customers were an elderly couple at a table in the rear of the room, the morning papers spread out on the Formica in front of them.

A ceiling fan whirred softly overhead, and easy listening classics played on a radio with the sound turned down low behind the counter. Most of the noise came from the kitchen, where Freddie, the cook, was prepping for brunch. The metallic clatter and banging of pans and the hiss and spit of the grill drifted through the open service hatch, along with the smell of food cooking that made Jessica's stomach growl.

Dylan stood behind the counter, wiping down the surface, with a look on his face that suggested friendly customer service wasn't on the menu today. At least not where she was concerned anyway. He glanced up briefly as Jessica dumped her bag on the floor and climbed onto a stool in front of him, then went back to his cleaning.

"I assume I'm still on the shit list?" she said.

A shrug. "The counter won't clean itself."

"Looks pretty clean to me."

Dylan sighed and tossed the rag aside. Pulled a mug from a hook on the wall behind him and filled it with strong black coffee from an almost-empty pot that had clearly been providing the elderly couple with their morning caffeine hit. He slid it toward her.

"You look rough," he said.

"Gee, thanks."

It was true, though. Jessica's pants and tee were rumpled, her short blonde hair greasier than Freddie's pan, yesterday's makeup smudged under red-rimmed eyes. She felt as bad as she looked. Her neck was stiff and her back ached from the impromptu sleepover in the Silverado. She took a sip of the coffee and pushed it away. It was lukewarm.

"Where have you been?" Dylan asked. "I stopped by the trailer yesterday afternoon, and you weren't there."

"That's because I haven't been home since yesterday morning."

She saw him stiffen, and his eyebrows lifted a fraction.

"Okay."

"Relax, Dylan, I haven't been out partying or picking up strange guys. I was working a case. Spent most of the day on the road, driving to Chowchilla to visit the women's prison up there."

"I'm surprised they let you back out again."

She rolled her eyes. "You're a real funny guy; anyone ever tell you that?"

Dylan smirked. *Almost a smile,* Jessica thought. Definitely thawing.

She went on, "Then I stayed over at Pryce's apartment after dinner. Or, to be precise, I stayed over in his parking lot. We had a fight."

"You seem to have a habit of pissing people off, Miss Shaw. What did you fight about?"

"This case I'm working on. The reason why I was in Chowchilla."

"Want to talk about it?"

"Sure, but first I want something to eat. I'm starving."

Dylan stepped over to the open service hatch.

"Hey, Freddie, can you stick some breakfast on for Jessica, please?"

"Sure thing, boss," she heard Freddie yell back. "Be with you in five."

"And some fresh coffee too," Jessica said, sliding the mug toward Dylan. "This sucks."

He smiled and shook his head. Tossed the tepid contents down the small sink behind the counter and set about making a fresh pot.

"Michelle's been looking for you," he said. "She seemed real pissed. Says you got her fired."

Dylan had asked Jessica out two days after she'd arrived in Hundred Acres—and just a week after breaking up with Michelle. With his fiery red hair, pale skin, blue eyes, and freckles, he wasn't Jessica's usual type, but he was cute in a Damian Lewis kind of way, so she'd agreed to the date. Michelle had never forgiven Jessica for wrecking her hopes of a reconciliation with her man, and there had been bad blood between the two women ever since.

"Michelle is a thief who got herself fired," Jessica snapped.

Dylan raised his hands.

"Hey, don't shoot the messenger."

"Did you know she was stealing from Jed Lockerman?"

"Nope."

His tone was light, but something in Dylan's expression made Jessica think he knew exactly what his ex-girlfriend had been up to while they were still together. But she didn't challenge him on it. She was tired and wasn't in the mood for another argument. Dylan placed Jessica's breakfast in front of her, and she shoved a forkful of pancake and bacon into her mouth and said nothing.

Dylan went on, "You also missed all the excitement yesterday. TV crews in town, interviewing folks about the murders that happened here back in '87. Anyone ever tell you about it? A teenage girl killed her two best friends up at Devil's Drop. Seems like she's gonna be executed soon. I heard most of the reporters got doors slammed in their faces, though. Have left town already."

Jessica chewed, then swallowed, took a sip of coffee. It tasted much better this time. Then she told Dylan all about Rose Dalton turning up at the detective agency, the prison visit with Rue Hunter, signing the contract and pocketing the twenty-five grand, the argument with Pryce because of his old partner's involvement in the original investigation. By the time she'd finished speaking, Dylan was frowning, concern written on his face.

"What?" she asked.

"You do know my dad worked the case too? He was the one who found the bodies."

Jessica suppressed a sigh. Having grown up in New York, she still couldn't get used to small-town life. The Hundred Acres locals all seemed to be connected to each other somehow. Here, everyone made it their business to know everyone else's business. Heck, you couldn't even break wind without someone two streets away knowing about it. It drove Jessica crazy.

"No, I didn't know he worked the case," she said. "But I guess it's not a surprise, seeing as he's been a cop here forever."

"He'll be pissed at you too."

"Yeah? Well, Pat can join the club. I might start handing out membership cards."

Dylan smiled. "And you'll probably get doors slammed in your face, just like those reporters."

"We'll see."

"Don't say I didn't warn you."

Dylan picked up the fresh coffee pot and wandered over to the elderly couple to offer them both refills. Jessica heard the three of them chatting and went back to eating her breakfast. She finished the pancakes and bacon, pushed the dirty plate to one side. Her cell phone pinged and vibrated across the counter.

"Who's texting you?" Dylan asked from over her shoulder. She hadn't heard him come up behind her.

"No one," she said. "It's a news alert. I set them up on my cell phone for any new stories on the Hunter case."

71

She picked up the phone and read the message on the screen.

Patty Meeks exclusive! Victim's mother blasts "evil" Rue Hunter ahead of killer's execution.

Jessica spun around on the stool and faced Dylan. Broke into a grin and held up the phone for him to see.

"Looks like someone in town is willing to talk about the murders."

11

JESSICA

Patty Meeks still lived in the same house she once shared with her daughter, Megan, before the murders took place.

It was a single-story country rancher on a quiet street that fell someplace between the good side and bad side of town. A wide, low structure with wood siding painted pale yellow and topped with a once-white sloping roof. The lemon-meringue-pie house stood lonely on an acre of land, ringed by six-foot chicken wire fencing. A **BEWARE OF THE DOG** sign was nailed to the front gate, but, thankfully, Jessica didn't spot any mutts prowling the yard.

Like most properties in Hundred Acres, there was no neat patch of lawn or vibrant sprouting flower beds or pretty rosebushes. Just a scrawny, naked tree without any leaves and some determined weeds sprouting from the dirt between gravel stones.

Jessica wondered if the house had always been this color or if the sickly hue had come after Megan's death. Lemon slicked over gravestone gray or bland beige in an attempt to add some cheer to dark times. Maybe it had worked once, but not anymore. The place was tired and had an air of inevitable sadness about it, like a faded Hollywood starlet long past her prime.

The place reminded Jessica of the house she'd shared with Tony in Blissville before he had died of a massive heart attack. They were both modest and a little rough around the edges, but Jessica thought the sorrow that filled every corner of a home following the loss of a loved one was what the two properties probably most had in common.

She sat behind the wheel of the Silverado and read the news article again. The reporter had done a hell of a job of spinning a handful of quotes into an eight-hundred-word piece. Patty Meeks spoke of how the two girls had formed a strong bond since meeting on their first day of kindergarten, how she'd feared Rue Hunter was a bad influence on her daughter as they grew older, and how she blamed herself for not forbidding Megan from continuing their friendship before it had all ended in tragedy. More than thirty years had passed since the murders, but Patty Meeks told the reporter she would never be able to forgive her daughter's killer, before adding that she welcomed the state's decision to finally execute Rue Hunter.

Jessica closed the web browser on her cell phone. She hesitated briefly, then pulled up the text messages app. Scrolled through her texts until she found the one she'd received just over a month ago:

Hey Jessica, how are you doing? Let me know you're okay. Been thinking about you a lot. MC xx

Matt Connor.

A fellow private eye whom Jessica had worked with in Eagle Rock last year as she'd investigated her biological mother's unsolved murder, as well as her own disappearance as a young child. She'd allowed herself to get close to Connor before discovering he'd been deceiving her, just as she'd found out her father had also lied to her for years. It was little wonder she was now so unable to fully place her trust in any man—including Dylan.

Jessica hadn't replied to Matt Connor's text, but she hadn't deleted it either, and each time she read it, her stomach did a weird little flip. Her finger hovered over the reply button now, like it had done at least a dozen times over the last four weeks. She shook her head and dropped the cell phone into her bag. She was still embarrassed by how easily she'd fallen for Connor's charm and his lies. He didn't even know she was back in California, had no idea she was staying just over an hour away from where he was based in Venice Beach, and Jessica decided that was the way it should stay. No point getting involved again, especially not with Dylan on the scene now.

Jessica flipped down the sun visor and appraised herself in the tiny mirror. The reflection staring back at her wasn't great. She smoothed down her hair, licked a finger and wiped day-old mascara and eyeliner smudges from under her eyes. Sniffed under her armpits and decided she'd do. Then she climbed out of the truck and made her way toward Patty Meeks's house.

The sun was high and hot and stung her tired eyes. It felt heavy and uncomfortable on skin that itched for a cool shower. Jessica rehearsed in her head what she'd say if the woman opened the door. Hoped it wouldn't be slammed in her face, like Dylan had warned. The gate creaked and groaned as she unlatched it and pushed it open. She paused, listening for the sound of barking, paws slapping on dirt, a warning growl. She heard nothing and quickly crossed the front yard, opened the screen door, and rang the bell.

She heard the chimes echo inside the house, followed by light foot-steps on the hallway floor. A pause just long enough, Jessica guessed, to press an eye to the peephole and decide whether to open the door or not. Then there was the harsh scrape of metal on metal as a security chain was fastened in place, before the door opened a few inches to reveal wary eyes above the taut chain.

"If you're a reporter, I already spoke to the press. I've got nothing more to say."

The woman was soft spoken, but there was steel in her voice.

"I'm not a reporter."

"I'm not interested in buying anything either."

"I'm not selling. I'm a private detective."

"Who do you work for? What do you want?"

"I'm employed by Ed Crozier. My client is Rose Dalton. Rue Hunter's sister."

The door slammed shut before Jessica could say another word, and she stood there, stunned, thinking Dylan would be delighted to be proved right. Then she heard the jangle of the security chain being unhooked, and the door was thrown open again to reveal Patty Meeks.

The newspaper article had used an old picture of Patty and Megan in happier times. Sitting in front of a Christmas tree, holding brightly wrapped gifts up to the camera, twinkling fairy lights and gaudy decorations in the background. A lifetime ago. The story carried no recent photography, so Jessica hadn't known what to expect when she came face to face with the girl's mother. But she could see now that Patty Meeks was still a striking woman despite the quiet fury radiating off her as she stood in the doorway. In the old photograph, the pair had looked more like sisters, sharing the same dark hair and blue eyes and fine features. Even now, Jessica would have placed Patty in her late fifties, no older than sixty, had she not known her daughter would have been almost fifty herself had she still been living.

"You're working on behalf of Rue Hunter?" Patty demanded. "You have ten seconds to explain what the hell you're doing on my doorstep before I drag you off my property."

Jessica's mouth suddenly felt as dry as the arid landscape surrounding Hundred Acres. She swallowed hard, worked up some saliva, and couldn't remember a word of the speech she had rehearsed just moments earlier.

"Technically, Rue Hunter isn't my client," she said. "But, yes, I'm being paid to look into the circumstances surrounding her conviction, and the deaths of your daughter and Lucas James, on her behalf. Honestly? I don't know if she's guilty or innocent. If my investigation supports her conviction, so be it. Her sister will be given a full report to that effect. If it casts doubt on her guilt, sheds some new light on what happened that night, wouldn't you rather know the truth?"

"That monster already confessed to what she did." Patty Meeks spat the words out like they were rotten food. "She already admitted to killing my baby. What else is there to find out? There's no mystery here."

"I met with Rue Hunter yesterday," Jessica said. "She says she's no longer sure she's guilty of the crimes she was convicted of."

Patty shook her head. "She would say that, wouldn't she? I bet Rue Hunter would say just about anything to avoid being put to death now that she finally has to pay for what she did."

Jessica shrugged. "It's possible. Likely, even. But if she goes to the death chamber claiming she might be innocent, there's always going to be that lingering doubt, isn't there? That tiny chance that maybe she wasn't guilty after all. Wouldn't it be better to know for sure?"

Patty Meeks stared at her for a long moment, and Jessica fully expected to find herself facing the white wooden door again. Then the older woman gave a small nod, turned, and walked down the hallway. Jessica hesitated, then stepped over the threshold and closed the door behind her.

She followed Patty into a living room that was furnished with mismatched and outdated items but was clean and neat. Patty perched rigidly on the edge of a faded floral armchair, and Jessica faced her on a matching couch that sagged in the middle when she sat on it. There was no offer of coffee or iced tea or lemonade. This wasn't a social call, and Jessica clearly wasn't a welcome guest.

She looked around. No dog bed or toys or hairs on the couch fabric. No smell of dog either—just a vague floral scent from a plug-in air freshener puffing out a fresh burst of perfumed air at regular intervals.

"Something wrong?" Patty asked, following Jessica's gaze around the room.

"I was wondering where the dog is."

"There is no dog."

Jessica was glad. She didn't like dogs. All that sniffing and licking made her feel uncomfortable. She was scared of them too. More than she was scared of people.

"Oh, right. I saw the sign on the gate and assumed you had one."

"My partner, Allan, had a dog. They both passed a couple of years ago. Allan first, then the dog." Her eyes met Jessica's. "I kept the sign to deter unwanted visitors."

Jessica nodded.

Hint taken.

The air freshener puffed out some fresh scent.

"What's your name?" Patty asked.

"Jessica Shaw."

"How long have you worked for Ed Crozier?"

"Around six months."

"What's he saying about you working for Rue Hunter?"

"He doesn't know yet. To be honest, I'm not sure he'll be happy about me digging around, asking questions, upsetting people."

"It's never bothered Ed in the past."

"What do you mean?"

"That's what private investigators do, isn't it? Dig around, ask questions, upset people." Patty Meeks gave a short bitter laugh. "In a place like Hundred Acres, everyone has secrets. And Ed's line of work means he knows most of them."

Jessica thought of the locked filing cabinets in the office that even she didn't have access to and figured Patty Meeks was likely right. Ed Crozier probably knew more about the private lives of the residents of Hundred Acres than anyone else in the entire town.

"What's she like now?" Patty asked suddenly.

"Who?"

"Rue Hunter. You said you met with her. What were your impressions of her?"

Jessica considered the question for a moment before answering.

"Quite a complex character," she said. "I spoke to her for around an hour, and in that time, I found her to be articulate, humorous, erratic, unsettling. Overall, I'd say intelligent but emotionally stunted. I don't think she's been unaffected by life in prison."

"How about manipulative?" Patty asked pointedly.

Jessica thought of Rue Hunter's parting comment, her own decision to sign Rose Dalton's contract as soon as the visit was over.

"Yes, I suppose she is."

"Will you be at the execution?"

"No," Jessica said. "Will you?"

Patty Meeks smiled coldly.

"Oh yes," she said. "I've been waiting for this day for more than thirty years. Wild horses wouldn't keep me away. The only thing that'd make me happier is if they let me stick the needle in her myself."

They both fell silent. Jessica could hear a clock ticking somewhere in the house.

"Do you mind me asking what you remember about that night?" she asked eventually. "The events of the evening as you recall them?"

Patty Meeks folded her hands onto her lap and stared at them. Then she looked up at Jessica and nodded. When she spoke, her voice was surprisingly strong.

"Megan was supposed to be going to a party. She'd mentioned it a few days earlier, asked if it would be okay to go with Rue and Lucas. The party was being held at the home of a girl from school. I knew the girl's parents, so I told Megan it would be fine to go along for a while so long as she was home by midnight, which was an hour later than her usual curfew. Lucas picked her up around eight thirty. He didn't come to the door or come inside. Just blasted the horn once, because they were picking up Rue next, and they were in a rush to get to the party. I remember Megan seemed excited, maybe a little edgy. Her cheeks were flushed, and she looked so pretty. It was summer, so she had a nice tan. She was wearing white jeans and a black silk blouse and high heels. A little more makeup than usual."

Patty inclined her head toward the sitting room's large front window.

"I watched from that window right there. She ran across the yard toward the car. Then she turned and gave me a wave before getting into the passenger side. It was the last time I saw my daughter alive."

"When did you realize something was wrong?"

"When Megan wasn't home by half past midnight, I started to worry. Then I phoned Lucas and Rue's parents. Steve and Heather James hadn't heard from the kids all night, but they weren't too worried. Barb Hunter wasn't at home—no big surprise there. I phoned the house where the party was taking place, but no one had seen Megan or Rue or Lucas the entire evening. Then I called the sheriff's station. I paced the floor, and I prayed to God, and I tried to convince myself Megan was absolutely fine. That she'd gone to some other party, had a little too much to drink, lost track of time. Sometime later, there was a knock on the door. When I opened it and saw the looks on Charlie Holten's and Pat McDonagh's faces, I knew Megan wasn't fine. They didn't have to say a word. I already knew my little girl was dead."

Jessica had been the one who'd found Tony's body, and it was something she'd never gotten over. Still, she could only imagine what that moment must have been like for Patty Meeks. That knock on the door.

"When did you find out about Rue Hunter's arrest?" she asked.

"The following day," Patty said. "Sheriff Holten was convinced she was guilty as soon as they found the knife. Hours before she confessed. I had no reason to disagree with him."

"You'd known Rue for years, since she was a little girl. She and Megan had been friends for a long time. Did you really believe she was capable of murder?"

"Yes, I did," Patty said matter-of-factly. "I didn't approve of their friendship, and I certainly didn't approve of the way Barb Hunter raised her kids. I never let Megan stay over at that house on Perry Street. Not once. Any sleepovers the girls had took place right here in this house. Don't get me wrong—I had no problem with Rue to begin with, even though I never liked her mother. As a little girl, she was sweet and polite. Then things changed. As she got older, she became sullen, withdrawn, downright odd at times. By the time she was a teenager, she was wild. Drinking, taking drugs, shoplifting. I know I was too strict with Megan, but I was terrified she'd wind up like Rue. I told her a dozen times I didn't want her being friends with Rue Hunter anymore, but Megan would get upset, and I'd always give in."

"I didn't realize Rue had a history of shoplifting," Jessica said. "Rose Dalton says she was accused of taking some items from Megan and Lucas the night they died. What was stolen?"

"Some cash and jewelry," Patty said. "Megan didn't have much money on her, probably around twenty bucks. Lucas had more, according to Steve and Heather, maybe fifty or sixty dollars. Both their wallets were empty when their bodies were found. Lucas's watch was also gone. It was a gift from his parents for his eighteenth birthday. A big, heavy gold thing. Very expensive. I remember noticing when Megan left the house she was wearing her diamond-and-emerald bracelet. It was also missing and also worth a lot of money."

"A gift for her sweet sixteen?" Jessica asked.

Unlike her friends, Megan had not yet celebrated her eighteenth birthday. Never would. Forever seventeen.

Patty shook her head. "No, it was originally a gift from Megan's father to myself for my own eighteenth birthday. Megan always liked it, so I passed it on to her once she was old enough to look after it."

"Allan, your partner, he was Megan's father? He bought the bracelet?"

"No, I met Allan several years after I lost Megan. Her father wasn't . . . around much when she was growing up."

"Did he know what happened to her?"

"Yes."

"Will he be at the execution?"

"No."

Another puff of scented air.

"Do you believe Rue Hunter stole those items?" Jessica asked. "They were never recovered."

"Yes, I do. I believe that's why she murdered them. I think Rue Hunter was probably very high on drugs and alcohol that night and wanted cash to buy some more. And, when Megan and Lucas refused to give her the money, she killed them and took it anyway."

"You don't think the motive for the murders was Megan and Lucas's relationship? It sounds like the police think the attack was sparked by jealousy, and the theft was simply opportune."

"My daughter wasn't allowed to date," Patty said. "I fell pregnant with Megan when I was seventeen, and I didn't want her to make the same mistakes as I did. Not that I ever regretted having Megan, not for a single minute. But I wanted more for my daughter. I wanted her to go to college and have a career and see the world. There was no relationship with Lucas James."

"It sounds like Megan lied about the party," Jessica said gently. "Maybe she lied about Lucas being her boyfriend too? Especially as he was dating Rue at the time."

"I was young myself once, you know," Patty said with a smile. "Was still young when Megan was a teenager. I remember exactly what it was like to be crazy about a guy. All those hours spent daydreaming, listening to romantic songs, suddenly making more of an effort with your appearance. I saw all the signs with Megan. I also saw her with Lucas plenty of times, and there was no change whatsoever in how they acted around each other in the weeks before they died."

"What are you saying?"

Patty Meeks smiled sadly.

"What I'm saying is, yes, Megan was in love with someone. But I don't believe for a minute she was in love with Lucas James, and I don't believe she was dating him behind Rue Hunter's back."

12

JESSICA

Jessica sat behind the wheel of the truck, yellow legal pad on her lap, scribbling notes from the conversation with Patty Meeks. Trying to get down on paper the key points before exhaustion wiped them from her memory.

When she looked at what she'd written, she realized she had more questions than answers. She slid the pad and pen into the bag sitting on the passenger seat, put the truck into drive, and headed for home. The question that occupied her thoughts the most for the duration of the short journey was the true nature of Megan and Lucas's relationship.

Patty Meeks struck Jessica as a woman who had been too over-protective of her daughter, who had treated Megan as though she was younger than her seventeen years. She wasn't allowed to date. She had an eleven p.m. curfew. She was expected to find a pay phone and call home if she was going to be out late. When she thought about it, Jessica wasn't surprised the woman didn't want to accept the girl had been dating Lucas.

Not only would Megan have been defying her mother by having a boyfriend; she would also have been lying to her best friend and hooking up with someone else's guy. A hell of a lot of deception for anyone, let alone a teenager who had probably just started dating. Then there was the visit to Devil's Drop. Jessica knew from personal experience that kids didn't always go to make-out spots just to make out—sometimes kissing led to a whole lot more. Maybe Patty Meeks couldn't accept the fact her daughter was more grown up than she'd wanted to believe.

But, if Patty Meeks's take on things was right, it threw up a whole bunch of other questions. Who was the guy Megan had been mooning over for weeks? Were they a couple? And what was she doing in the back seat of a car at Devil's Drop with Lucas James instead of her boyfriend?

Jessica rubbed her eyes. A headache was starting to bloom right behind her eyeballs, and she knew she was badly in need of some proper sleep after her uncomfortable night spent in Pryce's parking garage. As she turned onto her street, her heart sank as she realized a much bigger headache was waiting for her after spotting a familiar truck parked by the curb.

It was a dirty two-tone turquoise-and-cream Ford Ranger. Three-tone if you counted the rust patches holding it together. Ninety-two model, rear wheel hubcap missing.

Michelle Foster's daddy's truck.

Jessica had last seen the vehicle through a zoom lens out on a patch of wasteland on the edge of town. A load of illicit booze had been piled up high on its flatbed, and teenagers had crowded round placing orders. The truck and its contents had been the subject of a dozen photos slipped inside a brown envelope and stuffed into Jed Lockerman's mailbox Friday night.

"Shit," Jessica muttered under her breath.

She passed the Ford and turned into the driveway of a one-story concrete house with crazy paving siding. There was a two-car garage to one side of the property and a vintage Airstream trailer mounted on bricks on the other. The isolated patch of land, and everything on it, was owned by a woman by the name of Sylvia Sugarman, who had been Jessica's landlord for the best part of six months now.

When she'd first landed in Hundred Acres, Jessica had quickly realized a long-term stay at the Acres Motel wasn't going to happen after spending a few nights there. The place was so bad even the cockroaches had moved out. Unfortunately, it was the only motel in town.

She remembered Dylan telling her once about plans to build a big casino and hotel complex in Hundred Acres back in the eighties. Lucky by Lucchese had been the brainchild of a local businessman and would offer Angelenos all the glamour and fun of Sin City, without the long drive there and back across state lines. The project had fallen through, and visitors to the town ever since had been stuck with the Acres Motel instead.

When Jessica had been looking for a place to stay, committing to a rental on a house had felt too permanent, so Sylvia Sugarman's trailer had been the ideal compromise. The rent was cheap, it had all the space she needed, and, even though the wheels were long gone, Jessica liked what it had once represented. A mobile home designed with people, like her, in mind who didn't want to stay in one place for too long.

She parked in front of the garage and walked across the front yard, rounded the side of the house to where her own humble dwelling stood, and readied herself for yet another fight. It was shaping up to be quite a weekend.

Michelle was pacing back and forth in front of the trailer. Or at least she was pacing as much as anyone can pace on sunbaked mud while wearing a pair of acrylic-heeled mules and spray-on pants. A fulsome cleavage threatening to spill out of a low V-neck tee and too-black hair made longer and thicker by cheap clip-on extensions completed the look. *Kim Kardashian after falling on hard times,* Jessica thought.

The woman was sucking furiously on some sort of plastic vaping device, plumes of smoke streaming from her mouth and nostrils. The vape cloud drifted on the breeze toward Jessica as she approached the trailer. The smell was sweet and cloying, like cotton candy. The opposite of the sour expression on Michelle Foster's face. She stopped pacing and faced Jessica, one hand on her hip, the other stabbing the vaping device in her direction.

"I've been looking for you."

"Something I can do for you, Michelle?"

Jessica rummaged in her bag for the key to the trailer.

"You can explain why you got me fired from the liquor store."

Jessica sighed. She walked past the woman and inserted the key in the lock and opened the door. Turned to face Michelle.

"I didn't get you fired. You were stealing booze from your boss. That's why you got fired."

"It was a few lousy extra bucks," Michelle yelled. "A side hustle, no big deal. Everyone knew about it. Even Dylan and his daddy knew about it. But you had to ruin it for everyone, didn't you?"

"Jed Lockerman didn't know about it," Jessica pointed out. "He was losing money, and he didn't know why. He paid me to look into it, and that's what I did. It was a lot more than a few bucks, and you only have yourself to blame for getting fired."

Michelle shook her head in disbelief. "After what you did to me? I should be making your life hell. Not the other way around."

"So that's what this is really all about? You're still pissed about Dylan?" Jessica could feel herself becoming even more irritated. All she wanted was to climb into bed, go to sleep, and shut out the rest of the world for a few hours. Especially Michelle Foster. "You guys broke up before I even arrived in town. And Dylan said there was no chance of you getting back together anyway. You really need to move on, Michelle."

Jessica's neck snapped back suddenly, and her head connected hard with the side of the trailer, the blow from Michelle so rapid she didn't even register it happening until a searing pain shot through the base of her skull. Then Michelle's hand was around her throat, pinning her against the Airstream, acrylic nails pinching the delicate skin. Michelle's face was an inch from Jessica's own. Saliva foamed in the corners of her mouth; her breath was hot and fast and heavy. Not cotton candy, Jessica decided. Something fruity and sickly. Cherry or strawberry.

Lisa Gray

"You better watch that smart mouth, you little bitch," Michelle hissed. "Or someone might just shut you up permanently."

Jessica's headache had shot up from blooming to blazing in the space of five seconds, and she was light headed from the lack of oxygen reaching her brain. She clawed at the hand around her throat while trying to push Michelle off her. The woman had a few inches and at least ten pounds on her, and Jessica was no match for her physically. She fumbled under her T-shirt, pulled her Baby Glock from her waistband, and held it up. Not pointing it at Michelle, but making sure it was in her line of sight.

"Take your fucking hands off me," she gasped.

Michelle looked at the gun and let out a short, harsh laugh, but she removed her hand from Jessica's throat and took a few steps back.

"You have no idea who you're messing with, do you?" the other woman asked.

Jessica sucked in fresh air, felt her head begin to clear, her breathing return to normal.

"Oh, I've got a pretty good idea," she said. "A grown woman who acts like she's still in junior high."

When Jessica had first hooked up with Dylan, there had been a few petty incidents she'd had to deal with. Trash dumped outside her front door, the word *whore* scrawled in scarlet lipstick across her windshield, calls to her cell phone in the middle of the night. Stupid, childish stuff that she'd known Michelle Foster had been responsible for. It had stopped after a few weeks, but Jessica had a feeling the liquor store business had just reignited the feud, and then some.

Michelle smiled thinly. "That was just for starters."

"I'm not interested in your stupid games, Michelle," Jessica said. "Turn around and walk away now. If you don't, I might just be tempted to put a bullet through each of those plastic shoes. Then you won't be walking anywhere for months."

"You're not the only one with a gun, you know," Michelle said.

88

Then she turned and stalked toward her daddy's Ford Ranger, the acrylic mules slapping loudly against the hard mud. Jessica watched as Michelle climbed behind the wheel and turned the key in the ignition. Heard the engine cough and splutter, before catching and rumbling noisily. She waited until the truck drove off, leaving a cloud of dirty fumes in its wake. Then Jessica picked up her bag from the ground, where it had fallen during the altercation, and wearily climbed the two steps into the trailer.

Once inside, she locked the door, pulled down all the window shades, stripped off her clothes, and left them where they fell on the floor. She climbed into bed with a bottle of Scotch that Dylan had bought for her a few weeks earlier.

She wondered, as she drank what was left of the bottle, if it had been purchased from the back of Michelle Foster's daddy's truck.

13

PRYCE

Sunday afternoon. Even though it was his day off, Pryce was back behind his desk at Hollywood Division, three murder books spread out in front of him. None of them were his cases, but all had been weighing heavily on his mind since the night before.

The first one documented the slayings of Megan Meeks and Lucas James in Hundred Acres. A town he had been to only once or twice and an investigation he knew nothing about—other than being absolutely sure the work would have been carried out to the best of their ability by Holten and his team.

Pryce picked up his cell phone, scrolled through his recent call list, and tapped the number he was looking for. The call went straight to voice mail. He didn't leave a message, decided he'd try again later. He set aside the Hundred Acres murder book.

The other two files were more recent but still had to be retrieved from cold storage.

Charlie Holten's name was printed neatly in black marker on one of the yellowed sticky labels. On the other was the name Angel Henderson. A street kid turned prostitute who was widely believed to be the reason why Holten had ended up dead on a July night in 1997. The girl had been murdered less than a year earlier.

Holten had first come across Angel Henderson when he was a vice cop and she was a six-month-old baby. He'd carried her from a crack house following a drug bust, red faced and screaming, tiny fists punching air thick with gun smoke and residue. Her mother had been shot and killed during the raid. Not by Holten's bullet, but he'd felt some sort of connection to the child he couldn't explain as he'd held her in his arms. After she was placed in a children's home, he called regularly for updates and bought her a small toy each Christmas as she grew from a baby into a little girl and then an adolescent.

When she was fourteen, Angel Henderson walked out of the group home where she'd spent most of her life and never returned. Claimed by the streets of West Hollywood and those who prowled them after dark. Holten spent his days working cases and his nights searching for Angel Henderson. Using contacts, chasing leads, getting nowhere. After three years, he found her. Naked and beaten to death, her broken body tossed in a dumpster just off La Cienega Boulevard like a piece of trash.

What was known of her final hours was typed, hole punched, and filed in the depressingly slim three-ring binder lying open in front of Pryce now.

The first confirmed sighting on the night she died was early evening at Duke's on Sunset. A modest greasy spoon with a big reputation, the joint was always busy; there was always a line for food at all hours of the day and night. The $6.95 breakfast special it served until four a.m. was a big favorite with the regulars, but Angel Henderson wasn't eating the breakfast special. She was sitting at a table by the window, sharing a burger and fries with a skinny redhead with bad skin.

Angel was a knockout compared to her friend, according to those who'd seen the pair eating dinner. Afro curls burned blonde by drugstore bleach, a black fishnet cropped top hinting at a lacy padded bra underneath, silk harem pants slung low on the hips, a flat belly decorated with a diamante piercing. Her less memorable dining companion was never tracked down by the cops.

A couple hours later, Angel was spotted again, this time smoking a cigarette outside the Whisky a Go Go, on the corner of Sunset and

Clark, right next door to Duke's. There was a live band playing that night, and the place was heaving, so no one could say for sure whether Angel had been drinking in the bar or not. But more than one person had placed her on the sidewalk outside, after midnight, with a black guy in his twenties. Colored beads fastened to the ends of skinny, floppy dreads, baggy jeans belted halfway down his butt over designer boxers, an oversize baseball shirt, and two-hundred-dollar sneakers. Identified by witnesses as DaMarcus Jones, Angel's sometime boyfriend and occasional pimp and small-time gangbanger.

A guest at a motel on La Cienega later reported being roused from sleep around two a.m. by loud yelling from the street outside his first-floor window. He'd pulled back the curtain and watched as a young woman, probably in her late teens or early twenties, screamed and shoved at a white man in his midthirties. He had a stocky build and a shaven head and was wearing a short-sleeved white shirt and dark pants or jeans.

The couple were grappling with each other under the sodium glow of a streetlight, the deserted street still slick from an unexpected shower earlier in the evening. Illuminated like two actors in a spotlight on an empty stage. He was trying to haul the girl down the hill, south toward Santa Monica Boulevard, and she was trying to escape from his grasp. They appeared to be embroiled in a domestic dispute fueled by too much liquor. The motel guest had gotten bored after a while, dropped the curtain, and returned to bed.

It was the last known sighting of Angel Henderson alive.

The homicide investigation didn't land on Holten's desk—it wasn't his case—but he took an interest anyway. Too much of an interest, according to some, who said his obsession with the girl was what got him killed. Holten's murder was officially still unsolved, the case technically still open, but it was widely believed he'd been the target of a hit organized by DaMarcus Jones.

Pryce looked up from the murder book as his partner, Vic Medina, slumped into the seat at the workstation facing his own. Medina was dressed in his trademark outfit of Levi's jeans, tight white tee, black leather jacket, and Ray-Ban shades propped on top of long, dark hair. He nodded at the files on Pryce's desk.

"Working on your day off?" he asked. "Can't keep away from the place, huh?"

"I could say the same about you, Vic."

"Found myself at a loose end today and figured I might as well do some work. What's your excuse for working a Sunday?"

"Women trouble."

Medina raised an eyebrow. "You've not had another fight with Angie, have you? Don't tell me you're back on the couch again?"

Pryce shook his head. "Nope. An argument with Dionne this time. She has a boyfriend."

Medina winced. "Already? Ouch. Must make you feel old, pal. You run a check on him yet?"

"Don't be ridiculous, Vic. He's just a kid." Pryce smiled. "But his folks came up clean."

Medina grinned. "Nice work."

Pryce's smile disappeared. "I had a fight with Jessica too. Well, a heated exchange. Last night after dinner. Let's just say the evening didn't end well."

"Jeez, Jase. You know what your problem is? You've got too many women in your life, that's what. What did you fight about?"

Pryce told Medina about Jessica's decision to investigate the events surrounding the Devil's Drop murders, how his old partner was the one who had put Rue Hunter away for double murder, and how he and Jessica had clashed over whether the original investigation should be reexamined. He also told his partner how the whole business had gotten him thinking about Charlie Holten's murder again, more than twenty years after it happened.

It was a topic he and Medina didn't really talk about. Pryce had always believed being the partner of another cop was a bit like being in a marriage. You had your ups and downs, spent a lot of time in each other's company, got to know all the little things that made each other tick, and, ultimately, you had each other's back.

Often, as was the case with Pryce, there would be other partners along the way, like ex-wives lurking in your past after remarrying. Pryce had two before Medina came along—Charlie Holten and Rebecca Jensen, a detective he'd worked alongside for almost nine years before she'd transferred out from Hollywood to Topanga after being promoted to LT.

Pryce also knew, when one of those pairings was ended by a bullet, it was the one any subsequent partners found the hardest to live up to, the biggest boots to fill. He understood how tough it must have been for Medina having to follow in the footsteps of a ghost. Vic had joined the LAPD a good while after Holten's death, knew he'd met a violent end, but the details of the shooting weren't something he and Pryce had discussed at any great length in the more than a decade they'd worked together.

Until now.

Pryce slid the Angel Henderson murder book across his own desk toward Medina, gave him the background on Holten's loose association with the teenager during her formative years, how he had taken an even bigger interest in her following her death. Medina read the file, which didn't take too long because the investigation had gone nowhere.

Then Medina said, "Tell me about Holten and the night he died."

Pryce let his mind take a trip back in time to the midnineties and one of the worst periods he had ever experienced in his personal or professional life. The murder of Charlie Holten had had a heavy influence on both for a long time.

"Charlie was found behind the wheel of his car," he said. "Stopped at traffic lights, engine still running, both front windows rolled down.

A single bullet to the forehead. The shooting happened on an empty street in Echo Park, out by Dodger Stadium, just before midnight. No witnesses."

"Sounds like an execution to me."

Pryce nodded. "I wasn't given the case, of course. Charlie was my partner, so I was part of the investigation. I was interviewed twice by a couple of guys by the name of Hunt and Adams, both of them way before your time. They wanted to know about cases we were working together, Charlie's movements in the days leading up the murder, what his mood had been like, and so on. The case we'd been working at the time was a domestic homicide. Guy had offed his wife after finding out she'd been screwing around with a coworker. It didn't feel like the domestic 187 had anything to do with Charlie's shooting. As you said, it looked like an execution. Clean and professional."

"You're an astute guy, Jase," Medina said. "Did you have any inkling beforehand something might be wrong? That Holten might have gotten himself involved in something?"

Again, Pryce nodded. "I told Hunt and Adams that Charlie had seemed preoccupied for a few days. Like he was here, in the squad room, but he was a million miles away at the same time. Like he had something big on his mind."

"Did you ask what was bothering him? Did he talk to you about it?"

"Sure, I asked," Pryce said. "He told me he had something to sort out. Wouldn't say any more about it. We were pretty close so, if he didn't want to talk about it, I figured it was probably to do with his wife, Maggie. I knew they hadn't been getting on for a while. Then, after the shooting, I got to thinking about the letter."

"What letter?"

"I'm not sure when it arrived exactly. Maybe two or three days before the shooting. Delivered right here, to the office. More of a small parcel, really. Brown padded envelope, handwritten address on front. I remember Charlie pulling out a single sheet of paper, unfolding it, reading it; then all the color draining from his face. When I asked if he was okay, he said yes, shoved the note back into the envelope, and stuffed the package into the inside pocket of his sports coat."

"Any idea who the letter was from?" Medina asked. "What it was about?"

"It was never found," Pryce said. "Hunt and Adams looked into the whole marriage thing, whether Charlie could have had a secret mistress, if the letter was a possible blackmail attempt. I didn't think so. They checked out his call records, both incoming and outgoing. Office phone, home landline, cell phone. Nothing set alarm bells ringing. The mistress theory was quickly dismissed."

"What was your theory?"

"I always thought it was something to do with Angel Henderson."

"Why?"

"When Charlie was found in his car, he was a few blocks from a patch of wasteland. Nothing there but some derelict warehouses that had been shuttered for years. It was one of the places he would meet his snitches."

"You think the letter was arranging a meet?"

"I think it was a trap."

"Set by?"

"DaMarcus Jones."

"What happened to him?"

"He's been in the joint since '99," Pryce said. "A rap sheet with more entries than your little black book. Doing time for murder, attempted murder, and armed robbery after a liquor store raid went bad. The only way he's leaving the big house is in a pine box. Like Charlie with Angel Henderson, I took an unofficial interest in his investigation. Met with DaMarcus Jones two or three times shortly after his incarceration. No joy."

"What happened with the Holten investigation?"

"Officially, it's still open and subject to once-yearly reviews. Unofficially, no one's busting a gut anymore. Everyone thinks DaMarcus Jones is our guy, and he's never seeing daylight again. Different crime but still doing the time."

"What do you think?"

Pryce shrugged. "He never confessed."

They were both silent for a few minutes.

Then Medina said, "I don't think you're here on your day off to escape Dionne and all the boyfriend stuff." He nodded at the murder books still spread out in front of Pryce. "I think you want to take another proper look at the Holten case."

Pryce shrugged again. "Maybe."

Medina said, "Okay, I'm in."

Pryce stared at his partner in surprise.

"Seriously? You want to get involved?"

"Sure, I do. And it sounds to me like another visit with DaMarcus Jones is long overdue."

14

JESSICA

She was back in the prison in Chowchilla.

The stench of bleach and sweat filled her nostrils again. The smell of her own fear was stronger this time because Jessica wasn't in the visitation room. She was locked in a cell. A six-by-eleven-foot space designed for one person. But there were two of them. Rue Hunter stood in the corner, a needle hanging from her arm, blood dripping from her fingertips. She was laughing. Outside the cell, there was a rhythmic banging. Someone was calling Jessica's name.

She opened her eyes.

It took a few seconds for them to adjust to the gloom, to register she was safe in her trailer and not trapped within the concrete confines of the Central California Women's Facility. Jessica needed a further moment to register the banging hadn't ended with the dream. She grappled for the cell phone lying next to her on the bed to check what time it was, to see how long she had slept. She stabbed at the home button. Nothing happened. The phone was out of juice.

Another bang.

Jessica lifted the shade covering the window next to the bed a few inches and peered outside. Sylvia Sugarman was standing on the doorstep, a food tray in her hands.

"Jessica?" the woman called. "Are you in there? You okay, sweetheart?"

"Shit."

Jessica rolled off the bed, grabbed the empty liquor bottle, and threw it in the trash can under the sink. She picked up her pants and tee from where she'd dropped them on the floor earlier and pulled them on as she made her way to the door. Jessica threw it open as she was zipping up the pants.

"Sorry, Mrs. Sugarman, I was asleep. Didn't hear you knocking."

Sylvia liked to be called Mrs. Sugarman instead of Sylvia. She told Jessica once she thought it made her sound more refined, a little bit classy. And, according to Sylvia, Hundred Acres was badly in need of some class. It was the same reason why she drank her afternoon liquor from a crystal tumbler and always wore a full face of makeup even when she had no plans to leave the house.

Sylvia, fully made up as always, poked her perfectly coiffed head around the doorway. Jessica caught a whiff of her perfume. Something French, heavy and heady.

"I'm not interrupting anything, am I?" Sylvia asked, looking around. "The shades have been down all afternoon. I thought you might have had company."

"No, not at all. I was having a nap." Jessica stepped aside. "Come on in."

Jessica thought Sylvia looked disappointed as she squeezed past and dumped the tray on the dinette table and slid into one of the cracked leather seats.

"Chicken casserole and pecan pie," she said. "I knocked earlier, was going to ask if you wanted to join me in the house for dinner, but there was no response. You must have been dead to the world. And please don't take this the wrong way, sweetie, but you look like shit."

Jessica smiled. "You're not the first person to tell me that today. Rough night. Didn't get a whole lot of sleep. I guess I made up for it this afternoon. What time is it anyway?"

Sylvia waved her hand. "Who knows? Around six maybe?"

"Wow, I must have slept hard."

"Must have been a really rough night. How's that young man of yours, by the way?"

Jessica ignored the question. "Are you in a rush to get back to the house? I was actually hoping to have a chat with you. I wanted to pick your brains about a case I'm working."

Sylvia perked up. "One of your cases? Sounds interesting. Pick away."

"Thanks, I will. Can I get you something to drink?" Jessica opened the refrigerator and looked inside. "I have soda, water, beer. Or I could make you a coffee if you'd prefer?"

"Any ice?" Sylvia asked.

"Um, sure."

"If you're planning on cracking the seal on that bottle of whiskey on the counter, I'll have a large Scotch on the rocks. It'll help me sleep later."

Jessica rinsed out a tumbler, then opened the Talisker, poured a healthy measure, and dropped some ice cubes into the amber liquid. If she was a betting woman, she'd wager it wasn't Sylvia's first refreshment of the day and wouldn't be the last either, insomnia or not. She walked over to the table and handed the drink to the older woman.

"Sorry, no crystal tumblers."

Sylvia winked. "Oh, I don't mind slumming it occasionally, sweetheart. Just don't tell anyone."

Jessica grabbed herself a Diet Coke from the refrigerator, found a fork and spoon in the kitchen drawer, and slid into the seat facing Sylvia. She peeled the Saran Wrap from the casserole dish and savored the aroma of the food before digging in. She hadn't eaten since breakfast at Randy's.

"This is amazing, Mrs. Sugarman," she said between mouthfuls. "Thanks for saving me some."

"Just something I threw together." Sylvia's tone was nonchalant, but Jessica could tell she was pleased with the compliment. "And the pie is store bought before you go getting your hopes up for homemade. I lost all interest in baking when Mr. Sugarman passed a few years ago. He was the one with the sweet tooth. Plus, a gal has to watch her figure."

Sylvia patted a belly that was clearly flat under her slim-fit jeans and fitted blouse. Jessica realized she'd never seen the woman eat dessert.

"I'll take my chances," she said, moving on to the pie.

Sylvia drank some whiskey and waited for Jessica to finish eating. Then she said, "So what's the case you want me to help you with?"

"You remember the Devil's Drop murders that happened back in '87?"

"Sure, I do. Hard to forget a thing like that. In fact, I heard there were some reporters sniffing around town yesterday. Seems the Hunter girl is finally being executed. What's that terrible business got to do with what you're working on?"

"I've been hired by Rue Hunter's sister, Rose, to take another look at the case. Find out if there's any way Rue might be innocent."

Sylvia frowned. "I thought she confessed all those years ago?"

"She did. Now she's not so sure she's guilty after all."

"Really?" Sylvia sounded doubtful. "Innocent all of a sudden after thirty years of being guilty? How the hell does that work?"

"That's what I'm trying to figure out," Jessica said. "What did you think at the time? Did you believe she was guilty?"

Sylvia shrugged. "She confessed, so I guess so."

Jessica said, "What I wanted to ask you was how well did you know the Hunters? Did you have many dealings with the family when they lived in town? Is there anything interesting you can tell me about them?"

"I didn't know Rue particularly well, but I knew the mother," Sylvia said. "Hell, everyone in town knew Barb Hunter."

"Sounds like she was quite a character."

"Tragic, you mean." Sylvia shook her head, took a swallow of whiskey. "First came the beatings, then the drinking. And the drinking got a whole lot worse after her old man split town. You ask me? Him walking out should've been the best thing that ever happened to Barb. Leonard Hunter was one mean son of a bitch."

"What happened? Why'd he split town?"

"Apparently, he was none too pleased about becoming a daddy first time around. Made Barb's life hell after Rose came along. Blamed her for not taking the proper precautions. Just one more reason to justify using the poor woman as a punching bag, you ask me. When Barb realized she was pregnant again, with Rue, she was too far gone to do anything about it. This time, Leonard upped and left. Didn't want to face up to his responsibilities, like a real man would've done. Listening to Barb tell the story, after she'd had a bucketload of booze, you'd think it was the kid's fault her daddy left the family in the lurch, that she was somehow to blame for that jerk not sticking around."

Jessica said, "I guess it's easy to say now that Rue must have been damaged by the start she had in life, knowing how things turned out later on. But Patty Meeks says she was quite sweet as a kid, described her as being a polite little girl."

"You spoke to Patty Meeks?" Sylvia made a face. "You're braver than most folks around here. But Patty's right. From what I heard, Rue was a sweetheart—then she changed." Sylvia snapped her fingers. "Just like that."

"Changed how?" Jessica asked. "What did you hear?"

Sylvia said, "When Rue Hunter confessed to those murders, it was the talk of the town, as I'm sure you can well imagine. Not long after, I was having lunch with the girls. This was back when Hundred Acres still had a decent restaurant. Anyway, on this particular day, a friend of a friend joined us. She was a schoolteacher, and Rue had been one of her students when the kid was about ten or eleven. The woman was all cut up about what had happened at Devil's Drop. Told us Rue had been such a nice kid, like you said. Then, all of a sudden, she'd started acting differently. You know, terrible mood swings and the like. I got the impression the woman thought Rue might have been abused around that time, but she didn't come right out and say it." Sylvia drained the glass.

"Refill?" Jessica asked.

Sylvia nodded. "Please."

Jessica filled the tumbler again, cracked some ice into the Scotch, and then poured herself a double. She carried both drinks to the dinette table and slid back into the seat.

"Does the teacher still live in town?" Jessica asked. Sylvia shook her head, tossed back some Scotch, crunched an ice cube between her teeth.

"I'm pretty sure she left. Haven't seen her around for years."

"What was her name?"

"Nina, I think, but don't quote me on it."

"Last name?"

"Something foreign sounding. Spanish or Italian, maybe." Sylvia waved a hand dismissively. "You know I'm terrible with names, Jessica. And the woman wasn't really part of my crowd. I think I only lunched with her once or twice after that day."

They both fell silent, lost in their own thoughts, the only sound in the trailer the clink of ice against glass as they sipped their drinks.

Eventually, Jessica said, "What about Rose? Did you know her at all?"

"She waitressed at Randy's for a while. Otherwise, not really."

"I spent some time with her Friday evening. She seems nice, pretty normal. Lives in Arizona now, married with two kids. Sounds like she was the only normal one in the Hunter family."

"I'm not so sure about that," Sylvia said. "Maybe she wasn't as screwed up as the rest of them, but I think that girl had some issues of her own."

"Oh yeah?"

"I heard she broke a kid's nose back in high school once. Some little punk decided to impress his buddies by grabbing her ass. Instead of laughing about it or telling him where to get off, Rose Hunter turned around and whacked him hard with the book she was holding. Unfortunately for him, it was a huge, thick textbook, and she almost wiped his nose clean off his face."

"Good for her," Jessica said. "Do you remember who the guy was?"

"Sure, I do. Skinny guy, ugly as sin, although I don't suppose that broken nose helped his looks any. Works in the liquor store now. Still skinny and ugly." Sylvia waved her hand. "Jeb something."

"Jed Lockerman?"

"That's the one. Then it happened again."

"What happened again?"

"Another 'accident.'" Sylvia made bunny-ear fingers around the word. "This was after high school, years later, when Rose Hunter was waitressing at Randy's. This time, she dumped a pot of scalding coffee on some poor son of a bitch's crotch. Same thing. My friend Gloria saw the whole thing. Said the guy tried to cop a feel, and Rose didn't take too kindly to his direct approach. Then, a short time afterward, the whole Devil's Drop business happened, and it was all kind of forgotten about. Rue went to prison, Barb drank herself to death, and Rose up and left Hundred Acres for good."

"Anything else you remember about the Hunters?"

Sylvia shook her head. "I don't think so. If I do remember anything, I'll knock on the door." She drained her glass, slid out from the seat, and picked up the food tray with the empty dishes. "Catch you later, sweetheart."

"Thanks again for dinner."

After Sylvia returned to the house, Jessica remembered her cell phone was out of juice. She found the charger in her bag and hooked it up to the phone. The screen burst to life and pinged with an alert for a text.

The message was from Dylan, asking her over to his place. She tapped out a reply:

Sorry, crashed earlier. Just got your message. Give me a half hour to shower and change. See you soon.

She thought of the schoolteacher who had taught Rue Hunter as a child. Sylvia Sugarman might not be able to remember her name, but Jessica figured she knew just the person who might be able to help her track down the woman.

15

JESSICA

Dylan stayed rent-free in a studio apartment above his folks' garage. The McDonaghs owned the best house on one of the nicest streets in Hundred Acres, which was a bit like picking out the least wormy apple from a bad barrel, but still.

Pat's cruiser and Dylan's old station wagon were both parked in the drive, so Jessica found a space across the street, then jogged up the wooden staircase to the apartment. Dylan opened the door before she had a chance to knock and greeted her with a kiss.

"You eaten?" he asked, nodding to a brown paper bag on the tiny kitchenette counter. "I brought some burgers from the diner."

"I'm good, thanks. Sylvia made me dinner. But you go ahead and eat."

She flopped onto the double bed and kicked off her sneakers as Dylan unwrapped one of the burgers. The apartment comprised one large room, which acted as bedroom, living area, and kitchen, as well as a small shower room. The fact that Dylan still lived above his parents' garage had never bothered Jessica. She knew his focus right now was on making a success of the diner.

"Busy day?" he asked.

"Not busy enough," she said. "I spoke to Patty Meeks earlier, then crashed for way too long."

"How'd the chat with Patty go?"

"It was interesting, gave me some stuff to think on. Sad, too, I guess. I don't think she's ever gotten over what happened to Megan. I also spoke to Sylvia. Tried to pick her brains about the Hunters."

"Anything useful?"

"Maybe. She mentioned a teacher who taught Rue when she was a kid. Couldn't remember the woman's name, though. Say, I don't suppose you'd know who Sylvia was talking about?"

"So, you here to pick my brains too?" Dylan grinned. "And here was me thinking it was my body you were after."

Jessica grinned back. "Maybe I'm after both."

"Sylvia tell you anything about this teacher? Help narrow it down?"

"She thinks her first name was Nina. Said the surname sounded Spanish or Italian. Any ideas?"

"Sure," Dylan said without hesitation. "That would be Mrs. DePalma. She was one of my favorite teachers."

Jessica sat up straighter on the bed. "What happened to her? Sylvia says she moved away from Hundred Acres a while back."

Dylan nodded. "That's right. The DePalmas left town after they both retired, wanted to be closer to their daughter and grandkids." He trashed the burger wrapper and grabbed two beers from the refrigerator. Popped the tops and handed one to Jessica. "This would have been four or five years ago. My folks attended their farewell party."

"Do you know where the DePalmas moved to?"

"I'm pretty sure it was San Diego. I don't know where exactly, though."

Jessica placed her beer bottle on the floor and pulled her laptop from her bag and fired it up. A few minutes later, she had a hit.

"Was Mrs. DePalma's husband named Donald?"

"Yeah. Went by Don."

"Found them," she said triumphantly. "They reside in a senior living community in La Jolla."

Jessica checked the time on her cell. It wasn't quite eight p.m. Not too late to call, she decided. Dylan stood against the counter and drank his beer and watched as she punched in the number displayed on the laptop screen. After a couple of rings, a woman's voice answered.

"Mrs. DePalma?" she asked.

"That's right," the woman said. "May I ask who's calling?"

Jessica introduced herself and provided Mrs. DePalma with a quick rundown of the case she was working and how she was looking for information on Rue Hunter.

"How'd you track me down to San Diego?" the woman asked. "I left Hundred Acres years ago."

"A friend of mine, Dylan McDonagh, remembered you'd moved south to be closer to your family. I managed to find a listing online."

"Dylan!" There was delight in Mrs. DePalma's voice. "Such a nice, polite boy. How is he doing?"

"He's doing just swell." Jessica winked at Dylan. "My landlady, Sylvia Sugarman, said you once told her and a group of friends about an episode involving Rue Hunter when she was a student of yours? About how her demeanor seemed to change all of a sudden? Do you mind me asking what happened back then?"

"Oh, yes, I remember it well," Mrs. DePalma said, sounding sad. "Even now, after all these years. This would've been when Rue was in fifth grade, I think, when she was around ten years old. She'd always been a little shy, didn't like to speak up in class or answer quiz questions in front of the other students, but she worked hard. I got the feeling she was always seeking my approval. I felt sorry for her, wearing her sister's hand-me-downs, always a size too big, clothes that had been purchased from the Goodwill store in the first place. But she was never any trouble. Then things changed."

"In what way?"

"She'd missed school for a week or so. Her mother, Barb, said both Rue and her older sister, Rose, were sick; some kind of tummy bug had hit the whole household hard. When Rue finally returned to school, she was . . . different."

"Different how?"

"She'd always been quiet, but now she barely spoke at all. She lost all interest in schoolwork and became increasingly withdrawn. Often, I'd catch her staring out of the window when the other students were busy writing essays or completing pop quizzes. After a while, she began acting out, became disruptive in class. Back then, we didn't have school therapists or anything like that, but I did wonder if there was some kind of abuse happening at home. I tried to speak to Rue about it once or twice, but she wouldn't open up. I kept an eye on her for signs of cuts and bruises, but I never saw a mark on her."

Mrs. DePalma sighed heavily and said, "Looking back, maybe I should have done more, made some sort of an intervention. But I was young and inexperienced back then, a recently qualified teacher, and I didn't really know how to handle the situation. The school year came to an end, and Rue moved on to a different class. It's just . . ."

The woman fell silent.

"Just what?" Jessica prompted.

"That spell Rue Hunter was absent from class?" Mrs. DePalma said. "I always felt something happened during that time."

"What do you think happened?"

"I don't know. But it seems to me that little girl changed almost overnight."

Jessica felt a chill run down her spine.

"Did you have much involvement with Rue Hunter after that class year?"

"Not really. The next time I came across Rue, she was in high school. By then, there was a lot of talk about her wild behavior, how she seemed to be following in her mother's footsteps."

"You taught high school too?"

"No, I spent my entire career teaching elementary, but the two buildings were right next to each other, and I was on the social committee for both schools. You know, volunteering at events. I do remember being quite concerned about Rue's behavior at junior prom."

"Concerned how?"

"I was sure she'd been drinking alcohol, for a start. Then, I remember, she put on quite a show with her boyfriend on the dance floor. They were making out, and I mean *really* making out. I guess it sounds prudish now, but I was worried they were setting a bad example to the other students. It's hard to believe what happened to the boy just a year later . . ."

Jessica nodded, even though Mrs. DePalma couldn't see her. "Anything else you can tell me that might be useful?" she asked.

"I don't think so. If I do think of anything, I'll give you a call."

"That would be great."

Jessica recited her cell number and thanked the woman for her time. She killed the connection and dropped the cell phone on the bed.

Dylan was staring at her, an eyebrow raised.

"What?" she said.

"You told Mrs. DePalma I was a 'friend'?" he asked.

"Okay, maybe a friend with benefits. *Lots* of benefits."

"Much better."

He climbed on top of the bed, pushed Jessica back gently, and began nuzzling her neck.

Her cell phone pinged.

"Ignore it," she murmured, pulling his lips toward her own.

They kissed for a few seconds; then Dylan pulled back with a sigh. He picked up Jessica's cell phone.

"It's a voice message," he said. "Someone must have tried to call while you were speaking to Mrs. DePalma."

He tossed the phone at Jessica, got up, and made his way to the refrigerator for another beer.

"I guess it might be important," she said.

Jessica listened to the voice mail. It was from Pryce. She thought his voice sounded strained, like he was uptight about something. Probably still pissed at her after their argument the night before. She should have called him earlier to clear the air, prevented any bad feelings from festering. The message was short and straight to the point.

"Meet me at ten a.m. tomorrow at Bru Coffeebar in Los Feliz. There's something you need to see."

16

HOLTEN

1987

Holten watched through the two-way mirror as Dr. Ted Blume eased himself into a chair facing Rue Hunter across a small table in the brightly lit interview room. He offered her a hand to shake and a smile to put her at ease, and Holten remembered how much he disliked the man.

He'd only met him once before, at a police fund-raiser last fall, but once had been enough. The whole point of the evening had been to raise cash for local sheriff's departments to help them improve services in their local communities. Holten remembered how Blume—"Call me Dr. Ted!"—had schmoozed his way through the event, pressing the flesh, sipping free cocktails, and slipping business cards into jacket pockets. He lectured on psychology at community colleges and acted as a consulting psychologist for the very sheriff's departments that were badly in need of the funds being raised. Holten was pretty sure Blume, rather than the actual beneficiaries, was the biggest winner of the night.

Holten looked at him now from where he sat in his own tiny dark room. Midfifties, full head of blond hair, mustache, deep summer tan complemented by a neatly pressed cream linen suit and a light-blue dress shirt. The shirt was open necked, no tie, weekend casual even though it was Monday. Holten remembered how his wife, Maggie, had spoken to Blume for around five minutes at the fund-raiser. Not long, but long enough for her to declare Dr. Ted had the look of Robert Redford about him, with the same twinkly, crinkly, bright-blue eyes as the actor. Eyes, she said, that creased at the corners and made him look like he was smiling even if you couldn't see his lips moving under the mustache.

Holten *really* didn't like Dr. Ted Blume.

He didn't particularly like what the man did for a living either. Psychology. Holten snorted to himself. He'd always dismissed the whole thing as mumbo-jumbo nonsense. Fucking around with people's heads and making them worse than they'd been to start with. The problem was, Blume had been getting results in some high-profile cases recently, and the top brass were impressed by those results.

Holten didn't want the man anywhere near his investigation, but when Blume had shown up, uninvited, at the station this morning, Holten had felt like he had had no choice but to accept the services on offer. He and McDonagh had gotten nowhere with Rue Hunter, and she'd been in custody for more than twenty-four hours by then. They'd questioned her gently at first, then harder, but she wouldn't speak to them. She didn't want to exercise her right to a free public defender, she didn't want to talk about Devil's Drop, she just wanted to go home.

Holten had reluctantly agreed to let Blume have a try with the girl. He leaned back in his chair now, put his feet up on the desk, and watched what was happening on the other side of the mirrored window.

Rue had ignored Blume's offer of a handshake, but the man was unperturbed. He gave her his best Robert Redford smile, with the lips as well as the eyes, and clasped his hands together on top of a folder sitting on the table in front of him.

"Okay, no handshakes," he said. "But I should introduce myself properly. My name is Dr. Ted Blume."

"I don't need a doctor," Rue said. "I'm not sick. And I don't like doctors."

"I'm not a medical doctor, Rue. I help fix people's minds, rather than their bodies."

"I'm not sick in the head either."

He smiled. "No, of course not. I also help people who are a little sad feel better, and I help people remember things they might have forgotten. I promise, I'm not a scary doctor. In fact, most of my patients call me Dr. Ted or even just Dr. T. You know, like Mr. T off the TV? You ever watch that show?"

Rue eyeballed him for a few seconds, but his smile never wavered.

Finally, she said, "Sure, I've watched it. But you're nothing like Mr. T. He's black and has lots of jewelry. And he doesn't wear linen suits. You're more like the other one, who's always smoking the cigars."

Blume chuckled. "I guess I am. But Mr. T is cooler."

"You scared of flying too? Like Mr. T?"

"No, I like airplanes," Blume said. "Some of them even give you free booze during the flight."

"My sister, Rose, is scared of flying. Just like Mr. T. She says it's not normal, a machine that big moving through the air. She worries the airplane might drop right out of the sky if she ever got on one. Me? I can't think of anything better than floating above the clouds."

Holten was stunned. It was the most Rue Hunter had spoken since they'd brought her in early yesterday morning.

Blume said, "You'll get on that airplane one day soon, Rue. I'm absolutely sure of it. But, first of all, we need to get you out of this place, and I'm going to need your help to make it happen. Okay?"

Rue nodded. "Okay."

"I need you to tell me what happened at Devil's Drop."

Even from where he was sitting in the other room, Holten could see the girl stiffen.

"I already told those two cops I don't know what happened," she said. "I don't remember anything."

Blume said, "That's perfectly understandable, Rue. What happened to your friends was shocking, absolutely devastating. The police officers tell me there's some evidence to suggest you were at Devil's Drop when the murders took place, so it must have been very traumatic for you. And, sometimes, when we are subjected to violent or frightening events, the mind tries to protect us by hiding those memories from us."

Rue looked at Blume as though he was the one who needed a head doctor.

"What the hell are you talking about?"

"Okay, let me put it this way," Blume said. "Imagine your mind has lots of different drawers where you can store different thoughts and memories. If something bad happens, you might want to put that particular memory inside one of the drawers right at the back, close it tight, and try to forget all about it. The memory isn't gone completely. It's still there, just hidden away in a drawer. When trying to retrieve the memory, it's just about finding the right drawer to open. In your case, the drawer where the Devil's Drop memories have been stored. Does that make any sense?"

"What a load of horseshit," Holten muttered.

To his surprise, Rue nodded.

"I guess so," she said. "Like putting all your bad thoughts into a box and locking it?"

"Exactly." Blume beamed, looking pleased with himself. "Drawer or box. It doesn't really matter. It's pretty much the same thing."

"But what if you threw away the key, and you can't open the box anymore?"

"There are other ways to open the box."

"I'm not letting you hypnotize me, if that's what you're getting at." Rue folded her arms across her chest. "I saw a show about it once on TV. The folks who were hypnotized then started stripping and dancing around the stage like chickens. No way am I doing anything like that."

Blume laughed. "I'm not going to hypnotize you, Rue. There are other methods we can try. But being in a more relaxed state does help. Like when you're asleep. Sometimes memories can present themselves as dreams. Have you slept at all while you've been here at the station?"

"A little. Not much."

"Any dreams or nightmares? Anything about Devil's Drop?"

Rue looked away. "I don't know. Maybe."

"What did you dream about?" Blume asked gently. "What did you see in the dream?"

Holten held his breath.

"A knife," Rue said.

Holten breathed out slowly.

"Holy shit," he whispered.

"Tell me about the knife," Blume said.

Rue shook her head. "I don't remember much about it."

Blume opened the folder, pulled out a photograph, and placed it in front of Rue. It was a close-up shot of the murder weapon. A five-inch switchblade with an ornate wooden handle. The knife was caked in dried blood. Lucas's and Megan's blood.

Rue stared at the photo.

"Do you recognize this knife, Rue?"

She nodded. "Yes."

"From Devil's Drop?"

"No. I don't know. I bought the knife for Lucas. It was a gift for our one-year anniversary."

This was news to Holten. Rue had refused to discuss the knife when questioned by the sheriff and his deputy. He'd check it out. Find out where she bought it, when exactly the knife had been purchased.

"Did Lucas's parents know about this gift?" Blume asked.

"No," said Rue. "They'd freak if they thought he was carrying a knife."

116

"Is this the same knife from your dream? Take another look at the photo."

Rue did as she was told, shrugged helplessly.

"Maybe."

"Okay, close your eyes and try to relax," Blume said. "Then try to imagine the knife, this knife, in your hand. How does it feel?"

Rue squeezed her eyes shut. The silence hung heavy in the room for a full minute, then two minutes. Holten could hear deep, fast breathing, then realized it was his own.

"It feels heavy," Rue said eventually. "And it's wet. I need to grip it tight to stop it from slipping from my hand."

"Good girl," Blume soothed. "You're doing great. What else do you remember?"

Rue's eyes opened. "Nothing. I don't remember anything else."

Blume pulled some more images from the folder. Holten leaned forward for a better look. They were crime scene photos of Lucas James's car.

"I'm going to show you some photos taken at Devil's Drop," Blume said. "See if they help jog your memory, help you put yourself at the scene."

The first photo showed the driver's side of the vehicle. The rear door was shut. Smears of blood stood out a darker shade of red on the car's burgundy paint. There were red smudges on the window. The second photo was taken from the other side of the Toyota Cressida and showed a lifeless Megan Meeks hanging out of the open door.

Rue pushed the photos away.

"I don't want to see them. You can't make me look. Put them away."

"Okay, calm down, Rue. I'm putting the photographs away now."

Blume slid the crime scene photos back into the folder. Steepled his hands underneath his chin and stuck out his bottom lip. He was silent for a few moments, as though deep in thought.

"Let's try something else," he said at length. "No visual aids this time. What I want you to do now is to focus on the dream. How did you feel in the dream? How did you feel when you woke up? What were your emotions?"

Again, Rue closed her eyes.

"I was scared," she said in a small voice. "And angry."

"Let's focus on the anger. Why are you angry? Who made you angry?"

"I don't know. I don't remember."

"Were you angry with Megan and Lucas?"

She opened her eyes and stared at Bloom.

"I don't remember. I don't think so. Why would I be angry with Megan and Lucas?"

"Maybe they did something to make you mad?"

"No."

Holten could see the girl was becoming agitated again. Blume picked up on it too and quickly changed tack again.

He said, "Before Devil's Drop, did you have trouble remembering things?"

"Sure, if I have too much to drink, I don't remember much about the night before. Hell, I might not even remember my own name, depending on how much liquor I've had."

"Any other times? What about when you were younger?"

"Maybe," Rue said. "I don't know."

"The box you spoke about earlier? Did you ever put some bad thoughts in there and lock the box and throw away the key?"

"Maybe."

"Who told you about the box?"

Rue scrunched up her face, like she was thinking hard.

"My sister, Rose. She said if the bad stuff was locked in a box, it couldn't hurt me anymore."

"What bad stuff?"

Rue didn't answer him.

"Does your mom hit you, Rue?"

"A slap now and then. No big deal. It usually happens when she's drunk and wants to lash out at someone. Most of the time, she doesn't even remember doing it afterward."

"How does it make you feel when she lashes out at you? Does it make you angry?"

"I guess."

"Did your mom hit you when you were a child too?"

"Sure," Rue said. "Like I said, the occasional slap."

"Anyone else ever hit you?"

Rue frowned. "Anyone like who?"

"I understand your mom has a lot of, uh, male friends," Blume said. "Maybe you called them *uncles* when you were younger. Have any of these men ever hit you?"

"If you're talking about all the guys my mother screws when she's drunk, then no, I have never referred to them as *uncles*. And, no, none of them has ever hit me."

"Did any of them ever touch you in a way they shouldn't have?"

"No," Rue said firmly. "She never brings men home with her. They go to his place, or some cheap motel, or even do it on the flatbed of his truck in the bar's parking lot. But they never come to our house."

"Are you angry with your daddy for leaving you?"

"No, why would I be? I didn't even know him. As far as I can tell, Leonard Hunter wasn't worth knowing anyway. We were better off without him."

"Were you angry with Megan and Lucas?"

"You already asked me that question. I told you, I don't remember."

"But you do remember holding the knife?"

"Yes. It was heavy and wet. That's all I remember." She folded her arms in front of her chest again. "I don't want to do this anymore."

Blume nodded. "Let's stop for a while. You've done great, Rue. Really, really good."

She looked at him. "Really? You think I did good?"

As he'd watched the interview, Holten's opinion of Blume hadn't changed. He still thought the guy was an asshole. But, as much as he hated to admit it, he *was* impressed by how the shrink was getting Rue Hunter to open up to him. Surprised too. He decided to give Blume the benefit of the doubt awhile longer, see if the smooth-talking head doctor could come up with some real results.

"I think you've done very well," he heard Blume tell Rue. "Let's take a break. You must be exhausted. Why don't you try to have a little nap and see if anything else comes back to you? Maybe you'll remember more about Devil's Drop for me if you're able to get some sleep."

"Okay," the girl said. "I do feel pretty tired."

Holten jerked awake.

He must have dozed off himself after Rue returned to her cell to nap at Blume's suggestion. He didn't know what was going on in the girl's dreams, but his own were filled with the horrors of what he'd seen up at Devil's Drop—that was for sure. Memories he wouldn't be able to forget for a long time, no matter how many boxes or drawers he tried to shove them in. His neck ached and felt stiff, and he massaged it as he looked up to see Blume standing over him. The shrink was smiling the Robert Redford smile, with both the lips and the eyes. Hell, there were teeth as well this time. This must be big.

"What's happened?" Holten asked. "What time is it?"

Blume consulted his watch. "Almost ten p.m."

"Jesus." Holten sat up straighter. "I hope we're not paying you by the hour."

"I think you'll find my fee will be worth every cent, Sheriff Holten."

"Is that so?"

Blume pointed to the two-way mirror where Rue Hunter was sitting slumped in the chair in the interview room. The girl looked exhausted, deflated, defeated.

"Miss Hunter and I have had another chat after her nap," he said. "Well, when I say nap, she was asleep for quite some time. It would appear the slumber has done her good and has shaken loose some more memories."

The doctor paused for dramatic effect.

"And?" Holten snapped impatiently.

"She says she now remembers stabbing her friends to death at Devil's Drop," Blume said. "And she's ready to make a full confession."

17

JESSICA

Jessica pulled into a space in front of a 7-Eleven just off Franklin and noticed Pryce's midnight-blue Dodge Charger was already in the lot.

She thought about the message he'd left for her, how it had been blunt and straight to the point. The muscles in her stomach clenched. The visit to the prison in Chowchilla had been nerve racking. The prospect of a still-pissed Pryce was worse than a face to face with a double murderer.

Jessica glanced at the clock on the dash: 9:51. Pryce was always early; she was usually late. So, she figured, she had plenty of time for a smoke before their meeting. She reached for her pack of Marlboro Lights, sunglasses, and bag and climbed out of the truck. She leaned against the Silverado and smoked a cigarette, the nicotine gradually doing its job of setting her nerves at ease. A whiskey would've been better, but ten a.m. on a Monday morning was too early even for her.

She crushed the butt under the sole of her sneaker, popped a breath mint into her mouth, and slipped on the sunglasses. It was shaping up to be another glorious day. She wore a sleeveless black cotton dress, and the heat of the morning sun on her bare arms and legs felt good. The Converse had been a bad idea, though. Her feet squelched inside the high-top sneakers as she crossed the lot and turned onto North Vermont Avenue.

It was an eclectic street with a sprinkling of trendy bars and restaurants sitting comfortably alongside an old 1930s three-screen cinema and tiny handmade-jewelry boutiques. Millennials sipped lattes and green teas as they strolled the sidewalk or relaxed at outdoor cafés.

Bru Coffeebar was squeezed between a gym and a real estate agency. Pryce was sitting at one of the tables in the tiny, fenced-off outdoor seating area, and Jessica immediately felt the palms of her hands become as sweaty as her feet. He was wearing a black open-necked shirt, gray dress pants, and designer shades. She knew he would also have a gold badge clipped onto the waistband of the pants and a Beretta 92FS secured in a shoulder holster, but Jessica thought he would look like a cop even without the accessories.

She had to go through the coffee shop to reach the seated area via an open patio door, and Pryce glanced up from the menu he was reading and nodded a greeting as she passed him. He then stood as she lowered herself into the seat facing him. Pissed or not, he still had manners.

Turned out he wasn't pissed after all. Not anymore.

He handed her the drinks menu and said, "I'm sorry about Saturday night, Jessica. The way I spoke to you? I was way out of line."

"No, I'm sorry. When I agreed to take on the case, I didn't stop to think about the repercussions for other people. For you."

"You didn't know my old partner investigated the murders. You were thinking of Ed and the agency and the money."

"Partly it was about the money. But mostly it was about me. I wanted to feel challenged again. I wanted to prove to myself I could still handle more than infidelity cases and employee background checks. I jumped right in, size sevens first, without giving the whole thing enough damn thought."

"What's done is done," Pryce said. He drummed his fingers on the file in front of him. It looked like a murder book but not an LAPD one. "I may have a way for us to resolve the situation quickly and easily. But, first, we should order. I need to go pick up Medina shortly."

Jessica had forgotten all about the menu in her hand, hadn't so much as glanced at it.

"I'll have a black coffee," she said.

"Me too. I have no idea how to pronounce half of these drinks, never mind know if they taste any good."

She looked at the menu. The artisan selection included exotic concoctions such as Gihombo coffee, Sweet Tooth Shakisso espresso, and Ti-Kwan-Yin tea.

"Interesting choice of venue," she said, arching an eyebrow above the shades.

Pryce grinned. "Dionne likes the place, and it's close to home. I've got a field trip this morning, so no office for me today." He stood up and removed his Armani sunglasses, carefully folded them, and dropped them into his breast pocket. "Two black coffees coming right up—hopefully."

Pryce headed inside to place the order, and Jessica's eyes fell on the file again. She wondered if it was the reason Pryce had asked to meet, but she resisted the urge to open it and have a peek at the contents. Instead, she watched the steady stream of traffic rumbling past and the diners tucking into pancakes outside House of Pies across the street. She saw a battered old brown station wagon parked in the restaurant's lot that looked a lot like Dylan's car.

"Here you go." Pryce lowered a tray holding two large cups onto the table and slid back into his seat. "Some fancy Ethiopian name, but I *think* they're both basically plain black coffees."

Jessica took a sip and nodded approvingly. "This is pretty good. Maybe Dionne is onto something with this place after all."

She glanced across the street again as Pryce dumped the empty tray under the table. The brown station wagon was gone. She figured there must be hundreds of old cars similar to Dylan's on the streets of LA. In any case, he hadn't mentioned a visit to the city when they were together last night.

Pryce tried some of the coffee. "It is good," he agreed. Then he nudged the file toward her. "This is what I wanted you to see. Megan Meeks and Lucas James's murder book."

Jessica pushed her shades on top of her head and stared at Pryce. "I don't understand. Why are you showing me their file? Why do you even have a Hundred Acres murder book?"

"Don't ask where I got it from," Pryce said. "Let's just say I called in a favor. You have twenty-four hours with the file; then I need you to drop it off in my mailbox at the condo. Don't bring it to the station. I don't want anyone there seeing you with a police file you shouldn't have. And don't make any copies."

"Okay . . . I still don't understand why you're giving it to me, though."

"Look, Charlie was a damn good cop, and you're a good investigator, Jessica. I figure the quickest way to put this whole business to bed is for you to see for yourself how Charlie and his team carried out their investigation. Maybe if you look through the murder book, you'll realize there's no big mystery to unravel in Hundred Acres, no unanswered questions, nothing untoward going on. Maybe then you'll be satisfied Rue Hunter is guilty, just like she said she was thirty years ago."

"Thanks, Pryce. I appreciate it. This will be a big help."

Pryce checked his watch. "Shit, I have to go. Medina will be waiting for me. We gotta be someplace by lunchtime."

"New case?"

"Old case."

"I didn't think you worked cold cases."

"I don't. This one is personal."

"Personal?"

"Charlie's murder."

Pryce gulped down the rest of his coffee and nimbly climbed over the metal waist-high fence right onto the street. "Remember,

twenty-four hours with the file." Then he walked briskly in the direction of the 7-Eleven parking lot, turned the corner, and was gone.

Jessica decided to order herself another cup of the fancy Ethiopian
coffee and have a quick look through the Meeks/James murder book
before going through it again in more detail once back in Hundred
Acres.

She skimmed the transcripts of interviews carried out by Charlie
Holten and Pat McDonagh with Rue Hunter following her arrest, the
sheriff and his deputy clearly not having a great deal of luck with the
teenager. Then there were witness statements taken from Patty Meeks,
Heather and Steve James, and Rose and Barb Hunter, none of which
were particularly revelatory. Copies of pages from Megan's diary—which
had been found in her underwear drawer by Holten and McDonagh—
made several references to a secret romance with someone known only
as *L*, who was presumably Lucas James, despite Patty Meeks's doubts.

There were some other transcripts too from interviews carried out
by a Dr. Ted Blume, the "cop psychologist" Rue had told her about
during the prison visit. The woman was right; he did seem persuasive.
Jessica didn't like the sound of the man or his methods, both of which
came across as flaky and outdated to her, but she figured using visual
aids and analyzing folks' dreams were probably popular techniques back
in the eighties and early nineties.

She remembered what Nina DePalma had told her about a little girl
who'd been desperate for her teacher's approval, and Jessica felt like the
eighteen-year-old Rue Hunter had been just as needy for Dr. Blume's
approval. A copy of her confession followed, and Jessica decided to wait
until she'd returned to the detective agency to read over it properly.
After all, those were the words that had effectively sealed Rue Hunter's
fate.

Jessica noted there was no mention in the file of the guy Rue
claimed she was with the night of the murders. Rue had told her the
cops had asked lots of questions about the car ride before dropping their

interest. Jessica quickly flicked through the pages of the murder book again in case she had missed that part of the questioning. She hadn't. There was nothing. She was beginning to wonder if Rue had lied about a ride that night when she turned the page to the clear plastic folder containing the crime scene photos.

And alarm bells started to ring.

The first three images were held together by a paper clip and showed tire treads in the mud not far from Lucas James's Toyota Cressida. Scribbled on a faded yellow Post-it note stuck on the top photo were the words *No further action required.*

Jessica then turned to the prints of the two bodies in the back seat of the vehicle. Megan was wearing white jeans and a black silk blouse, just as Patty Meeks had described in their conversation at her home yesterday. And Jessica knew from the prison visit with Rue Hunter that Lucas had been wearing blue jeans and a black-and-white plaid shirt. The woman had spent the last thirty years being haunted by nightmares of herself ripping apart those clothes, and the flesh that lay underneath them, with a bloodied knife.

Jessica stared at the crime scene photo of Lucas James again.

He wasn't wearing blue jeans or a black-and-white plaid shirt.

18

PRYCE

Pryce drove north for seventy miles, deep into the Antelope Valley on the western tip of the Mojave Desert. Medina had spent most of the journey reading up on the murders of Charlie Holten and Angel Henderson.

A cop and a street kid. Worlds apart in life, but their deaths both compressed into a bunch of pages in three-ring binders to be pored over by strangers.

Dry, bleached scrubland stretched as far as the eye could see on either side of the car until a large compound made up of more than two dozen squat gray-and-white buildings appeared on the shimmering horizon up ahead. Like a desert mirage under a baking sun. As they got closer, they could see high razor-wire fencing enclosing the facility that was home to more than three thousand male inmates.

Once inside the building, Pryce was reminded again how prisons always smelled like hospitals, a gut-churning mix of cleaning products and bad food and piss and shit. The only pop of color in the gray concrete interview room was provided by the orange jumpsuit worn by the inmate who was waiting for them. The man was shackled to a table by his handcuffs. He was tall and muscular, the bright uniform stretched tight across wide shoulders. The floppy dreads were long gone, replaced now by graying hair cropped close to the scalp.

DaMarcus Jones regarded Pryce with a hint of amusement in his brown eyes.

"Long time no see, Detective Pryce," he said. "To what do I owe the pleasure after all this time? Must be, what, almost twenty years since we last spoke?"

"Think of it as a pleasant surprise," Pryce said.

DaMarcus Jones had clearly looked after himself throughout his incarceration. Pryce guessed the toned physique was down to daily cell squats, push-ups, sit-ups, and lunges. A man who made full use of the exercise yard by actually walking around it, instead of huddling in corners smoking and plotting and hustling like other inmates when granted their daily hour of fresh air.

From what Pryce had heard, DaMarcus Jones had been working on his soul, as well as his body, during his years inside. The former gangbanger and pimp was now the unofficial prison chaplain after apparently turning his back on the devil and finding religion. Pryce spotted a cross crudely inked on the back of his right hand, its lines blurred by a blunt needle and the passage of time. He wondered if DaMarcus Jones was Catholic and how he felt about confession.

"You know why I'm here, DaMarcus," he said. "Someone put a bullet in my partner's head a long time ago, and I'm not going to rest until I find out for sure who did it. Maybe it's time you finally helped me out."

DaMarcus smiled. "I may have changed over the years, Detective, but my answer remains the same. I didn't shoot your partner, and I didn't order no one else to do it either."

Pryce held his gaze. "You sure about that, DaMarcus?"

"Positive. I was involved in a lot of bad stuff back then, and I'm paying for it now. Have been for almost two decades. But taking out a cop? That's a whole different level altogether."

"What about Angel Henderson?"

The smile disappeared, and Pryce saw something flicker behind the man's eyes. Pain, sorrow, regret. Whatever it was, he wondered if she was the reason DaMarcus Jones had turned to God, why he felt the need to permanently mark his skin with religious symbols, why he tried to steer other prisoners back onto the right path after they'd taken a wrong turn in life.

"I didn't kill her either." He lowered his eyes. "At least not directly."

"What do you mean?"

DaMarcus continued to stare at the table, wouldn't look at Pryce.

"She didn't die by my hands, but I sent her to her death. I ask for God's forgiveness every day, but I'm not sure I'll ever be able to forgive myself for what happened to Angel."

"A john?" Pryce asked.

DaMarcus nodded.

"What happened to him?"

DaMarcus raised his eyes and, this time, there was a hardness to them.

"Let's just say he didn't get the chance to hurt another girl after what he did to Angel."

Pryce knew DaMarcus was talking about street retribution. Something, as a cop, he shouldn't condone. But he'd seen the photos of Angel Henderson's broken body, and he was pretty sure he wouldn't be losing a whole lot of sleep over the punishment handed out to the guy responsible for her ending up dead in a dumpster.

"What about Charlie Holten? He liked you for it, DaMarcus. Took an interest. It must have made life difficult for you considering your line of work back then."

A nod and another smile.

"True."

DaMarcus turned his attention to Medina, who hadn't spoken so far during the visit.

"You don't say much, do you?"

"I'm the strong, silent type."

"Is that so? First time I ever met a cop who didn't like the sound of his own voice."

"It's you we want to hear talking, DaMarcus."

"I said all I got to say."

Medina glanced at the cross on DaMarcus's hand. "You know, they say confession is good for the soul."

"I already confessed my sins to God."

"Maybe he wasn't listening," Pryce said. "Why don't you try me? I'm all ears."

DaMarcus sighed. "Put a Bible in front of me right now, and I'd happily place my hand on it and tell you I had nothing to do with your partner's death."

"But you know something, don't you? I can see it on your face. You say you've changed, DaMarcus. Prove it."

"I have changed."

"So do the right thing."

"Okay, but I want something in return."

Pryce shook his head. "You know I can't cut you a deal, DaMarcus. There's no way I can get you out of this place."

"That's not what I'm asking."

"What then?"

"I want you to go find Angel's grave. Lay some flowers there. I mean good ones from a proper florist; none of that cheap garbage from the grocery store. And then you tell her I'm sorry."

Pryce nodded. "I can do that. No problem."

"Thank you."

"Tell me about Charlie Holten."

"You're right," DaMarcus said. "Your partner was a problem for the crew. Sniffing around, asking questions, sticking his nose in places he don't have no business sticking it. We needed to know what he knew about our operations, so we turned the tables and kept eyes on him. The night he got whacked, two of my guys followed him to the warehouses out by Dodger Stadium. Thought he was meeting a snitch up there. The boys kept well out of sight, waited a half hour or so. Then a truck pulled up next to Holten's car, and he got in the truck. They sat there for a while. Not going anywhere, just talking, I guess. Fifteen minutes later, Holten was back in his own car. They both drove off separately, Holten first, then the truck following a minute or so later."

"Who was in the truck?" Pryce asked.

"No idea, and that's the God's honest truth. If it was a snitch, he wasn't from our crew or any of the others we knew back then. It was too dark to make out the driver, but my guys didn't recognize the wheels."

"Then what happened?"

"The boys held back for a few minutes, then decided they'd try to pick up the tail on Holten again. Just in case he had any more meets planned. They heard a single gunshot, turned the corner, and your man was stopped at traffic lights, head on the steering wheel, horn blaring. The truck was already burning rubber, and my guys pulled a 180 and did the same in the opposite direction."

"I don't suppose your guys got a plate? A make or model for the truck?"

DaMarcus laughed. "You're not talking about cops, Detective. They weren't hanging around long enough to note down a tag or admire the wheels. What I can tell you is that it was a dark-colored dually covered in mud. Definitely not a sleek city ride like those favored by the crews at the time. If it was a hit, it was nothing to do with me or any of my crew."

"A dually?" Pryce asked.

"Dual rear wheels," DaMarcus explained.

Pryce looked at Medina and saw from his face he was thinking the same as him. If what DaMarcus Jones told them was true, then Holten knew his killer. Had spent time with the shooter just moments before he'd fired a shotgun into Holten's face.

It was as much as they were going to get from DaMarcus, so Pryce and Medina both stood and headed for the steel door to alert the guard outside that the interview was over.

"Detective Pryce?"

Pryce turned to face DaMarcus before stepping through the open doorway.

"Yes, DaMarcus?"

"Don't forget about the flowers."

19

JESSICA

Pryce had told Jessica she couldn't make any copies of the Hundred Acres murder book, but he hadn't mentioned anything about showing the contents of the file to other people. As well as Lucas's clothing, the tire tracks bothered her, and she wanted to know more about the vehicle that had left the treads behind in the mud at Devil's Drop.

Her own knowledge of cars and tires was fairly limited. Sure, she could change a flat if need be. The amount of time she'd spent behind the wheel of a truck these past few years, it was a necessary skill. After all, being stranded alone late at night, waiting for roadside assistance with nothing more than a cell phone with patchy reception and some misplaced optimism about a quick response, wasn't an ideal scenario for any young woman to find herself in.

But, when it came to identifying a vehicle just from its tread marks, she didn't have a clue where to start. Had no idea if it was even possible.

Acres Tire & Wheel Mart comprised a shop front with a garage space out back, about a half mile along the highway from the detective agency. Tires were piled four high on either side of an open front door with sale signs propped on top of each bundle. Shiny steel rims were displayed on glass shelves in the window. A chubby guy who looked to be around the same age as Jessica stood behind the counter. He was wearing coveralls and a greasy baller cap with the name *Jerry* stitched on the front. The shop smelled of rubber.

"Nice truck." He looked past Jessica to where the Silverado was parked outside. "You after a new set of tires?"

"I'm actually hoping you can help me out with something else." She'd already removed the crime scene photos of the tire tracks from the file's plastic folder, and she placed them on the counter now. "What can you tell me about the kind of vehicle that would leave behind tracks like these? Is it possible to ID a make and model?"

The guy—she assumed his name was Jerry—frowned.

"You a cop or something?"

"Something," Jessica said. "Can you help or not?"

"Look, lady, you want mounting, balancing, reconditioning, repair, replacement, inspection, or upgrades, I'm your guy. But I must've missed the day we got the CSI training."

"You can't tell my anything at all?" Jessica pointed to the large sign screwed to the wall behind the guy. It was illustrated with a smiley-faced tire wearing a big gold crown. "I thought you were supposed to be the 'King of Tires'?"

"My boss, Mr. Slater, is the 'King of Tires.' He's on vacation, so I guess you'll have to make do with me."

"And who are you? The Joker?"

Jerry shrugged, and she moved to collect the images from where they were spread out on the counter.

"Hang on, not so fast," he said with a sigh. "Let me have another look at those. I'm no Columbo, so I can't give you a definite answer on the exact make or model or anything, but I should be able to tell you the tire manufacturer and possibly narrow down the car manufacturer from there." He scooped up the photos and studied them one by one. Held them up close to his face. Frowned again. "Nah, I don't recognize these treads at all. Certainly not a match for any of the manufacturers we stock in here. When were these photos taken?"

"Summer of 1987."

He smiled. "Ah, that explains it. Tread patterns change over time, so a manufacturer's style thirty-some years ago would likely be totally different now. If Mr. Slater was around, he might recognize these treads, but it'd still be a long shot. What I can say is, from the width of the tracks, I don't think we're talking about off-road or truck tires, so my best guess is they were made by a regular vehicle. Maybe a sports coupe."

"Okay, thanks." Jessica tried not to show her disappointment.

"One other thing. You have two long treads made by the front and rear wheels on each side of the vehicle." Jerry swung one of the photos around so Jessica could see it and pointed to one of the treads. "But see how the right tread differs from the left?"

Jessica peered at the image. He was right; there was a slight difference in the pattern that she hadn't noticed before.

"One of the wheels on the right side had a spare installed," Jerry explained. "Often, the spares folks keep in their trunks are different than the factory wheels."

It was true. Jessica's own spare was a cheaper alternative to the Silverado's original tires.

Jerry went on. "A spare is a temporary fix, so this was installed not long before these photos were taken, before the driver had the chance to have the spare replaced at a garage."

"I don't suppose you keep records of tire installations carried out on-site at your garage out back?"

"Sure, we do, but not from 1987. We only keep customer files for ten years; then they're shredded."

"Okay, thanks for your help."

Jessica picked up the photos and headed for the exit. The information Jerry had given her might be nothing, or it might be something. Her gut told her it could be helpful down the line, and she felt a prickle of excitement at the thought of making progress in the investigation no matter how small.

"Hey," Jerry called after her. "I could offer you a good deal on some new tires for the Silverado, if you'd like?"

"Maybe some other time."

Jessica figured she might just take him up on the offer when the time came to get the hell out of Hundred Acres.

◆ ◆ ◆

Back in the truck, Jessica returned the crime scene photos to the murder book lying on the passenger seat, then drove the short distance to the agency.

She parked, grabbed her bag, and slid the folder under her arm. Smoked a cigarette and then pushed open the front door. She was pleased to see Ed behind his desk and was looking forward to filling him in on the Hunter case and what she'd found out so far. Before she had the chance to speak, Jessica heard the muted sound of a john flushing, and then the door to the small bathroom opened. Sheriff Pat McDonagh emerged, zipping up his fly. Dylan's father frowned as his eyes went to the file under Jessica's arm. She quickly slipped it into her shoulder bag.

"Hello, Pat," she said. "Didn't notice your cruiser outside."

"Parked outside the diner. Thought I'd treat myself to some lunch courtesy of my boy and then take a stroll along here and have a chat with his girl." McDonagh inclined his head toward Crozier. "We were just talking about you, in fact."

Jessica glanced at her boss.

"I take it the sheriff filled you in on our latest case?"

Ed nodded but said nothing. He was usually as bright and loud as the garish Hawaiian shirts he always wore, but he seemed subdued right now. His demeanor was completely at odds with the pineapple-and-palm-tree print that was today's sartorial choice.

137

Jessica flopped into the chair at her desk and turned her attention back to McDonagh. Dylan had clearly inherited his blue eyes and red hair from his father, albeit Pat's hair and mustache were both now sprinkled generously with gray. He was a few inches shorter than Dylan and thicker around the middle. Sweat rings stained the underarms of his silver-tan uniform shirt.

She said, "If you're here to try to convince me to drop the investigation, you're wasting your breath. I already accepted payment from Rose Dalton to take on the job, and that's exactly what I'm going to do."

"Who's Rose Dalton?" McDonagh asked.

"Rue Hunter's sister. Dalton is her married name."

McDonagh shook his head and sighed. "And what exactly does the job involve, Jessica? Folks are already upset by those reporters hanging around during the weekend. You really think it's a good idea to go upsetting people further?"

Jessica shrugged.

"I don't get it," he went on. "I thought you were happy here? Enjoyed being part of the Hundred Acres community? You're well liked in town, Jessica. Why jeopardize it?"

She was genuinely baffled as to where McDonagh had gotten the crazy idea she was happy in Hundred Acres. Her stay in town was always going to be temporary, but she figured it was information best not shared with her almost-boyfriend's dad.

"I don't want to upset anyone, okay?" she said. "It's a job is all. The agency could do with the money, so I agreed to take on the investigation. I know you were involved with the original case, but it's really nothing personal. Rose Dalton just wants a clearer understanding of what happened the night Lucas and Megan died."

"I was more than just involved," McDonagh said. "I was the one who found those kids' bodies at Devil's Drop. Kids I knew. And what I saw up there is something I'll have to live with for the rest of my life. I can assure you, Holten and I both investigated those murders by the book. You can dig all you want, Jessica, but you won't find anything. Rue Hunter is guilty. End of story."

Jessica was desperate to challenge McDonagh on the tire tracks. Ask him why the cops had decided "no further action" was needed in tracking down a car driven by a possible key witness. But she couldn't ask the question without revealing she'd seen the murder book and landing Pryce in trouble.

She said, "If I'm wasting my time, then I guess it's my time to waste."

"I really can't convince you to drop all this nonsense?"

"Sorry, Pat, but no. You can't."

"In that case, I have work to be getting on with." McDonagh picked up his sheriff's hat from where he'd dropped it on Crozier's desk, fixed it tight on his head, and strolled toward the door. Tossed them a wave. "I guess I'll see you both around."

Jessica waited until the door had closed fully behind McDonagh, then turned to face Crozier.

"I had hoped to speak to you about the case myself. I guess Pat beat me to it."

"You sure this is a good idea, Jessica? Maybe Pat has a point about upsetting people."

"Oh jeez, Ed. Not you too? Since when did you develop a conscience?"

"That's a bit harsh."

"Is it? How long have you been doing this job? Forty years? More? And how many divorces have you been responsible for in that time? How many folks getting fired?"

"None," he said. "If someone's marriage ended or they lost their job, it was the result of their own actions. Not mine. All I do is provide information to people willing to pay for it. I don't make folks do the stuff they do."

"Exactly. That's all I'm doing for Rose Dalton. Providing information."

"I get what you're saying, Jessica. I really do. It's just . . ."

"Just what?"

"Steve and Heather James left Hundred Acres a long time ago. I'm not sure if they're even still living. But Patty Meeks is still in town, and rooting around in the past is going to be painful for her. I just think the woman has been through enough."

"I already spoke to Patty Meeks. Sure, she's none too pleased about my investigation, but I think she understands why I'm doing it."

Crozier's eyebrows shot up in surprise.

"You spoke to Patty? When? What did she say?"

"Yesterday, at her home. She told me what she remembered about the night Megan died." Jessica held Crozier's gaze. "And she also said you never cared too much about upsetting folks in the past if it meant getting the job done."

"Patty really said that?"

Hurt was etched across Crozier's face. It was a brief moment of vulnerability Jessica had never seen before from her boss. Usually his eyes sparkled with mischief; his chubby, weather-beaten face was pink with laughter. Now, he looked sad and serious.

"What did she mean, Ed? Was she an old client of yours?"

"No, Patty was never a client." He offered Jessica a smile that looked forced. "Okay, this case, what have you found out so far?"

Jessica told Crozier about seeing the murder book, how Holten and McDonagh had apparently decided against following up on the car that had left behind the tire treads, how the crime scene photos showed Lucas James wearing different clothes than the ones described by Rue Hunter during the prison visit.

"Good work getting a look at the police file," Crozier said. "I'm impressed. The tire treads are interesting, although it's possible Holten and McDonagh discovered they'd been left behind on a different night.

Maybe that's why no further action was needed? Worth trying to find out who the driver was, though. As for the clothing being different, are there any statements from Rue Hunter in the murder book where she describes Lucas wearing a black-and-white plaid shirt or blue jeans?"

Jessica quickly skimmed the statements provided by Rue, as well as the signed confession. There were no mentions of the clothing worn by Lucas James at the time of his murder.

"No, nothing at all."

"Okay, just be careful where Rue Hunter is concerned. Keep digging, but don't trust everything she tells you."

It was good advice. Jessica was about to ask Crozier about his own recollections of the Devil's Drop murders when her cell phone buzzed. The caller ID showed Jed Lockerman's name. She swiped to answer.

"Hey, Jed. How's it goin'?"

"Not too bad, thanks. Was wondering if you could stop by the store when you have the chance?"

"Sure. What's up?"

"Coupla things. Bottle of Talisker here with your name on it. A thank-you for sorting out the Michelle Foster business. Still can't believe she was stealing from me. I've known that gal since she was a baby."

"No problem. What else?"

There was heavy breathing on the line all of a sudden, as though Lockerman was holding the phone too close to his mouth. When he spoke again, his voice was lower.

"I hear you're looking into that business from '87? That right?"

"Word sure travels fast around here."

There was a pause, and Jessica could hear background chatter from customers in the store. More heavy breathing. Then, almost in a whisper, Lockerman said, "I saw something that night, Jessica. Something I ain't never told anyone else. Now I'm thinking maybe I ought to be telling you what I saw."

Jessica felt that familiar tingle of knowing she could be close to making a breakthrough in a case. She took a steadying breath, tried to keep the excitement from her voice. She didn't want to spook Lockerman.

"You're right, Jed," she said. "You should tell me. Don't speak to anyone else. I'm on my way."

20
PRYCE

Holten's widow had remarried in the late nineties, a year or so after her husband's murder. She'd been Maggie Barclay ever since and had moved out to Studio City shortly after the wedding.

She lived in a small Spanish-style hacienda house on a tree-lined street called Sunshine Terrace, where residents actually had white picket fences surrounding their manicured lawns and well-tended properties. Maggie's home was no exception. Pryce had visited a few times in the past, and he wondered now, as he had done on those previous visits, if her Hallmark Channel lifestyle post-Holten was a deliberate antidote to the years spent as a cop's wife. If the house had been determinedly built on happiness to replace the anxiety and sorrow of her previous life.

Two lawn chairs sat empty under the shade of a giant oak tree in the front yard. Pryce had met Maggie's second husband, an accountant by the name of Harry Barclay, once or twice. He was ten years younger than Maggie and, as far as Pryce knew, still took on private jobs. His car wasn't in the drive, so Pryce assumed Harry was out meeting with a client, which was probably for the best, given what the topic of conversation would be.

Pryce and Medina both got out of the Dodge Charger and made their way up the gravel driveway to the front door. Pryce and Maggie still swapped cards every Christmas, but several holiday seasons had passed since the last time they'd seen each other. Even so, there was no surprise on her face when she opened the door to find him on her doorstep.

"Jason." She smiled warmly. "How lovely to see you."

"Good to see you too, Maggie."

She was smaller than he remembered, and she looked older too. He guessed she must be in her late seventies now. Her gray hair was cut short, and she wore a pink T-shirt with a crochet neckline, navy slacks, and cream loafers. She glanced at Medina, a question in her eyes, although the smile remained firmly in place.

"This is my partner, Vic Medina," Pryce said.

Maggie nodded. "I see. Official business. You'd better come in."

They followed her into a brightly decorated living room. Two ivory leather sofas were positioned on either side of a light-wood coffee table and were adorned with cheerful cushions and throws in paint box colors. Large vibrant sunflowers filled a crystal vase on the sill of the picture window. An afternoon talk show blared loudly from a flat-screen television in the corner. Maggie picked up a remote control from the coffee table and muted the volume. Pryce and Medina sat at either end of one of the couches.

"I was just about to put some coffee on," she said. "Still plain black for you, Jason?"

"Sure is. Thanks, Maggie."

"Detective Medina?"

"Please, call me Vic. Two sugars and plenty of cream for me, thanks."

She retreated to the kitchen, and they could hear cupboard doors and drawers opening and shutting, the clink of cutlery and crockery, the gurgle of the coffee machine. A rich aroma drifted through to the living room.

As he waited for Maggie to return, Pryce gazed around the room. A dozen photo frames topped a sideboard in the same light-wood finish as the coffee table. In one frame was a picture of a much-younger

Maggie and Holten at a barbecue. He was laughing and brandishing metal tongs at the camera, while she smiled shyly from behind a wineglass. Pryce felt a jolt of grief hit him all of a sudden. Grief for himself and for Maggie.

She reappeared just then, carrying a tray with three steaming mugs and a plateful of cookies, which she carefully placed on the coffee table. She handed them a mug each and invited them to help themselves to the cookies, an offer Pryce declined and Medina accepted. Then she sat on the couch facing them, took a sip of her own coffee, and placed it on the table.

"Is this about Charlie?" she asked. "Did DaMarcus Jones finally confess to killing my husband?"

"We are here about Charlie," Pryce said. "But I'm afraid I still can't provide you with the closure I know you want, Maggie. The closure we both want. Vic and I visited Jones in prison earlier today. He still says he had no involvement in Charlie's shooting."

Maggie nodded. "He's still sticking to the same story, huh? After all this time?"

"The thing is, Maggie, I think he's telling the truth."

Again, if she was surprised, she didn't show it.

"You're a smart man and a good cop, Jason. If you no longer believe DaMarcus Jones was responsible for my husband's death, you must have a good reason for changing your mind. Tell me."

He told her about Jones finding religion and helping younger prisoners. About his guilt over Angel Henderson's death and the punishment he'd handed out to the man who killed her. How his fellow gangbangers had followed Holten the night he was murdered on Jones's instruction and had witnessed a meeting between Charlie and a mysterious truck driver late at night in Echo Park.

And Pryce told Maggie how he had come to the conclusion that Holten must have known his killer.

She listened to his story without interruption. By the time he was done, silent tears stained her cheeks.

"You really don't think Charlie's murder had anything to do with what happened to Angel Henderson?" she asked.

"I don't know for sure, but I don't think so."

Maggie wiped at the tears, then reached for the coffee, took a sip, and cradled the mug in her hands.

She said, "You know, I used to get so angry when he'd go out looking for that girl. I'd be on my own, lonely, desperate to feel my husband's arms wrapped around me in our bed, needing to know he was safe at home with me so I could sleep soundly. Instead, he'd be out all night, fraternizing with goodness knows who, cruising the streets searching for a stranger, while his wife was home alone.

"Of course, I knew the reason for his obsession with Angel Henderson, even if he didn't want to admit it to himself. I always believed Charlie thought of Angel as the daughter he never had. Ever since the day he carried her out of that drug house. He was desperate to be a father, and I couldn't give him the children he so badly wanted. You probably already know we tried for a long time, Jason. That we spent thousands of dollars on fertility specialists.

"Much later, we discussed fostering or adopting, but I think we both knew our marriage was all but over by then. When the girl died, he spent even more time away from home trying to find her killer. By then, the anger was long gone. All I felt was sadness. For her, for him, for myself. For what had become of our marriage."

"I'm sorry things weren't so great between you and Charlie toward the end," Pryce said. "And the last thing I want to do is upset you, Maggie, but I do need to ask you some questions."

Maggie hesitated, just for a second, then said, "Okay."

"Like I said, we're now looking at the possibility Charlie knew his killer. Someone unconnected to DaMarcus Jones. Is there anything at all you can think of that happened in the days leading up to Charlie's death that could be helpful? It may be something that seemed unimportant or insignificant at the time?"

She shook her head. "No."

"Is there anyone Charlie might have spoken to or met with during that time frame? Someone we don't know about? Something that didn't come up in the original investigation?"

Maggie shook her head again and placed the mug on the table. Her hand trembled, and some of the coffee sloshed over the side. Pryce shot a look at Medina, who raised his eyebrows. It was the first time Maggie had appeared shaken during the visit.

Pryce leaned forward on the couch. "Maggie, is there something you're not telling us? You know it could be important to the investigation, right?"

She said nothing.

"It could help us catch Charlie's killer," Pryce pressed.

"I don't think it will," she said, her voice not much louder than a whisper.

"Why not let us be the judge of that?" Pryce said gently.

Maggie looked away, pressed a fist to her mouth to stifle a sob. A fresh wave of tears rolled down her cheeks. Pryce thought she suddenly looked even smaller than she had when she'd first answered the door.

"Please, Maggie."

She turned to face him, and Pryce could see the turmoil in her eyes.

"I've never told anyone, other than Harry."

Pryce just nodded, waited for her to continue.

Maggie took a deep breath, let it out slowly.

"Shortly before Charlie died, I found out he was staying out all night for a different reason," she said. "A reason that had nothing to do with Angel Henderson."

"What are you saying, Maggie?"

"I'm saying I lied to those detectives who investigated Charlie's murder. And I lied to you too, Jason."

Pryce felt like all the air had been sucked out of the room. Like he had just taken a punch to the gut. He could see Medina shifting awkwardly next to him on the couch from the corner of his eye, as he stared at Maggie.

"What did you lie about?"

"Charlie did have another woman. I don't think it was really serious enough to call it an affair or to refer to her as his mistress, but he was having sex with someone else. In the weeks before he died."

Pryce was stunned. He'd known the mistress theory had been explored during the investigation, but he'd never believed it was true. Not for a single second. Now, he didn't know what to say, how he was supposed to react.

Maggie said, "From the look on your face, I'm guessing you didn't know, Jason?"

"I had no idea. How long was it going on for?"

"Not long. A month or so."

"Why didn't you tell us, Maggie?"

"I didn't want the state of my marriage to be the subject of gossip at the station." There was a hint of defiance in her voice now. "Don't forget, I knew a lot of those cops. I knew their wives and their families. I was sure Charlie's infidelity had nothing to do with his murder, and I decided our private life was no one else's damn business."

"But how could you be sure this woman had no involvement in Charlie's death?"

"Those two detectives, Hunt and Adams, came to me with their theories about Charlie being blackmailed by a mistress, which was just ridiculous. For a start, we had no money. We were surviving on a cop's salary, and any savings we did have had been eaten up by fertility treatment payments. And even if it wasn't about money, even if she was blackmailing him for some other reason, the woman had no hold over him, as far as I could tell. I knew Charlie was sleeping with her, and she knew that I was aware of what was going on, had been since the first night they got together. Then Hunt and Adams mentioned DaMarcus Jones, and his connection to Angel Henderson, and I was convinced she was the reason Charlie was murdered. So I kept quiet about his other woman."

"How did you find out about her?"

"He told me. We were already sleeping in separate rooms by then. He came home late one night, drunk and sobbing and stinking of her perfume, and he shook me awake and told me what he'd done. Said he still loved me, but he'd needed to feel the kind of physical intimacy we hadn't shared for a long time. I held him in my arms as he cried like a baby, and I told him to do what he had to do. He spent the night with her a few more times before he died."

Pryce had known nothing about the affair. Realized now just how little he'd really known about his partner. The revelation was like a brick to the face.

"Can you tell me anything about this woman?" he asked. "You know we'll have to try to track her down and speak to her about Charlie's murder, right? Especially now that we're looking at other angles not involving DaMarcus Jones."

"Of course," Maggie said. "I truly am sorry for not telling you the truth, Jason. I was ashamed, and I genuinely thought DaMarcus Jones was behind Charlie's death. But I'm afraid there's not much I can tell you about the woman other than her name was Marie, and she worked in a bar called the Raeberry over in the Eastside."

"We'll check it out," Pryce said. He nodded at Medina, who withdrew a small notepad from his jeans pocket and wrote the names of both the woman and the bar. "Is there anything else you can tell us about the days leading up to the murder that might be useful? Anything else you felt you couldn't tell us at the time?"

Maggie shook her head. "I told Hunt and Adams everything else I knew. How Charlie had been anxious and agitated in the days before the shooting, how I was sure he had something on his mind but wouldn't discuss it. How he'd shut down any attempts at a conversation."

"Any ideas at all about what might have been bothering him?"

"None whatsoever." She looked at Pryce. "All I can say is, it must have been something big if he felt he couldn't confide in you or me."

21

JESSICA

Jessica reached the liquor store in under five minutes, eager to hear what Lockerman had to tell her.

It was a straight run, east along the highway, in the opposite direction from the tire mart. The building was low and detached and had a kind of disheveled appearance, like the drunks it serviced every day. Once-white paint flaked off in chunks, like dry skin on sunburned shoulders, the result of decades spent baking in fierce heat and being roughly swept by desert winds. The midafternoon sun glinted off the yellow store sign propped on the flat roof, unlit now, but a beacon for those cruising the highway after dark.

Jessica ignored the "no parking" warning, mounted the curb, and pulled up between a black plastic trash receptacle and an empty newspaper dispenser. A plastic banner advertising an energy drinks offer flapped in the soft breeze. She put the truck into park and watched as a guy in a dirty wifebeater stumbled out of the store clutching a brown paper bag, looking like his purchase was an attempt to recover from last night's drunk.

One of the double doors was propped open. The other had a crude cardboard sign taped behind the glass, under the red blinking LED **OPEN** sign, advertising the assistant manager's job. At first glance, the place appeared empty. No customers, no Jed Lockerman, the counter unmanned. Jessica wandered down the center aisle, snacks and candy bars and potato chips stacked on one side, freezers filled with packs of ice on the other. Then she spotted Lockerman in the warped reflection of a circular convex security mirror nailed high on the back wall.

She turned the corner into the next aisle and found him on his knees in front of an open refrigerator, stacking bottles of Bud and Coors and MGD onto the bottom shelf.

"Hi, Jed."

He glanced over his shoulder. "Hey, Jessica. I didn't expect you to get here quite so soon." He pushed himself to his feet with a groan, left the rest of the beers in the cardboard boxes on the floor, and started making his way toward the front door. "Let me just lock up for ten minutes. I don't want anyone to interrupt our conversation, and I don't have staff cover in order to have a chat out back since firing Michelle."

"Sure thing."

Jessica wandered back the way she had come and waited for Jed next to the cash register. He secured the front door, hurried back along the aisle, and slipped behind the counter. Pulled a bottle of Talisker from the shelf behind him and handed it to her.

"This is for you," he said. "As promised."

"You really don't have to." She grabbed the bottle and slipped it into her bag. "But thanks anyway."

Jessica leaned on the counter and appraised him. She wasn't one for judging people on looks alone, figured a guy who could make her belly laugh was worth a hundred Brad Pitts, but Sylvia Sugarman was right—Jed Lockerman was not an attractive man. Reed thin, receding hair, acne-scarred skin, eyes a little too close together. And not forgetting that long, bony nose, now pointing southwest instead of south, courtesy of Rose Hunter's textbook.

He asked, "You really trying to get Rue Hunter off the hook for those murders?"

Jessica smiled. "Not exactly. I'm being paid by her sister to take a fresh look at the case, see if I can find any evidence to suggest Rue might be innocent before her execution. If she's guilty, there's not a whole lot I can do to help her." Jessica stared right at Lockerman's nose and arched her eyebrows. "Speaking of Rose Hunter, I heard you two have a bit of history?"

His face burned red. "Whatever that woman told you is a lie. What happened back in high school was an accident."

"I heard the story from someone else. Rose didn't say a word about it."

"Well, it didn't happen the way she claimed back then." His voice was steadily rising. "I bumped into her is all. Trust me, that gal had problems, just like her crazy, murdering sister."

"Chill, Jed," Jessica said. "I get it—it was an accident. Now, why don't you tell what you saw at Devil's Drop? What's this big secret you've never shared with anyone else?"

He chewed his bottom lip. "It might not be important. Although I think it probably is a big deal. I mean, I ain't never heard anyone else mention it. So I don't know if that means it's important or not."

Jessica huffed impatiently. "Oh, for Chrissake, Jed. Just spit it out, will you?"

He glanced around, as though worried someone might overhear them, even though the store was empty and the locked front door meant they wouldn't be interrupted by customers. When he spoke again, his voice was lower, like it'd been on the telephone. Thankfully, there was no heavy breathing this time.

"Back in the summer of '87, I was a bartender at Cooper's. I was working a shift the night of the murders. It was Fourth of July, which meant double pay and a ton of tips. The place was packed, and it was hot and sweaty. Later in the evening, around nine p.m., I took my break and stepped outside for some air and a cigarette. That's when I saw her."

"Rue Hunter?"

Lockerman nodded. "She was in the phone booth right outside Cooper's. When I'd seen her earlier in the bar, she'd looked totally out of it. Now, she seemed real mad. She slammed the receiver hard into the cradle, left the phone booth, and paced in front of it for a while, muttering and cussing. Then a car pulled up next to her."

Jessica's skin prickled; adrenaline shot through her veins.

"Tell me what happened next," she said.

"The driver rolled down the window, and Rue stormed over to the car and started yelling at him for being late. Called him an asshole a couple times and told him he'd wrecked their plans. He said something about car trouble. She still looked real pissed. Then he mentioned having some beer and pot and how there was still plenty of time to party. Asked if she wanted a ride or not. Rue climbed in the passenger side, and they drove off."

The car.

The treads.

The flat tire.

The driver Holten and McDonagh had decided not to bother tracking down.

"I don't suppose you know who was driving the car?"

"Sure, I do."

"Who?"

"Tom Lucchese."

Lucchese.

Where had she heard the name before? Then she remembered. The plans for a luxury Vegas-style casino and hotel complex in Hundred Acres that never came to fruition. Dylan had told Jessica the story months ago, when she'd bemoaned the lack of decent accommodation options in town.

"The guy who was going to build the casino?" Jessica was confused. "He was driving around on a holiday weekend, with booze and drugs in his car, picking up teenage girls?"

"Nah, you're thinking of Bruce Lucchese," he said. "Tom was his son."

"And you're absolutely sure it was him?"

"No doubt about it. For one, I saw him real clear when he leaned out the window to speak to Rue. And, second, no mistaking those sweet wheels."

"Why? What kind of car was he driving?"

"Toyota Supra Turbo. Cherry-red metallic, pop-up lights, less than a year old by the looks of it."

"You seem to remember an awful lot about a car from more than thirty years ago."

Lockerman grinned. "As I said, it was a sweet ride. Lucchese was a few years younger than me, probably twenty or twenty-one. While I was pulling shifts at Cooper's, he was driving around in a smart piece of Japanese machinery. I hated his guts."

"Fair enough," Jessica said. "Why didn't you tell the police what you saw?"

"They didn't ask."

"You could've volunteered the information."

"By the time I found out about what happened to Lucas and Megan, Rue had already confessed. Lucchese's name was never mentioned, so I figured he was in the clear. Had nothing to do with the murders. In any case, I didn't want to go upsetting the big boss man. Everybody in town was hoping to land a job at the new casino when it was built, and I was no different. Didn't see how causing unnecessary trouble for his boy would help anyone. Especially me."

"What happened to the Luccheses?"

Lockerman shrugged. "They packed up and left town around six months after the murders when the casino project fell through. Not sure where they went. Back to Vegas probably. Or maybe LA." He chewed his bottom lip again. "You think what I saw was important, Jessica? Tom Lucchese giving Rue Hunter a ride that night?"

She thought of the tire treads in the mud at Devil's Drop, just yards from where Lucas's and Megan's bodies had been found.

"Yeah, Jed. I think it was important."

22
PRYCE

Pryce and Medina grabbed a late lunch in a small, no-frills eatery in Silver Lake before taking a stroll down the street to the Raeberry.

It was late afternoon and baking hot. All blue skies and no clouds. The kind of day better spent enjoying the salty breeze coming in off the sea at Malibu or Venice, instead of pounding sizzling sidewalks in the Eastside.

Medina said, "So what do we think the chances are of us finding the mysterious Marie still behind the bar here? Just waiting for us to wander in and ask her questions twenty-some years after the event?"

"Pretty much zero," Pryce admitted. "But we don't have anything else to go on right now."

"Agreed. You want me to take the lead on this one?"

"Why not? Looks more like your kind of place, Vic."

The Raeberry was a small shop front at the end of a block tagged with graffiti. In the lot around the side, discarded shopping carts were parked next to vehicles presumably belonging to staff and patrons. Inside, it could have been midday or midnight. It was impossible to tell once the door closed behind them, shutting out the daylight. The ceiling and lighting were both low, and there were no windows. The bar area was softly lit by red fairy lights, the pool table in the rear of the room illuminated by a branded Corona Extra lamp. A Patsy Cline record could just about be heard playing on an old-fashioned jukebox over the thwack of cue tips striking pool balls.

It wasn't a cop hangout, and Pryce knew they'd both been made as cops as soon as they walked through the front door. He also knew the bartender wasn't Marie. The woman was at least twenty years too young, her dyed blue hair swept back in a ponytail exposing a shaved undercut. She wore tight jeans and a tank top, showing off tattoo sleeves on both arms, and had a silver ring hooked through her nose that, Pryce thought, made her look like a bull. Clearly not Holten's type, he decided. But Pryce had thought Maggie was Holten's type, and, apparently, he had been wrong. At least in those final days of his ex-partner's life.

The bartender eyed them suspiciously as they both took a seat on the padded leatherette stools in front of the bar and ordered a beer each. She wordlessly walked over to the refrigerator, pulled out two Buds, popped the tops, and placed the bottles in front of them. Medina handed over some cash and told her to keep the change. She didn't bother to thank him.

"You cops?" she asked.

"Yep, detectives," Medina said.

"Is there a difference?"

"Well, we're not here to chase an unpaid parking ticket."

"What are you here for?"

"To enjoy a beer."

"Okay."

"And to speak to someone who used to work here," Medina said. "Maybe she still does."

The bartender narrowed her eyes. "Who?"

"Marie."

"Marie who?"

"Just Marie. Does she still work here?"

"No, I've never even met anyone called Marie."

Medina shrugged. "I guess it was a long shot. This would've been back in '97."

Pryce wondered if the woman had some coke hidden in her purse, or really did have an unpaid parking ticket, something to explain the hostility he'd picked up from her the moment they'd walked through the door. Then again, maybe she just didn't like cops.

The bartender asked, "Is she in trouble, this Marie woman?"

Medina shook his head. "She's not in any trouble. We just want to speak to her. She might be able to help with an old case we're working on."

"Sorry, I can't help you."

Pryce said, "Anyone who *can* help? Someone older? Someone who's worked here longer?"

She stared at him for a long moment. Finally said, "My boss will be in later."

"How much later?"

"Maybe an hour or so."

Medina said, "Great, in that case, we'll have two more beers, please."

◆ ◆ ◆

A little under an hour later, Medina was on his third Bud, and Pryce had switched to club soda because he was driving.

They were nursing their drinks when a shaft of early-evening light spilled momentarily across the dim room as the door opened. They turned to see a woman in her fifties glance at them briefly before heading for a door off to the side of the bar, which Pryce assumed was some kind of staff area or break room. The bartender followed the older woman through the door, leaving the bar unattended.

A minute or so later, the door opened, and they both reappeared. The bartender with the blue hair began cleaning glasses and tried to look like she wasn't eavesdropping, while the woman in her fifties made her way toward Pryce and Medina.

She was small and wiry and capable. Short dark hair and alert blue eyes. Dressed plainly in blue jeans, a tee, and black ankle boots. She had the air of someone who didn't take any shit from anyone. A trait no doubt honed over years working in places like this one, whether dealing with drunk customers or cops asking questions. She glanced over her shoulder at the two guys shooting pool, then motioned Pryce and Medina farther along the bar, away from the pool table.

"Cathy," she said, by way of introduction. "I'm the bar manager. What can I do for you, Detectives?"

Blue-hair had clearly given Cathy the heads-up, but they showed their badges and introduced themselves anyway.

"We're trying to track down a woman who worked as a bartender here around 1997," Medina said. "We were hoping you might be able to help us find her. Her name is Marie."

"Uh-huh? And does this Marie have a last name?"

"I'm sure she does, but we don't know what it is."

"Do you have a photo of her?"

"No."

"What does she look like?"

"We don't know."

Cathy raised an eyebrow. "You don't have shit to go on, do you?"

Medina smiled. "No, we don't."

"Why do you want to speak to her? Has she done something wrong?"

"Not that we know of. We're looking into an old case, and we believe Marie may be able to help us. That's all."

"This case you're working on? What is it exactly?"

Medina said, "A police officer was shot and killed."

"What's it got to do with Marie?"

"We believe Marie knew the police officer and may have spent time with him in the days before his death. She might be able to tell us something important. His killer has never been found."

Cathy's eyes narrowed. "And this took place in '97?"

"Yes."

"Why are you looking into it now?"

"The officer who was killed was my partner," Pryce said. "I just want to know what happened to him. And I don't care how long it takes to find out."

Cathy's face softened. "Charlie Holten was your partner?"

Medina and Pryce looked at each other.

"Yes, he was." Pryce said. "You knew Charlie?"

Cathy smiled sadly. "Sure, I knew Charlie. He used to come in here a lot. Pretty quiet, seemed to have a lot of sadness about him, like he might find the answers to all his problems if he stared hard enough into his bourbon glass. I guess you could say the same about a lot of the customers who drink in here. Seemed like a nice guy, though. None of us even knew he'd died until it was in the newspaper."

Pryce said, "Look, Cathy, I know Charlie had some sort of . . . relationship going on with a woman called Marie who worked here. Do you know who I mean? Did you work with Marie?"

Cathy shot another look over her shoulder at the pool guys and lowered her voice.

"Yes, Marie worked here. But it was a long time ago. I really don't think she'd appreciate the past being dragged up again now."

"Please, Cathy," Pryce said. "It might be important."

The pool guys had stopped their game and were now watching the exchange between Pryce, Medina, and Cathy.

"I don't know where Marie is. I'm sorry; I can't help you."

"You must know something," Pryce pressed. "A last name. The name of the street where she lived. Something. Anything."

"I think you'd better leave now."

Her voice was louder, and the hardness was back; all the softness of earlier, when she'd spoken about Holten, was gone.

Pryce saw the pool guys lay their cues on the table and slowly walk toward them. They were in their twenties, both wearing wifebeaters, both muscular and mean looking.

"Hey, Marie," one of them called. "Are these guys bothering you?"

Pryce stared at the woman.

He didn't know whether to laugh or be pissed at himself for being too dumb to realize what—or who—had literally been staring him in the face this whole time.

"Marie?" he asked.

"Shit," Marie said.

23
JESSICA

A while back, a missing persons case had taken Jessica to Vegas, to the parts of town where most tourists didn't venture.

She'd been hired by the family of a young woman who had left behind her small town in Idaho for the bright lights of Hollywood. When Polly Perez stopped calling and writing her parents, and they found out she had left the apartment she'd shared with other wannabe actresses after failing to make the rent, they had gotten worried, asked Jessica to track the girl down.

Turned out, when Polly had failed to make it anywhere near the silver screen in Tinseltown, she'd tried her luck with the big shows in Vegas. When that roll of the dice didn't work out either, she'd wound up working in a strip bar in the older part of town. The kind of grubby establishment that offers five-dollar pitchers during happy hour and ten-dollar table dances until dawn. Situated next to the pawnshops, and title loan places, and twenty-five-bucks-a-night motels. A five-minute drive, and a million miles away, from the Strip and its casino megaresorts and huge gambling floors and dancing fountains.

Polly hadn't come to any harm, wasn't in any real trouble; she'd just been too ashamed to tell her folks what she was doing to pay the bills. Too ashamed to admit her dreams had crashed and burned in the Nevada desert.

It was on this same stretch of road, at the north end of Las Vegas Boulevard, where Jessica found Tom Lucchese, following a database search of properties registered in his name.

He owned an old-fashioned casino and slot machine parlor called Lucky's, a detached one-story where you could eat prime rib for under six dollars and play Keno and video poker until you ran out of cash.

As she walked through the front door, Jessica swapped gentle dusk for a dimly lit room with garish carpeting and plastic potted plants. Her senses were immediately assaulted by the flashing lights and beeps and chimes and incessantly repetitive jangles of the machines. There was a whiff of hope and desperation in the air, along with the prime rib.

Thankfully, there was also a fully stocked bar in the rear of the room, and Jessica headed straight for it and settled on a stool. The bartender was a petite blonde with a ready smile. Not beautiful but pretty enough to guarantee decent tips from those with pockets weighted down with slot machine winnings. Her name was Shawna, and she was the bar manager, information Jessica had already garnered from the staff page of Lucky's website, which also included a photo and short bio about the owner, Tom Lucchese.

He was in his early fifties, tan, with brown wavy hair worn a little too long, and a smile clearly enhanced by expensive cosmetic dentistry. A self-proclaimed successful businessman who was happily married to Jeanne and who had two adorable kids. He'd bought the casino in late '97, funded a major refurbishment, changed the name to "Lucky's," and thrown open the doors to the public in early '98. It might not occupy a prime spot on the Strip, but the place was busy on a weeknight and, Jessica guessed, turned over a pretty profit for Lucchese.

Following in his father's footsteps, she thought, right down to the name of the casino.

She ordered a Scotch on the rocks and watched Shawna pour the liquor and drop some ice in the tumbler.

"Are you here on vacation?" she asked.

"Business."

Shawna frowned ever so slightly, as though wondering what kind of business might take a young woman to the industrial part of Vegas on a Monday night, but she didn't ask any more questions, just slid the drink across the counter, the frown replaced by a smile.

"Here you go. Just holler if you want a refill."

Jessica handed over some bills and took a sip of whiskey. It was house stuff but passable. "I was hoping for a quick word with your boss, if he's around?"

"Mr. Lucchese?" Shawna said. "Sure, I think he's still in his office. Haven't seen him leave for the evening. Do you have an appointment? What's your name?"

"I don't have an appointment, and he won't know my name."

The frown returned. "Oh, in that case, I don't think I should disturb him."

"I think he'll want to speak to me," Jessica said. "We know some of the same folks from the time he lived in Hundred Acres."

"Okay, let me give him a try."

Shawna walked over to a wall phone behind the bar, picked up the receiver, and hit a button. Waited a few seconds, then whispered something, nodded even though the person on the other end of the line couldn't see her, hung up, and approached Jessica.

"Sorry, Mr. Lucchese says he's busy right now. I guess you'll have to catch up some other time."

Jessica smiled. "Give Mr. Lucchese another call and tell him I'd like to discuss the events of Fourth of July 1987. I think he'll want to hear what I have to say."

Shawna hesitated, then sighed and wandered over to the phone again. Went through the same motions as a few moments earlier. Lifted the receiver, hit the button, waited, whispered something, nodded. This time, when she hung up, she motioned Jessica to follow her to a door next to the bar marked "Staff." She swiped a key card hooked to her belt across a sensor and pushed open the door to reveal a small, narrow corridor.

"Mr. Lucchese's office is right at the end of the hallway," she said. "He says you can have five minutes."

Jessica passed a brightly lit break room that stank of stale micro-waved food and coffee on one side of the hallway, and male and female restrooms that stank of stale urine on the other. She rapped her knuckles on the last door she came to.

"Come on in."

Jessica opened the door to reveal a cluttered, cramped office space mostly taken up by a desk, a couple chairs, and shelves stuffed full of magazine files. Behind the desk sat the real-life version of Tom Lucchese, which was rougher around the edges than the airbrushed one on the website. He didn't bother standing up, just gestured for Jessica to take a seat facing him, and gave her a wary look.

"I'm sorry—I didn't catch your name."

"I didn't give my name. It's Jessica Shaw. Thanks for agreeing to see me. I know you're a very busy man."

He stared at her for a moment, then grinned, exposing teeth that were also less impressive than in the website photo.

"This place sure does keep me busy," he agreed. "Shawna mentioned we have some friends in common? I'm intrigued. I haven't been to Hundred Acres for years. Decades, in fact."

"More of a mutual acquaintance than a friend," Jessica said. "At least, as far as I'm concerned. Her name is Rue Hunter."

A shadow passed across Lucchese's face, followed by a nonchalant expression.

"I know who she is, of course, but I never met her. We certainly weren't friends."

"But friendly enough to offer her a lift to Devil's Drop the night of the murders?"

Lucchese's face paled under his tan, and he blinked a few times before regaining his composure.

"I have no idea what you're talking about or why you're interested in something that happened thirty years ago, but you've clearly mistaken me for someone else." He began to rise from his seat. "As you said, I'm a very busy man, so if you don't mind . . ."

"Actually, I do mind," she said. "I'm a private investigator who has been hired to look into the Devil's Drop murders. I have an eyewitness who saw you pick up Rue Hunter outside Cooper's shortly before the murders took place."

"Whoever this 'eyewitness' is, he's lying."

Jessica placed her cell phone on the desk in front of Lucchese and swiped the screen to show each of the crime scene photos of the tire treads.

"I also have an expert who has verified these tire treads, photographed at Devil's Drop on the night of the murders, are a match for the Toyota Supra Turbo you were driving that summer. That is, there's a match with the wheels on the left side that still had the original manufacturer's tires. You installed a spare on the right side shortly before these photographs were taken."

Jessica figured referring to Jerry from Acres Tire & Wheel Mart as an expert was stretching things, but the store assistant *had* confirmed the tread patterns matched Toyota tires from the late eighties when she'd returned to the store after her conversation with Lockerman.

Lucchese was fully out of his seat now.

"Okay, you need to leave."

Jessica scooped up her cell phone and dropped it in her bag.

"Maybe I should've just gone straight to the Hundred Acres Sheriff's Department with what I've found instead of coming here first."

"You trying to blackmail me? Is that what this is all about? Well, too bad, because the cops already know. They've known all along."

"I'm not trying to blackmail you," Jessica said calmly. "I have no interest in your money. I'm simply trying to establish what happened that night and your role in it all."

Lucchese settled back into the chair. Ran his fingers through his too-long hair.

"I tell you what I know, and then you leave, okay? I don't have any more surprise visits from cops at my place of work. Agreed?"

"I'm a private investigator, not a cop. But, sure, feel free to off-load."

He said, "I didn't know Rue Hunter, had never met her before that night, and that's the truth. I was passing Cooper's and saw her outside. She seemed in a bad way. I stopped and asked if she was okay. You know, like a Good Samaritan. She was upset, said she had to meet her friends at Devil's Drop and didn't have a ride. Asked if I'd take her. I felt sorry for her, so I said yes. Worst decision I ever made. So I dropped her off at Devil's Drop, like she asked. The place was deserted. No other cars, no sign of those kids who wound up dead. Then I left. A couple of days later, I heard the bitch had confessed to butchering her friends. I knew it looked bad for me, so I told my dad what happened, and he sorted it out."

"Sorted it out how?"

"We paid a visit to the sheriff's department. Explained what happened, how it would be beneficial for everyone involved if the Lucchese name was kept out of the investigation. The girl had already confessed to the murders by then. It made perfect sense. For the good of the town and all."

"So Holten and McDonagh both agreed to cover up a key witness, an important part of the investigation? For the sake of the *town*? What about Rue Hunter? What about what was best for Lucas and Megan?"

Lucchese shrugged. "What can I say? My father was a very persuasive man. What Bruce Lucchese wanted, Bruce Lucchese got."

24
HOLTEN

1987

Holten was reading over Rue Hunter's confession again when the phone on his desk buzzed. It was his receptionist, Sandy.

"I have Bruce Lucchese and his son at the front desk," she said. "He says they both need to speak to you immediately."

"Can you check the planner and ask him to make an appointment, please, Sandy? I'm up to my ears in paperwork right now."

"I already did. He says it's important."

"I'm sure he's aware we're in the middle of a big case. Tell him it'll have to wait."

"He says it's about the case."

Holten sighed and rubbed his eyes. He'd endured another sleepless night following the Hunter girl's confession. A meeting with an asshole businessman and his arrogant son was the last thing he needed.

"Okay, show them through to the interview room. I'll be there shortly."

He hung up the phone and saw McDonagh give him a quizzical look from across the office.

"Who's being interviewed?"

"Bruce Lucchese and his kid. Says he has information about the Hunter case."

"Seriously? What could Lucchese possibly know about the murders?"

"Exactly," said Holten. "My guess is he's fishing for information. Probably wants to figure out how much damage the bad publicity might do to his big casino project."

"Yeah, I guess it could be a problem for the development."

Holten thought McDonagh seemed worried, and he had a pretty good idea why but didn't say anything. Now wasn't the time.

"Okay, let's get this over and done with."

The Luccheses were sitting side by side on one side of the table, and Holten and McDonagh slipped into the two vacant seats facing them. Holten appraised father and son.

Bruce was dressed casually in tan chinos and a navy Ralph Lauren polo shirt and deck shoes. He looked like he planned to spend the afternoon on a yacht as soon as the police interview was over. He was in his midforties and very tan and muscular. The type who spent a lot of time outdoors playing tennis or running. He reminded Holten a lot of Dr. Ted Blume—smooth and charming and manipulative. Like Blume, Holten had disliked Bruce Lucchese on sight the first time he'd met him.

Tom Lucchese was basically a younger version of his father. The same muscular build, the same dark wavy hair, and rich good looks. He was dressed in denim cutoffs and expensive sneakers and a Harvard tee, even though Holten was pretty sure the kid never went to college, never mind an Ivy League one. He'd had fewer dealings with Tom than he'd had with Bruce, but Holten wasn't keen on the kid either. From what he'd seen, Tom Lucchese seemed to spend most of his time tearing around town in his Toyota Supra acting like an asshole.

Father and son both usually wore their arrogance like expensive Armani suits, but not today. Bruce was tapping his fingers nervously on the table, while Tom sat slumped in his chair with his eyes fixed on the floor, like he didn't want to make eye contact with the two cops.

Maybe the interview would be more interesting than Holten had first anticipated.

He said, "Bruce, we believe you want to speak to us about the incident at Devil's Drop. Is this correct?"

"That's correct. We have some, uh, information."

"Okay. Just to make you aware, we are going to record this interview. Would you like to call your lawyer? You're entitled to have a legal representative present before answering any questions."

Bruce stopped tapping his fingers on the table and held up his hands.

"God, no," he said. "No recordings and no lawyers. What we've got to say stays between us four. It doesn't go outside of this room."

Holten shot McDonagh a look, but his deputy just shrugged.

"That's not how it works, Bruce," Holten explained. "If you have information relating to the murders, we really ought to be carrying out a formal interview."

Bruce shook his head. "No way. You do it my way or we leave."

McDonagh said, "Why don't we hear what they have to say off the record? Then we can decide if they should make a formal statement."

Holten sighed. "Okay, shoot."

Bruce looked at his son. "Tom?"

Tom shook his head. "You tell them," he mumbled.

"Tom, uh, gave the Hunter girl a ride to Devil's Drop the night of the murders." Bruce held up his hands imploringly. "Hear me out. It's not as bad as it sounds."

"Shit," McDonagh said.

"It sounds pretty bad from where I'm sitting," Holten said.

A rich, older kid like Tom Lucchese was the last person he'd expected to be Rue Hunter's mysterious ride, and he was even more surprised that Bruce was offering up this information about his son.

But any relief Holten might have felt at having the missing piece of the puzzle was tempered with wariness. Bruce Lucchese didn't do anything unless it benefited himself. Holten thought of the confession he'd been reading just moments earlier. He had a feeling his investigation had just gotten more complicated.

"Tom didn't see anything," Bruce said quickly. "He wasn't involved in what happened to those kids. He was only trying to help the Hunter girl."

"Tom?" Holten said. "Why don't you tell us what happened?"

The younger man nodded and sat up straighter in the chair. His hands, which were clasped together in his lap, were trembling. Finally, he looked at Holten.

"I was out cruising around town in the car," he said. "You know, just seeing who was out and about. Thinking of heading to a party or two. I drove past Cooper's, and I noticed the girl standing outside."

"Rue Hunter?" Holten asked.

"Yeah, I guess so. I'd never met her before. She looked totally wasted, so I pulled over and asked if she was okay. She was upset because she was supposed to be hooking up with her friends and didn't have a ride. She asked me if I'd take her to Devil's Drop, where she was meeting them. I thought maybe some sort of secret party was happening up there, so I said yes."

"Then what happened?"

Tom glanced at Bruce, who gave his son a small nod of encouragement.

His gaze drifted to the floor again. "Nothing happened. When we got there, there was no one else around. Definitely no sign of a party, so I dropped her off, and I left. I know I shouldn't have left her on her own up there in the middle of nowhere, after dark, but she told me she'd be fine. She was expecting her friends any minute, and, like I said, I didn't even know her."

"Where did you go after dropping her off?"

"I went home."

Bruce nodded. "That's true." He drummed his fingers on the table again. "Tom was back at the house pretty early."

Holten said, "I thought you were out cruising for parties? Looking for fun on a holiday weekend? So why go home so early?"

"I guess I changed my mind."

Holten looked at Tom and his trembling hands. Then he looked at Bruce with his nervously tapping fingers. He had the feeling neither of them was giving him the full story.

"Why are you here? Why are you telling us all this, Bruce?"

"It's the right thing to do, isn't it?"

"It would be the right thing to do if your son was here to make a formal statement about his involvement in the events that led to the deaths of two teenagers. But that's not the case."

Bruce said, "I know you have your fancy crime scene guys these days who could probably place Tom's car at Devil's Drop. And maybe someone saw the Hunter girl in the car. It's a nice ride, after all. Eye catching. Expensive. I should know; I paid for it. But we've told you what happened. Tom wasn't involved. He wasn't even a witness. So why drag him into all of this mess? The Hunter girl confessed, didn't she?"

"She did," Holten agreed. "She also said someone gave her a ride out to Devil's Drop."

"Did she say who?" Bruce asked.

"No, she doesn't remember."

Bruce slapped his palm on the table. "There you go! If my boy had anything to do with those murders, she would have remembered, wouldn't she?"

"That makes no sense, Bruce," Holten said.

Bruce ignored him. He went on. "In any case, his prints would be on the knife. They'd be all over the car those kids were found in. Run some tests, or whatever it is you do, and you'll see my son wasn't there when the murders took place."

Holten said, "Look at it from my point of view. I have a suspect who claims she was with someone the night of the murders. I have crime scene photos of unidentified tire treads at Devil's Drop. I can't just make them go away."

"Sure, you can," Bruce said. "Cops make stuff go away all the time."

"What's that supposed to mean?"

Bruce looked pointedly at McDonagh.

Holten turned to his deputy. "What's he talking about, Pat?"

McDonagh squirmed uncomfortably in his chair. "The kid was driving a little too fast one night. I, uh, decided to let it go."

Holten sighed and rubbed his eyes. "Shit." He turned back to Bruce. "Making a speeding violation disappear is very different from covering up evidence in a murder investigation."

"Okay, cards on the table time." Bruce adopted the no-nonsense persona of a businessman trying to close a difficult deal. "How much is it going to cost to make this mess go away?"

"What?" Holten was incredulous. "You're seriously trying to bribe a police officer?"

"Look, Sheriff Holten, I've already got two investors talking about pulling out of the casino project on the back of the murders. If the Lucchese name becomes linked in any way to this shit storm, it could shut down the development completely."

"I won't compromise a murder investigation because of some damn casino." Holten eyeballed Bruce angrily. "And I won't be bought either."

Bruce stared back at Holten. McDonagh shifted uncomfortably in his chair again.

"This isn't just about me or Tom or a casino," Bruce said. "This is about the whole goddamn town. Take a look around you, Sheriff. Businesses are shuttered, homes are in foreclosure, the town is dying. There is nothing here for our kids. No future. Lucky by Lucchese could change all that. The casino and hotel complex means jobs, prospects, money, security, tourism. Can't you see that?"

"He's right, Charlie," McDonagh said quietly. "The Hunter girl has confessed. She hasn't implicated Bruce's son in any way. Why let what she did ruin any more lives?"

"Are you serious, Pat? You're really suggesting we cover up crucial evidence in a murder investigation?"

"There is no investigation," McDonagh said. "Not anymore. We have the killer in custody. She will go to jail, and, God willing, Patty Meeks and Heather and Steve James might be able to rebuild their lives one day. It's over. Why not let it go?"

Holten had heard rumors McDonagh was gunning for the chief of security gig at the casino, and now he was beginning to think they were more than just rumors.

"Why do you care so much if the casino goes ahead or not?" he asked his deputy.

"Bruce is right," McDonagh said. "Hundred Acres is on its knees. But it doesn't have to be, not once the casino is open for business. I'm just thinking of my family, my boy, his future. You'd be on the same page as the rest of us if you had kids of your own, Charlie."

It was a low blow, and McDonagh looked as though he wished he could have shoved the words back into his mouth as soon as he'd spoken them.

Holten just nodded. He felt bone tired all of a sudden. Tired of the town, the people, the job. Hundred Acres had been a mistake. He'd known it for a long time now, and Holten simply no longer had the strength to fight anymore. He scraped back his chair, headed toward the door, and opened it. Then he turned and looked at McDonagh.

"Do what the hell you want, Pat," he said. "But when the shit hits the fan, it's all on you. Just you remember that. I'm done here."

Holten closed the door before McDonagh could respond. He meant what he'd said. He was done here. And he was done with Hundred Acres. Leaving Los Angeles for small-town life was supposed to have been the start of the next chapter in his life. One with kids, a growing family. Now, every single day he spent here was like a punch to the gut. A reminder that that dream wasn't going to happen. He decided he would talk it over with Maggie when he got home; then he would put in for a transfer back to the LAPD and take the first opening that became available.

Maybe there was still a chance to rekindle the passion for his marriage and his career—a chance to save them both.

Holten walked out of the station into the desert night, stood there, and watched as a blood sunset slashed the darkening sky with deep red and orange.

He thought about the three men he'd left in the interview room to conspire on their own, and he shivered despite the heat that still hung heavy in the air.

25

JESSICA

It was after midnight when Jessica returned from Vegas.

The sky was black and vast and empty. No stars and no moon. Sylvia's house was also dark, lying silent and dormant behind curtains drawn tightly across all the windows. She had clearly turned in for the night, the landlord's belly warmed and her mind numbed by the liquor that helped her drift off to sleep. The dull yellow glow from a streetlight in front of the house provided just enough light for Jessica to find the trailer's lock. She opened the door, stepped inside, and flipped the switch.

She froze.

The tiny hairs on her arms stood on end, and goose bumps popped out on her skin.

Something wasn't right.

Jessica looked around. The interior of the trailer was mostly open plan. To her right was the unmade double bed, the sheets still bunched and twisted. Jeans, T-shirts, and dresses hung in the open-fronted closet in the sleeping area. The rest of her clothing spilled from an open suitcase at the foot of the bed. Straight ahead was the small kitchen, dirty plates and cups piled on the counter, fat drops of water dripping into the sink. To her immediate left was the dinette, where her laptop sat on the table. Beyond the dinette, at the far end, was the bathroom, the only separate room in the trailer.

Her eyes scanned the entire space again. Then she saw what was wrong.

Two things.

The laptop.

And the bathroom door.

The laptop's cover was raised, at an angle of twenty-five degrees to the base. Jessica always closed the laptop fully when she was finished working, and she always powered off the machine.

She glanced at the bathroom door. It was closed. In contrast to the laptop, she always kept it open. The only exceptions were if she was taking a shower or using the toilet, just in case Sylvia made an unexpected appearance at an unfortunate moment. At all other times, the bathroom door was kept open, especially when she was leaving the trailer.

The reason was simple—to prevent situations like the one she was in right now. Jessica didn't like walking into a trailer, apartment, or motel room and being confronted with a closed door. She wanted to be able to tell immediately that she was alone, to be reassured a stranger wasn't hiding in the shadows, waiting to attack.

Now the bathroom door was shut, and Jessica had a bad feeling about it.

She dropped her bag to the floor, pulled the Glock from the waistband of her jeans, and raised the weapon in front of her. Walked slowly in the direction of the bathroom. Five small, careful, silent steps. Jessica held her breath and pressed an ear to the door. She heard nothing. Then she took a deep breath, hit the light switch, and kicked open the door. Leading with the gun, she quickly took in the room. Her heart rate rocketed when she saw a face staring at her before realizing it was her own startled reflection in the mirror above the washbasin.

"Get a fucking grip, Jessica," she muttered.

She glanced around the small room. The shower stall was empty, and the toiletries on the counter were undisturbed. She crouched down and opened the door of the cabinet underneath the sink and saw toilet paper rolls stacked neatly and a box of tampons and a pile of spare hand towels. Nothing appeared to be out of place.

Then Jessica remembered she'd left the front door wide open.

She sprang to her feet and spun around, the gun pointed straight ahead of her. She was alone. She took several deep breaths. Then she retraced her steps back through the trailer and closed the door and locked it. She placed the gun on the dinette table, next to the laptop, and she checked inside the kitchen cupboards and the overhead storage cabinets and every inch of the open-fronted closet.

Nothing appeared to be missing.

Could she have left the laptop open herself? Closed the bathroom door? Possibly. But Jessica didn't think so.

Sylvia changed the trailer's towels and bedsheets once a week. Every Saturday without fail. If Jessica wasn't home, the landlord would use her own key. But today was Monday, not Saturday. Could Sylvia have made an unplanned visit? Jessica's eyes fell on the messy bedsheets. No, she didn't believe the woman had been inside the trailer in her absence.

Jessica placed a hand on the seat in front of the laptop, where the old leather was wrinkled and slightly sunken. It felt cool to the touch. No warmth from recent body heat. She placed a finger under the lid of the computer and slowly pushed upward until the screen was fully visible. Then she hit the space bar. The screen lit up, showing a password prompt. Two-step authentication was installed, so she was confident the computer's security hadn't been breached. Jessica shut down the laptop and closed the lid.

She looked around the room again. Sniffed the air. There was the faint aroma of the perfume she'd spritzed earlier in the day mixed with the slightest hint of hair spray and deodorant. All floral, feminine scents. She thought she could detect a whiff of something else too. Musk and old sweat. Something unmistakably masculine.

Jessica shivered even though it wasn't cold inside the Airstream. Someone had been in her trailer. She was sure of it. Someone who had no business being in her home without her permission. Then a name popped into her head.

Michelle Foster.

Dylan's ex-girlfriend spent a lot of time driving around in her daddy's old truck, which would explain the smell. But Jessica wasn't convinced. This didn't feel like Michelle. It wasn't her style. Too subtle. So if not Michelle, then who? And why? Was it merely an attempt to take a look at the files stored on her laptop? Jessica thought of the closed bathroom door and shook her head. You didn't break into someone's home, attempt to access their computer, then decide to take a leak. Someone had been looking for something other than computer files. But what?

Jessica's eyes fell on her shoulder bag, lying on the floor where she'd dropped it. The folder poked out of the top of the black leather hobo. The Hundred Acres murder book. She had kept it on her person at all times since her meeting with Pryce. Didn't want to risk losing it and landing the detective, or his contact, in big trouble.

She racked her brain, tried to think of those who knew she had the police file or, at least, access to some of its contents. Ed Crozier knew about the murder book for sure. Pat McDonagh might have spotted it during his unexpected visit to the detective agency. Likewise, Jed Lockerman when she'd visited the liquor store. Jerry from Acres Tire & Wheel Mart and Tom Lucchese both knew she had access to crime scene photos from Devil's Drop. Jessica tried to remember if she had told Dylan about Pryce loaning her the Hundred Acres file, but she didn't think so.

If trying to find out what information Jessica had about the Devil's Drop murders was the reason for the break-in, the next question was, how did the intruder manage to gain access to the trailer? She had used her key to unlock the front door. The lock hadn't been jimmied, and the door hadn't been busted. Jessica found a miniflashlight in her bag and shoved the gun into the waistband of her jeans. She opened the door, stepped outside, shined the flashlight on the lock, and inspected it. There were some superficial scratches, metal on metal, left by years of the teeth of the key trying to find the lock. Maybe a picklock set had been used to gain entry on this occasion, but the lock wasn't damaged in any way, clearly hadn't been forced.

Jessica pointed the flashlight at the ground around the trailer entrance. The beam showed several overlapping shoe prints, all different sizes, different treads, some more defined than others. A mix of prints left by herself, Dylan, and Sylvia. Even now, a light breeze sent swirls of dust in the air, disturbing the prints and making it almost impossible to identify if anything had been left behind by the intruder.

She removed the Glock from her waistband and held the gun and flashlight in front of her as she slowly circled the tin can she called home. She checked each of the windows as she went, making sure they were closed and locked. When she reached the rear of the trailer, Jessica suddenly felt exposed and vulnerable. Beyond the backyard's chicken wire fence, she knew there was nothing but miles and miles of empty scrubland, stretching out toward distant mountains. The streetlight didn't reach this far back, and, right now, all she could see was inky blackness straight ahead, the flashlight's beam illuminating no more than ten feet in front of her. She stood with her back pressed against the cool metal of the Airstream and listened for the sound of another presence, but other than an electrical hum in the air and her own breathing, the silence was as thick as the darkness that surrounded her. She completed the rest of the circuit around the trailer and confirmed no windows had been left open or unlocked.

So how had the intruder gotten inside her home?

Jessica's own key had been stashed in her bag the entire time she was in Vegas. Sylvia had a key, the one she used to access the trailer with fresh towels and bedsheets when Jessica wasn't at home, but she kept it on a chain with her house keys, so it was unlikely she'd misplaced it.

Then Jessica remembered the third key.

It was taped beneath one of the potted plants by the door to Sylvia's house. There were begonia and dead nettle and viola and coral bells. The spare key was hidden beneath a vibrant and vigorous fuchsia plant. Its purpose was to provide access to the trailer in the event of the tenant accidentally locking themselves out or losing the key, especially if Sylvia wasn't at home or it was too late for her to be disturbed. She'd had the third key cut after one of the Airstream's previous inhabitants got roaring drunk one night; lost his keys, cell phone, wallet, and dignity; then decided to wake an extremely pissed Sylvia in the middle of the night to gain access to the trailer so he could promptly pass out.

Jessica made her way toward the house and lowered herself onto her haunches next to the assortment of plants on either side of the front door. There was no sensor light for visitors, so she laid the gun down and used the flashlight to locate the fiery pink and purple leaves of the fuchsia. Then she carefully lifted the heavy terra-cotta pot and looked underneath. There was no key. She lifted the begonia and the dead nettle and the viola and the coral bells, and she inspected the base of each of the potted plants in turn. Again, she found nothing.

The key was gone.

26
JESSICA

Tuesday morning. Three full days and change until Rue Hunter's execution.

Jessica still didn't know if the woman was guilty or innocent, if her memory was as scrambled as she claimed it was, or if she was playing Jessica like a Steinway piano. But she was sure that what really happened at Devil's Drop was only just becoming clear now. And, more than thirty years later, Jessica suspected some folks still weren't telling her the full story.

Following last night's discovery about the missing key, she had endured a restless night. There was no security chain attached to the trailer's door. No chair she could wedge under the doorknob. Hell, there wasn't even a proper doorknob even if there had been a chair. In the end, she'd settled for dragging her suitcase in front of the door, a makeshift barrier constructed of plastic, cotton, and denim that would offer no real resistance to an intruder but would at least alert Jessica to their presence if anyone did attempt to gain access.

It didn't work. She tossed and turned for most of the night and eventually gave up on sleep around dawn, damp with sweat, bedsheets discarded on the floor, her mood as dark as the new day was bright.

The commute to Los Feliz did nothing to boost her spirits. Jessica arrived at Pryce's apartment complex at 9:56. Four minutes to spare until his twenty-four-hour deadline expired. Dionne buzzed her into the apartment complex lobby, and Jessica dumped the murder book in the mailbox as agreed.

The return to the neighborhood had reminded her of the station wagon that had been parked near the coffee shop when she'd met with Pryce the day before, and she made a mental note to ask Dylan if he'd been in LA when she saw him later.

Back in the truck, Jessica pulled out her cell phone and searched for the number for the prison in Chowchilla. She needed to quiz Rue Hunter about Lucas's clothing and ask her about Tom Lucchese. She tapped her fingers on the steering wheel impatiently and waited for the call to connect.

"Central California Women's Facility. How may I direct your call?"

"I'd like to speak to Rue Hunter, please. One of your inmates."

"Are you a family member?"

"No, I'm not. But I'm employed by her sister to investigate her case."

"Are you her lawyer?"

"No, I'm not. I'm a private investigator."

"In that case, this is a prison; it's not a hotel. We can't just page you through to a room."

"So how do I speak to her? It's important."

"There's a process."

"What process?"

"You submit a request for telephone access to an inmate, and we review the request."

"How long does this process take?"

"It depends."

"The inmate is being executed on Friday."

"I'm very sorry to hear that. But we still have a process. I can take your details and submit a phone call request if you'd like?"

Jessica huffed a sigh, left her details, and killed the connection. She put the truck into drive and headed for I-5 and Hundred Acres. As she drove, Jessica called her old boss, Larry Lutz, on hands-free mode. She needed to hear a friendly voice. The call connected, and Larry's familiar Brooklyn accent filled the truck's cab on the speaker system.

"Hey, Jessica! How's my favorite PI?"

"I bet you say that to all the girls. I'm good, Larry. How's the agency?"

"Not the same without you. When you coming home?"

She smiled. "Maybe one day. Just not yet."

Every time she spoke with Larry, he asked when she'd be returning to New York. Jessica had sold her father's house, quit her job, and taken off soon after Tony had died. She couldn't face being surrounded by painful memories, so she'd spent more than two years trying to outrun her grief instead. Recently, she'd begun to feel the pull of home again. She missed the noise and bustle and dirt and grime and the unrivaled charisma of her city.

As if reading her thoughts, Larry said, "You know there's always a job for you here, don't you?"

"You replaced me, remember?"

"Yeah, well, we can always make room for a little one. Seriously, kid, you sound down. Like you got a touch of the blues. You sure everything's okay?"

Jessica sighed. Larry knew her too well. She told him about the Devil's Drop case, how she'd upset Pryce and Dylan's dad, how even Ed Crozier had reservations about her digging up the past.

"What do you think, Larry? You think I'm doing the right thing?"

"Trust your gut, Jess. It's never let you down in the past, and you ain't never been scared to ruffle a few feathers to get the right result."

"I guess."

"Tell me something," he said. "Why'd you take the case on?"

"At first, it was about the money and the thrill of the investigation."

"And now?"

"Now it's about what it should have been about right from the start."

"Which is?"

"People. Those who need answers. That's what you always taught me, huh? We do what we do to help people who can't find those answers for themselves."

She thought of Rue Hunter, Rose Dalton, Patty Meeks. They all needed answers. The events at Devil's Drop had denied each of them, in their own way, the chance to share the kind of mother-daughter moments most families take for granted—college graduations, weddings, special birthdays. Just like Jessica. She'd grown up believing her mom had died in a car accident when she was a baby, before discovering last year the truth was way more sinister. She knew she'd never have closure, not really, but at least Jessica had some answers.

"I think you got this, kid," Larry said.

"Thanks, I guess that's what I needed to hear."

"You take care of yourself. You hear me?"

"I will. Speak soon."

Jessica ended the call and pressed her foot down harder on the gas.

Three days and change until Rue Hunter's execution.

A woman's life—and possible death—depended on her, and Jessica knew time was fast running out to find out the truth.

27

PRYCE

Pryce and Medina ate a late breakfast at the same place on the Eastside where they'd had a late lunch the day before, only this time they both opted for the challah french toast rather than the Cobb salad.

They finished their food, wiped their mouths with paper napkins, and ordered more coffee. Pryce glanced at his watch and realized the tiny hand had moved only three minutes since the last time he had checked.

"You worried she won't show or just admiring your fancy time-piece?" Medina asked.

"I need to pick up something at the apartment and drop it off someplace very soon. But, mostly, I'm worried she won't show."

Marie Conlon had reluctantly agreed to the breakfast meeting after her identity had been inadvertently revealed by the wannabe knight in shining armor at the Raeberry. She'd refused to discuss Holten further with Pryce and Medina at her place at work. The two pool-playing muscle heads had then suggested the detectives both leave without even finishing their drinks.

At twenty-two minutes past the hour, twenty-two minutes later than agreed, the door to the diner opened, and Marie Conlon walked into the room like a welterweight might enter the ring—prepared for a fight and determined to win. Small and capable. Still dressed plainly in jeans, a tee, and black ankle boots.

She spotted the detectives at a table in the rear of the room. Wove past other diners and took a seat facing them.

Pryce said, "Thanks for coming, Marie. I was beginning to think you wouldn't show."

"I almost didn't. Part of me hoped you'd both have left already."

"So why come?"

"I knew you'd keep hounding me at my bar if I didn't show. I figured this way, at least I could get it over and done with. Like pulling off a Band-Aid real fast. Not pleasant but necessary."

"I'm glad you did decide to meet with us," Pryce said. "We'll make it as painless as possible."

"You know, I've been waiting twenty years for you to show up asking questions about Charlie. Still doesn't mean I want to talk to you, though."

Medina said, "The bartender with the interesting blue hair didn't even bat an eyelid when we asked if she knew someone called Marie. Did she forget your name or something?"

Marie smirked. "A couple of cops come into a bar like mine and start asking questions, you don't give up the answers too easily. She texted me as soon as you asked to speak to whoever was in charge."

"Why speak to us at all?" Pryce asked.

"I guess I was curious. I wanted to know how much you knew about me. Turns out, not so much."

Pryce said, "We didn't even know you existed until yesterday, when we spoke to Charlie's widow. She told us about you."

Marie's face flushed at the mention of Maggie, and she was saved by the timely intervention of the waitress asking to take her order. She waved away Pryce's offer of breakfast. Just wanted coffee, no food. They all sat in silence and waited for the waitress to return with the latte and move on to another table before they resumed their conversation.

"How long were you and Charlie having an affair?" Pryce asked.

"I'd hardly call it an affair. More like a fling. Five weeks at most." She stared at the table, her cheeks burning again. "I know it was wrong. The whole thing was a mess. He was a cop, and a sad cop at that, but he was a nice guy, and I guess one thing led to another. What can I say? It's the biggest cliché in the bartenders' handbook."

"There's a bartenders' handbook?" Medina quipped.

Marie looked at him. "No."

Pryce threw Medina an exasperated look. Now wasn't the time for dumb jokes.

Marie turned to Pryce. "I have a question for you."

"Shoot."

"Why now? Why are you suddenly investigating Charlie's murder after all this time?"

"Something came up recently that got me thinking about him again," Pryce said. "Not that I ever stopped thinking of Charlie. But I always believed a man who's been in prison for a very long time was responsible for his murder. I visited him yesterday, and he swore he didn't kill Charlie. I guess maybe I believed him this time, and now I want to find out who did shoot my partner."

"Who is this man you met with?"

"A former gangbanger by the name of DaMarcus Jones."

Marie nodded. "Charlie mentioned him a few times. He believed this Jones guy killed a young girl."

"Charlie spoke to you about Angel Henderson?"

She nodded again. "Usually when he had a bellyful of booze. He felt guilty for not saving her. That was Charlie—always trying to save people." Marie smiled sadly. "The one person he couldn't save was himself."

"How did Charlie seem to you in the days before his death?" Pryce asked. "Was he acting differently? Did he say or do anything out of the ordinary? I appreciate you only knew each other for a short time, but it sounds like your relationship was fairly intense. Is there anything at all you remember that could help us?"

Marie took a sip of coffee.

"One night, he came into the bar, and he seemed really down," she said. "Even more sad than usual, and he was drinking a lot more too. Double bourbons all the way. I was worried about him, so I finished early and took him back to my place. Asked him what the hell was going on."

"What did he say?" Pryce prompted.

"He wasn't making a whole lot of sense. He mentioned something about receiving a letter and how his actions had ruined lives. Said he'd made a huge mistake, and now he had to put things right regardless of the consequences."

"Did you ask what he was talking about? What letter? What mistake?"

"Of course I did," Marie said. "He just kept saying people had to know the truth. He wouldn't tell me anything else."

"Did he mention any plans to meet someone? A rendezvous in Echo Park?"

Marie frowned. "I don't think so. But he might've said something about a phone call he wasn't looking forward to making."

"He say who the call was to? When it was taking place? Where he would be making the call from?"

Marie shook her head. "He didn't. I'm sorry, there's really not much more I can tell you. Charlie passed out soon after. I must have fallen asleep next to him because when I woke up he was gone. It was the last time I saw him."

28

JESSICA

Hundred Acres was surrounded by a kind of barren beauty that Jessica had never really explored in the six months she'd been in town.

Not until now.

She drove west along the main highway until she spotted the turn for an unmarked dirt trail, then bumped the truck down off the steaming blacktop onto the rough terrain. The Silverado's big tires navigated the small rocks and boulders and twigs and dry leaves with an easy elegance as the trail gradually rose on a steady incline.

In town, the flat yellow landscape was punctuated by the occasional burst of green flora. Here, Joshua trees and California juniper were bunched together in dense clusters, and there were hills and mounds and strange jagged sandstone rock formations. On the higher slopes and peaks in the distance, Jessica could see tall, proud white firs silhouetted against an impossibly clear blue sky. The trail, all sand and dirt and bordered by wildflowers and desert chaparral, was just wide enough to pull over to the side to allow any oncoming vehicles to pass. But there were no other cars or trucks on this stretch of road today.

Jessica was alone.

She continued on the same path for another mile or so, and then the wild, hilly trail suddenly flattened out, and a large clearing appeared ahead of her.

Devil's Drop.

The opening was wide enough for four or five cars to park in a row next to each other, while allowing for a respectable distance between each vehicle for the purposes of privacy that had been necessary back in the days when the place was regularly frequented by amorous adolescents. From what she'd heard from Dylan, no one visited this spot anymore, other than the occasional hiker unaware of the place's tragic history.

Jessica parked right in the middle of the clearing, nose facing out toward the hundred-foot drop. In roughly the same position as Lucas and Megan had met their violent ends, from what she could tell from the crime scene photos. She climbed out of the truck and just stood there for a moment, the midday sun hot on the back of her neck. She closed her eyes and tried to soak up the atmosphere. The air smelled musky and earthy, almost like rainfall, despite the heat. A hawk flapped its heavy wings somewhere overhead and unleashed an almighty ear-splitting screech.

Jessica thought of the screams that would have ripped apart the silence here on a July night more than thirty years ago and shivered.

She opened her eyes and looked around. Imagined what this spot would have been like in better times. Horny teenagers, intoxicated by booze and lust. Car windows steamed by heavy breaths and wet kisses. Gently rocking fenders acting as do-not-disturb signs. Devil's Drop should have been remembered fondly as a place where you came of age, where you made silly mistakes or moments of magic, where you took that next tentative step toward adulthood. Not someplace where your life was ended by the sharp point of a blade before you'd even had a chance to grow up.

Jessica walked slowly toward the plunging drop that gave the former make-out spot its name, her sneakers disturbing the dust, a hand raised to protect her eyes from the sun's harsh glare. The drop itself was a large sandstone syncline, dipping deep in the center before the layers of sedimentary rock formations rose upward again on the other side of the canyon. She reached the edge and looked over. Glimpsed reedy weeds, and ragged ruts and ledges, and craggy, sunbaked stone. Her stomach lurched, just as it had done the first time she'd peered over Pryce's balcony at Los Feliz Towers, and she quickly took a step back.

She heard a noise behind her.

It was a sharp crack that tore through the peaceful silence, as loud and unexpected as the report from a shotgun.

Jessica spun around and saw Pat McDonagh standing in the clearing, hands on his hips, watching her. He was around forty feet away. Even from that distance, she could see he was sweating heavily, like an enthusiastic but inexperienced hiker who'd just completed a particularly tough trek.

"Sorry—didn't mean to scare you, Jessica," he called out. "Especially with you standing so close to the damn edge." He kicked roughly at the ground, sending a puff of dirt into the air. "Must have stood on a twig or something."

She walked toward him. "It's fine, Pat. You didn't scare me, just startled me a little."

"Trying to get a feel for the place?" he asked when she'd reached him.

"Something like that. I've never been up here before."

McDonagh smiled, but his eyes remained stone cold. "I'm guessing you're still carrying out your little investigation, huh? Those Hunter women still filling your head with nonsense?"

"Yes, I'm still trying to find out what happened here in 1987, if that's what you mean."

"You already know the full story, Jessica. Everybody knows the full story."

Jessica thought of Tom Lucchese and his claims that the sheriff's department not only knew about his involvement in the Devil's Drop murders but had gone as far as covering it up at the request of his rich daddy. She wondered what else she—and everybody else—still didn't know about what really happened that Fourth of July.

"Maybe," she said. "We'll see."

"What's that supposed to mean?"

"It means my investigation isn't over. Not by a long way."

"It'll be over on Friday when they stick a needle in Rue Hunter's arm and she finally gets the punishment she deserves. Sure, it's a sad story, but it's also a pretty straightforward one. A girl had a lot more alcohol and drugs than she could handle, killed her friends, then robbed their dead bodies. That's all there is to know."

"Maybe," Jessica said again. "It's just that some things don't really add up as far as I can see."

"Oh yeah? What things exactly?"

Jessica hesitated, unsure whether she should push McDonagh just a little bit on Rue Hunter's ride the night of the murders. Decided she could ask the question without mentioning Tom Lucchese's name or that she'd already spoken to him.

"Rue didn't have a car," she pointed out. "In fact, she didn't even have a license. So I can't help but wonder how she managed to get to Devil's Drop all by herself? I've just driven the trail myself, and it seems to me it'd be pretty tough to navigate in the dark and on foot. Especially if wearing inappropriate footwear or no shoes at all."

"She was able to make her way back to town on foot after murdering two people," McDonagh shot back. "We have a witness who spotted her walking barefoot along the highway, covered in Megan and Lucas's blood."

"I guess," Jessica said. "I just figure it's way tougher hiking up a hill than it is to make your way back down."

"People do crazy stuff when they're full of drink and drugs. Trust me on this one, Jessica. Rue Hunter acted alone. No one else was there that night."

Jessica held his gaze for a long moment. "You know why I'm here. What brings you to Devil's Drop today?"

He shrugged. "Sometimes I come up here to think, other times to plink a few tin cans and let off some steam. No one here to bother me, other than the hawks."

Jessica had first learned how to fire a gun herself at the shooting range on West Twentieth Street while growing up in New York. After what happened in Eagle Rock, she'd decided to sharpen her skills again and regularly shot a few rounds at the range over in Silverdale. She didn't plan on adding Devil's Drop to her shooting spots.

"Where's your cruiser?" she asked.

McDonagh pointed behind him, farther up the trail.

"I'm parked there. There are a few nooks just wide enough for a single vehicle if you know where to look."

"This place doesn't bring back bad memories for you?"

"Nah, not anymore. It's quiet and peaceful, and usually there's no one else around. I like it here, despite its past. All that bad stuff was a long time ago."

Jessica nodded. "Okay, then I should let you get back to your contemplation or your shooting. Whatever it was that brought you out here today."

He smiled. "I wasn't hinting for you to leave. There's plenty of space for both of us."

"I have to get back to town anyway."

"You have a date with Dylan?"

"No, I have a date with a locksmith."

"A locksmith? Why?"

"I'm having a new lock fitted on the trailer."

McDonagh frowned. "Have you had a break-in?"

"It's nothing I can't handle."

"Was anything stolen? You should come by the station and make a report."

"It's fine, Pat. Don't worry about it. I'll catch you later."

Jessica made her way toward the Silverado. She climbed inside and backed slowly away from the cliff's edge. As she rolled the truck toward the rough trail that would take her back to the highway, she saw McDonagh in her rearview mirror, still standing on the same spot, watching her drive away. She had no idea how anyone, let alone the person who had discovered the bodies, could enjoy solitude or find any kind of contentment in a place where lives had been taken in such a violent way.

Devil's Drop gave her the fucking creeps.

Jessica pressed her foot harder on the gas, felt the big tires crunch over twigs and leaves and dried wildflowers, her butt bouncing on the seat, as the truck careened down the steep incline.

Suddenly she wanted to put as much distance between herself and Devil's Drop—with its ghosts and secrets—as she possibly could.

29

JESSICA

Jessica met with the locksmith, picked up the new keys, and felt a whole lot better about sleeping in the trailer.

Sylvia would be provided with the spare, of course, but Jessica had decided against telling her landlord the real reason for the new locks. If someone had been inside Jessica's Airstream, it meant they'd also been snooping around on Sylvia's land when she'd likely been home alone. Jessica didn't want to alarm the woman. She'd come up with a story about snapping her key off in the lock and how it was time for a security upgrade anyway. Sylvia wouldn't care as long as Jessica was picking up the check for the replacement. She'd also suggest a better hiding place than the plant pot for the new key.

Jessica then spent a few hours at the agency catching up with other jobs that had been left languishing in her in-box while she'd been focusing on Rue Hunter. They were both basic background checks. The first was an employer requesting the lowdown on a new employee; the second was a fledgling relationship in which the woman wanted to know about any dirt on her new man.

True love for you right there, Jessica thought.

She was just finishing up the reports when the door opened, and Ed bustled into the office. He spotted her behind her desk, and, this time, his smile was as bright as the Hawaiian shirt he was wearing, his mood clearly improved since the visit from McDonagh the day before.

"Hey, Jessica."

She peered at the green-and-purple monstrosity he'd teamed with his cream slacks.

"Let me guess. Mangosteen?"

Ed grinned. "Very good."

"Haven't seen it before."

"It's new. You like it?"

"*Like* is a very strong word, but it's certainly eye catching. Or maybe I mean eye watering. What're you doing here anyway? Isn't it a little late for you to be at the office?"

Ed nodded toward the paperwork in his own in-box.

"Work's starting to pick up again. Thought I'd grab some files to look over at home later. How's the Hunter case? Found anything interesting?"

"I found out whose car left the tire tracks at Devil's Drop the night of the murders."

Ed's bushy gray eyebrows shot up to meet his receding hairline.

"Really? Who?"

"Tom Lucchese."

Ed frowned. "The rich kid?"

"That's the one."

He whistled. "No need to ask how he managed to cover it up. I'm guessing his daddy's checkbook had something to do with it."

"You reckon the cops were on the take?"

"Holten? I don't think so. The guy had a lot of integrity, as far as I could tell. Pat, on the other hand, has always been a little more willing to bend the rules if there's something in it for him."

"We're talking about more than bending the rules, though, Ed. We're talking about the murder of two teenagers."

Like a kid slipping on a Halloween mask, Ed was suddenly wearing the same serious expression as yesterday when McDonagh had stopped by the office.

He said, "That's why you need to be careful where the sheriff is concerned, Jessica."

"I will be," Jessica said. "Cross my heart."

"Have you managed to track down the Lucchese kid?"

Jessica smiled. "He's not a kid anymore. I met with him last night. He owns a small casino in Vegas."

"Like father, like son, huh? What's the connection between Lucchese and Rue Hunter? Bit of an age gap between them. Wouldn't have figured them for friends back then."

"He claims he didn't know her. Says he picked her up outside Cooper's when she asked him for a ride. According to Lucchese, she was wasted, and he was just trying to be a Good Samaritan."

"Do you think he was involved with the murders?"

"I really don't know, Ed. That's what I'm trying to find out. But time is fast running out for answers, at least as far as Rue Hunter is concerned."

"Did you find out about the clothing discrepancy?"

Jessica shook her head. "I've got a request for a phone call with Rue pending with the prison."

They were both silent for a few moments.

Then Jessica asked, "What did you know about the Luccheses?"

"What do you mean?" Ed asked sharply.

Jessica frowned at his tone. "The usual stuff. What they were like, who their friends were, if they were popular around town."

"They were popular with anyone hoping to land a job at the new casino complex, which was most folks around here. I don't think many people actually liked Bruce as a person, though. To put it bluntly, the guy was an asshole. Hundred Acres' answer to Gordon Gekko. Typical eighties yuppie businessman. He liked to get his own way, and he liked to own nice things, and he was happy to show the color of his money to get whatever the hell he wanted."

Jessica remembered Tom Lucchese using almost the exact same words to describe his father.

"What about the son?" she asked.

"As I said, like father, like son. A rich asshole who liked nice things, just like his daddy. A guy who cared more about possessions than he did about people."

"What happened after the casino and hotel complex fell through? Where did the Luccheses go? What did they do next?"

"Last I heard, the family moved back to Vegas, although I had no idea the son went on to open his own casino there."

"Why did the Hundred Acres casino project fall through? Was it a direct result of the murders?"

"Partly, yes. Investors began to pull out almost immediately after what happened to Megan and Lucas. Bruce and his remaining financial backers did try to carry on with plans for the development for another six months or so. The diggers moved in, and foundations were laid, and everything appeared to be back on track for a while. Then a body was found on the land where the new complex was to be built."

"Holy shit," Jessica said.

"Exactly," Ed said. "I guess people started to believe the whole project was cursed, which isn't ideal for a casino where patrons are relying on good fortune. The corpse proved to be the final nail in the coffin for Lucky by Lucchese and, in many ways, for the town as a whole."

"Tell me about the body," Jessica said. "Who was it? What happened?"

"The guy had been in the ground for a long time. Not much left of him other than rotting bones. Turned out to be some drifter from Arizona, a small-time criminal, who'd disappeared sometime in the late seventies. I don't think they ever did find out who whacked him."

"And here was me thinking nothing interesting ever happened in a place like Hundred Acres."

Ed winked saucily. "There's always something interesting happening in small towns. You just need to know where to look." He picked up the files from his in-box and tucked them under his arm. "I'm outa here, kiddo. See you tomorrow?"

"Sure, thing, Ed. See you then."

She heard Ed's car start up outside and drive away; then she opened her laptop and pulled up a Google search page. Jessica didn't hold out much hope of finding any information on the mysterious drifter online, considering how much time had passed since both his death and the discovery of his body. But there was no local newspaper in Hundred Acres where she could search through old back copies, so she thought the online search was worth a shot anyway.

She typed the words *Hundred Acres* and *dead body* and *drifter* and *Arizona* and tapped "Enter." She found one hit that was relevant. It was an article published a little over ten years ago in the newspaper that served a small town in Arizona called Calhoun. A local woman had issued a fresh appeal for information on the unsolved murder of her brother. The man's name was Clayton Manners, a forty-one-year-old salesman and petty criminal who had traveled the West Coast selling cleaning products. He'd been reported missing in the spring of 1979, and his body was eventually discovered on the site of a new casino being built in a desert town in the Antelope Valley in December 1987.

According to the sister, the last known sighting of Clayton Manners was in a bar in Southern California, located just six miles from where his body was later found buried in a shallow grave. He'd spent the evening drinking whiskey, shooting pool, and chatting with a number of women.

Eyewitnesses described Clayton Manners as wearing blue jeans and a black-and-white plaid shirt the night he disappeared.

30
JESSICA

Jessica should have been able to sleep more soundly after the new lock was installed on the trailer. Instead, she'd endured another restless night filled with dreams of decaying yellow bones wrapped in blue denim and black-and-white plaid.

What she couldn't understand was how Rue Hunter's own nightmares for the last thirty years had been haunted by a man wearing identical clothing.

Jessica kicked off the bedsheets and had strong black coffee and a cigarette for breakfast. After showering, she dressed in gray skinny jeans, a black tee, and Converse sneakers, then drove the ten minutes to the station. She pulled into the lot next to McDonagh's cruiser just as her cell phone pinged with a text message. It was from Dylan.

Hey, my dad said you'd had a break-in at the trailer? Why didn't you tell me? Are you okay?

Jessica sighed and tapped out a response.

It's no big deal. Nothing was taken.

Dylan replied immediately.

Even so, I'm worried about you. Maybe you should move in to my place for a while?

There it was. The dreaded next step. Moving in together. The offer may have been presented as a solution to her safety and security issues, rather than an acknowledgment of how they felt about each other, but the end result was the same.

Jessica had had two long-term boyfriends in the past—one while at college, the other when she lived and worked in Blissville. The second one had broken her heart, and there had been no one serious since. Sure, she'd had flings, and she'd definitely had some kind of feelings for Matt Connor. She'd then hoped that what she felt for Dylan might develop into something more over time. Now Jessica knew it wouldn't.

She had no desire to crash at Dylan's place for a night or a week or a month or a year. His affection was suffocating at times, and, if she was being totally honest with herself, she felt their relationship—or whatever it was—had run its course. Like a strawberry milkshake topped with whipped cream, it had been fun and naughty to begin with but had curdled over time. She had known whatever they had going on together was fast approaching its expiration date the day a thirty-year-old murder investigation got her blood pumping faster than her man did. A serious talk was coming all right, but it had nothing to do with moving in together.

Jessica's fingers flew over the phone's tiny keyboard.

Thanks for the offer but I'm good. New lock installed.

She dropped her cell phone into her bag and headed for the station entrance.

Sandy, the elderly receptionist who'd worked for the sheriff's department forever, told Jessica to go straight on through to the squad room. She strolled past the three cells and caught a whiff of urine and vomit from the drunk tank, which reminded her of the prison at Chowchilla. She found McDonagh behind his desk, sitting on a swivel chair, talking on the desk phone. The other workstation, usually occupied by the deputy on duty, was empty. The sheriff finished his call and motioned for Jessica to take a seat.

"Morning, Jessica. You here to make that report on the break-in?"

"No, I'm here for information on Clayton Manners."

McDonagh's expression was blank; then recognition slowly dawned as his brain plucked the name from the dark recesses of his memory.

"Why on earth would you be asking about Clayton Manners?"

"I'm interested is all."

"Has his sister hired you too?" he demanded. "Just like Rose Hunter did? Are you here to question another one of my investigations?" McDonagh spun sharply on the chair's wheels and gestured angrily at a bank of gray steel filing cabinets. "Hell, why not have a good root through all of my cases? See if there's anything else that takes your fancy."

"Clayton Manners's sister is not my client," Jessica said calmly. "But—you know what?—maybe it's not such a bad idea. Maybe the poor woman still wants to know who killed her brother. You never arrested anyone for his murder, right?"

McDonagh spun the chair back to its original position. He steepled his fingers under his chin, elbows on the desk, and stared at her for a long, uncomfortable moment. She refused to flinch under the weight of his heavy gaze.

"What's going on, Jessica?" he said. "Why the sudden interest in Clayton Manners? He has nothing to do with the case you're working on."

Except, the night he disappeared, he was wearing clothing that fit with Rue Hunter's memories. And he's connected to the Luccheses, who are connected to the Devil's Drop murders.

"It's like you said. Hundred Acres is my home now. Maybe it's time I knew a little more about the place. But, I've got to say, three dead bodies—murder victims—in less than a year isn't exactly what I was expecting to find in the town's history books."

McDonagh's jaw worked, and a vein throbbed in his temple like a warning sign.

"You really want to know about Clayton Manners? I'll tell you all about him. Clayton Manners was a thief and a con man and a drunk. Worst of all, he was a sick son of a bitch who had a thing for young girls."

"He was a pedophile?"

"Yes, he was," McDonagh said. "Young teens—rather than little kids—were more his taste, but that doesn't make it any more right."

Jessica felt sick. "How did you find out?"

McDonagh said, "When we finally identified the body, we made a call to our law enforcement colleagues in Calhoun. Let me tell you, those boys down in Arizona weren't shedding too many tears over Clayton Manners. Quite the opposite. He'd served jail time for petty theft and small-time fraud, mostly conning old folks out of their life savings. But there had been plenty of rumors about other stuff—predatory behavior around young teens—for a long time. Then, about eighteen months before he disappeared, there were accusations he'd raped a thirteen-year-old girl. The poor kid was too traumatized to make the complaint official, so he was never arrested or charged, but everybody in town knew he was an animal."

Jessica was horrified. "He got away with it? Didn't have to pay for what he did to that girl?"

"Not exactly," McDonagh said. "One night, while making his way home from the local bar, Manners was given a hell of a beating. Left for dead. It was dark, and it was late, and there were no witnesses, so no arrests were ever made. The assault may or may not have had something to do with the girl's daddy and his buddies. Who knows? Manners left

Calhoun as soon as he was well enough to check himself out of the hospital. Then he started selling cleaning products in California and Oregon."

Jessica said, "And, just like Calhoun, no arrests were ever made after his body was discovered in Hundred Acres, right?"

"Right," McDonagh said. "We suspected something similar to what had happened in Arizona, only, this time, whoever wanted revenge for their kid didn't stop at a beating. Officially, the Hundred Acres Sheriff's Department did all we could to investigate his murder with the limited resources at our disposal. Off the record? Clayton Manners deserved to rot in hell. Whoever dumped him in that hole in the ground did the world a favor as far as I'm concerned."

Jessica was on her way to the detective agency when her cell phone chirped in the holder on the dash. The caller ID showed an unknown number. She pulled over onto the dirt shoulder, grabbed the phone, and swiped to answer. Listened as a recorded message from the Global Tel Link inmate telephone service asked if she would accept a collect call from CCWF inmate Rue Hunter. Jessica hit the key to accept and heard some static and clicks as the call connected.

"Rue? Are you there?"

"Hi, Jessica. Yes, I'm here. I got your request for a phone call. Do you have news?"

Rue's voice sounded small, less assured than it had been during their face-to-face visit, but maybe it was just the connection. Jessica could hear the prison's usual orchestra of cell doors slamming and prisoners hollering in the background. She switched off the engine, cutting off the AC, and pressed the phone tight against her ear to hear better. Heat filled the truck like switching on an oven.

"I've made some progress," she told Rue. "But I have some more questions for you."

"Okay. Ask away."

"Can you tell me again what Lucas was wearing the night of the murders?"

Rue answered without hesitation. "Blue jeans and a black-and-white plaid shirt."

"The thing is, Rue, I've seen the crime scene photos. Lucas was actually wearing tan Bermuda-style shorts and a white T-shirt."

There was a long silence.

"That's impossible," Rue said. "You must be mistaken."

"There's no mistake."

"I don't understand. I told you about the flashbacks and the nightmares. If I were to close my eyes right now, I'd still see those clothes. The jeans and the shirt."

"Uh-huh," Jessica said. "Tell me about Clayton Manners."

"Who?"

"Clayton Manners."

"I don't know anyone by that name. Who is he?"

"He was a traveling salesman from Arizona. His body was found in a shallow grave in Hundred Acres around six months after the Devil's Drop murders."

"Why would I know this guy? I was already in prison by then."

"He was wearing blue jeans and a black-and-white plaid shirt the night he disappeared. He was reported missing by his sister in 1979. He'd been murdered."

There was an even longer silence this time, and Jessica thought the call had been disconnected.

"Rue? Are you still there?"

When Rue Hunter spoke again, her voice was low and furious.

"Are you trying to fuck with me, Jessica? Because I don't have a whole lot of time left for stupid games."

"I'm being deadly serious."

Jessica heard fast, wet breathing, followed by a soft thud.

"Rue? Are you okay? What was that noise?"

"I had to sit down. I'm on the floor. All this stuff you're telling me . . . all these questions . . . I don't feel too good. I don't think I want to have this conversation anymore."

"This can't be a coincidence," Jessica said gently. "How could you possibly know what Clayton Manners was wearing the night he was murdered?"

"Maybe I saw something about his disappearance on a news bulletin? Or read about it in the paper years ago? I don't know. You're confusing me with all these questions. I thought you were trying to help me."

"I *am* trying to help you."

"I don't need this kind of help. I'm hanging up now."

"Rue, wait," Jessica said quickly. "I need to ask you one more thing."

A sigh.

"Okay."

"Tom Lucchese—do you know that name?"

"Uh, yeah, Lucchese sounds familiar. I think it was going to be the name of a new hotel or casino or something."

"I have an eyewitness who says Tom Lucchese gave you a ride to Devil's Drop the night Lucas and Megan died. The guy himself admits he picked you up outside Cooper's. You were standing next to the phone booth outside the bar at the time."

A long pause.

"Was the car a cherry-red color with fancy pop-up lights?"

"Yes!" Jessica couldn't keep the excitement from her voice. "That's exactly what it was like. Is there anything else you can remember about Tom Lucchese? Anything at all? It could be important."

Jessica could hear the woman mumbling the word *Lucchese* over and over again.

Then Rue said, "Lucky."

"That's right. His dad's casino, the one you mentioned earlier, it was going to be called 'Lucky by Lucchese.'"

"No, I meant the guy in the car. His name was Lucky. Or, at least, that's what folks called him. Lucky Lucchese. I can picture him now. Dark wavy hair. Good looking. A little older, maybe early twenties."

Jessica barely dared breathe.

"Yes, that's him."

"Fuck," Rue said.

"What?" Jessica asked.

"Lucky was Megan's new boyfriend."

31

MEGAN

1987

It was the last day of May and the last day of school.

An ending but also a new beginning. The first day of the rest of Megan's life.

So far, it sucked big time.

Walking out of Hundred Acres High School for the final time wasn't how she'd imagined it would be. She wasn't expecting a big hoo-ha, nothing like the final scene in *Grease*, when Danny and Sandy and the rest of the Rydell seniors hit the carnival, jumping on rides and eating hot dogs and cotton candy and spontaneously bursting into song and dance routines.

But she hadn't envisioned walking home from school on her own either. Just like every other day.

Rue had dropped out completely weeks ago, and she'd persuaded Lucas to cut his afternoon classes so they could drive out to the beach at Santa Monica. Celebrate high school being over, just the two of them. Sure, they were still her best friends, and they made an effort to include Megan as much as possible, but everything had changed the night Rue and Lucas got together.

Megan thought back to last year's junior prom and the strange emotions she'd experienced at the dance itself and in the weeks afterward.

For a while, she'd even considered the possibility she might have had a crush on Lucas she hadn't even been aware of until he'd hooked up with Rue. That their new relationship had somehow shaken loose feelings for him she'd subconsciously been suppressing. Eventually, she realized it wasn't Lucas she wanted—it was a return to the way things used to be.

Their friendship—once made up of three equal parts—had splintered and become something else. She was no longer the most important person in Rue's life, or Lucas's life, because they were the most important people in each other's lives now. Megan could only ever hope to be second best. The third wheel.

Then there was the question of what she was going to do with the rest of her life now that school was over. She liked the idea of working with children, but becoming a teacher would mean college and coursework, and Megan wasn't particularly academic. She wasn't the dumbest in class, but she was nowhere near the smartest either. She could apply for a maid's position at the new hotel being built in town, but it wouldn't be open for a while yet, which didn't leave a whole lot of options for gainful employment in Hundred Acres in the meantime. Maybe she'd just pack up her stuff and run away to Vegas and become a showgirl. Megan smiled and shook her head. That was more Rue's style.

"Hey, what's so funny?"

Megan jumped at the sound of the deep male voice. She'd been so lost in her own thoughts she hadn't noticed the car rolling slowly alongside her as she'd strolled along the sidewalk. She didn't know the first thing about cars, other than this one was cherry red and fancy and looked real expensive. Kinda sexy, just like its driver, who was leaning out of the open window and grinning at her.

Megan stopped and turned to face him, and the guy behind the wheel slowed the car to a stop too. A key chain shaped like a four-leaf clover hung from the rearview mirror; "With or Without You" by U2 played on the radio. She'd never met the driver, but she knew who he was. Older. Gorgeous. Rich.

Tom "Lucky" Lucchese.

The afternoon sun had been pleasantly warm on her skin, but now Megan could feel her face and chest burning. Why was Lucky Lucchese talking to *her*? He hadn't lived in town long, so maybe he was looking for directions or had confused her with someone else.

"Um, sorry, did you say something?" she asked.

"You were smiling. I asked what was so funny?"

"Oh nothing. I was just daydreaming. Stupid, really."

"Last day of school, huh?" He nodded to the book bag she was holding.

"Yeah." Megan clutched the bag to her chest in an attempt to conceal the blotchy red rash she was sure was spreading rapidly all over it.

Lucky smiled. "Shouldn't you be out celebrating with your friends?"

"I guess they're busy with their own celebrations."

"Hey, that sucks. Doesn't seem right to me, you being left all on your own."

Megan shrugged and forced a smile. "I really don't mind."

"It's Megan, right?"

She nodded, felt a thrill course through her. Lucky Lucchese knew her name!

He said, "Why don't we go grab a burger someplace? My treat."

Megan's heart knocked gladly inside her chest, and she felt a little light headed. She looked around, thinking she must be the victim of a joke or a bet or a prank, but there was no one else on the street other than herself and Lucky. Then she thought about her mom and how strict she was about Megan dating boys. But this wasn't a date, was it? Of course it wasn't! Lucky Lucchese wasn't interested in her. He could have his pick of the girls in Hundred Acres. Probably Silverdale, Shady Bluff, and Ingleby too. In any case, her mom wouldn't be home from work at least until six p.m. Even so, Megan hesitated.

"Um, I don't know . . . I should probably get home."

Lucky pushed open the passenger door and grinned at her in a way that turned her insides to mush, just like the first time she'd seen Tom Cruise in *Top Gun*. But this was real life, and she felt sick and excited and nervous all at the same time.

"Come on," he said. "Live dangerously."

Megan paused a beat before answering.

"Sure, why not?"

She had the rest of her life to be sensible.

32

PRYCE

With their boss, Lieutenant Sarah Grayling, out for the rest of the day, Pryce and Medina were able to set aside their other, official, caseloads for an hour or two so they could turn their focus back to Holten.

How the Echo Park meet had been arranged was key to finding out who Holten had met with the night he'd died. Pryce was still convinced the letter his partner had received in the days before his death was significant, but he no longer believed it contained details of the late-night rendezvous at the abandoned warehouses.

He thought of what Marie Conlon had told them about a phone call Charlie hadn't been looking forward to making.

It made sense. After all, this had all gone down in the 1990s, not the 1890s. If two people were going to arrange a meet, they'd do it by phone, not letter. Certainly not correspondence mailed to a police station for what had clearly been a clandestine meeting. If you were being really careful, you'd use a pay phone or a burner, but Pryce couldn't recall if burner phones were even a thing back in '97.

They'd decided to go over all the call records, both incoming and outgoing, relating to Holten in the days leading up to his murder. Home, office, and cell. Hunt and Adams, the two detectives who'd investigated the homicide, had already checked out the lists, but Pryce and Medina both felt it was worth another shot.

They agreed that Medina would check out the Holtens' home phone records, and Pryce would go through the calls Charlie had made from his desk phone and cell.

It didn't take long to establish many of the numbers on both of their lists were no longer in use. Had probably been attached to residential properties, where the homeowner had swapped out the old line as part of a television/internet/phone bundle or had ditched the landline completely in favor of a cell phone. If need be, they could trace who the number had last been registered to before being disconnected.

Most of the numbers still in use belonged to businesses—a pizza delivery place, an optician, the local library, a window cleaning service.

Medina completed his list and went in search of chocolate and soda from the station's vending machine. Pryce asked for a Hershey's bar and a Dr Pepper. He tried to stick to a healthy diet as much as possible, but right now, he was heading for a slump and needed a sugar hit.

He had two more numbers left to try. He punched in the digits for the penultimate entry on Charlie's cell phone call list. Heard static, followed by ringing. No dead tone. Good, Pryce thought, the number was still in operation.

A woman answered.

She offered a greeting she'd probably uttered a million times before.

Pryce sat up straighter in the chair. He was suddenly alert. Heart pumping. Just like those tension-packed seconds before the starter gun went off ahead of a big race during his college track days.

He asked the woman to repeat what she'd just said. Wanted to be sure he hadn't misheard her. She repeated the words. Pryce had heard correctly the first time.

Holten had used his cell phone to make a call just hours before he'd gotten into his car, driven to Echo Park, and climbed into a truck outside some deserted warehouses at midnight. The same night some-one had put a bullet in his forehead.

Pryce mumbled something about a wrong number and hung up. His mind was racing faster than his legs used to during those track meets more than thirty years ago.

He circled the second-to-last entry on his list.

It was a Hundred Acres telephone number.

33

JESSICA

Jessica called Ed on the truck's hands-free mode to inform him there had been a change of plan. She wouldn't be in the office today after all.

She was already on the Antelope Valley freeway—the Silverado swallowing up mile after mile of blacktop, the rugged, rolling peaks of the San Gabriel Mountains growing smaller in her rearview mirror.

The call connected, and Ed's voice boomed over the speakers.

"Hey, kiddo, how you doin'? Where you at?"

"Right now, I'm on Highway 14 heading north toward Chowchilla."

"Some new developments?"

"You could say that," she said. "I found out who Megan's secret boyfriend was. The mysterious *L* whom she wrote about in her diary."

Ed sounded confused. "We already know who the secret boyfriend was. It was Lucas."

"Apparently not."

"Who then?"

"Tom Lucchese. Although, back then, he was known by the nickname 'Lucky.'"

Jessica heard nothing but the hiss of the speakers for a quarter mile. She assumed the cell signal had dropped out, but when she glanced at the phone's screen, she saw the call was still connected, and the signal was strong.

"Ed? Are you still there?"

When he answered, his voice sounded weird.

"What you're telling me is impossible. There's no way Megan and Tom Lucchese were an item."

"Why is it impossible?"

"It just is. Trust me. Where did this new piece of information come from anyway?"

"Rue Hunter. I spoke to her earlier on the phone."

"Rue Hunter?" Ed snorted. "Now there's a surprise. Megan and Lucas were dating each other—that's why Rue killed them. Although it sounds like she's still not willing to accept they were romantically involved. Now she's coming up with this fantasy nonsense about Tom Lucchese."

"Patty Meeks didn't think Megan and Lucas were dating either," Jessica pointed out. "She told me she would have known if they were a couple."

Ed snorted again. "Patty ought to know better than most how kids that age get up to all sorts of stuff their folks don't know about. She's a prime example."

"What does that mean?"

"Nothing, forget it," he said quickly. "Just don't go trusting everything Rue Hunter tells you."

"There's something else," Jessica said. "I discovered more about the body you told me about. The one they found buried on the site of Bruce Lucchese's casino. His name was Clayton Manners, and he was a pedophile."

"Sounds like he was a piece of shit. But I'm guessing there's a reason why you're interested in this guy?"

"There sure is. The night he disappeared—and was most likely murdered—he was wearing blue denim jeans and a black-and-white plaid shirt. Clothing identical to what Rue Hunter claimed Lucas James was wearing the night of the Devil's Drop murders. Except we know Lucas was wearing different clothes entirely."

"Holy shit."

"My thoughts exactly."

"Has Rue Hunter offered an explanation?"

"She claimed she'd never heard of Clayton Manners. Got real upset when I told her about him and mentioned the clothing."

"Seems like a hell of a coincidence to me. What do you think, Jessica? Do you think she's lying? You think she's playing you?"

"I really don't know. But I don't like coincidences as big as this one. I'm planning on finding out what exactly is going on."

"You on your way to the prison?"

"No, I'm on my way to pay a surprise visit to Rose Dalton."

It was midafternoon when Jessica arrived in Chowchilla.

She cruised along Avenue 26, passing yellow sunbaked fields and a red tractor parked on the dirt shoulder, and headed, from memory, for the motel where she'd met Rose on Saturday when she'd signed the contract following the prison visit with Rue.

Only four days ago, but it felt like a lifetime.

Rose's temporary home was located behind a small shopping plaza, which housed a liquor store and a Mexican restaurant and a vacant unit up for lease. The motel was a medium-size two-story structure, whitewashed with navy-blue trim and railings, bringing to mind a sailor's uniform. Despite the nautical color scheme, the building was a hundred miles from the nearest ocean, surrounded on all sides by the driest of land. The motel was probably kept in business all year round by families visiting loved ones incarcerated at the nearby Central California Women's Facility or Valley State Prison.

Jessica pulled into the lot next to Rose's metallic-blue Audi. A central staircase took her to the upper level, and she found Rose's room at the end of the walkway. Jessica knocked on the blue door and waited.

When there was no answer, she retraced her steps, then walked around the building to the small pool area out back, where she found Rose sitting at a table on her own, face upturned to the sun. Despite the huge Jackie Kennedy sunglasses, she could see the woman was surprised when Jessica dropped her bag on the tiled flooring and slid into the empty seat facing her.

"Jessica, what are you doing here? Has something happened? Is everything okay?"

"I thought it was time I checked in. Provided you with an update."

Rose removed the sunglasses and frowned.

"You drove all this way to give me an update?"

"Kind of. There's also some stuff I want to ask you about."

"Sure. Anything I can do to help."

"I found out who gave Rue a ride to Devil's Drop the night of the murders. A guy called Tom Lucchese."

"Really? I remember him. He was a year or two younger than myself. Kind of an asshole. I didn't realize Rue knew him."

"She didn't," Jessica said. "Not really. But Rue claims Megan and Lucchese were dating. She says Lucchese was the secret boyfriend, not Lucas."

"Wow. Why hasn't Rue mentioned this Lucchese guy before?"

"I guess she didn't remember him until now."

"But this changes everything," Rose said, excited. "Don't you see? If Tom Lucchese was Megan's boyfriend, then it blows apart Rue's so-called motive for the murders."

"If Rue is telling the truth, that is. Tom Lucchese drove Rue to Devil's Drop, that much I do know for sure, but there's no real evidence to suggest Lucchese and Megan were a couple."

"Maybe Lucchese will confirm it himself?" Rose suggested hopefully.

"I don't think so. I spoke to him a couple of days ago. He says he gave Rue a ride because she was late meeting friends, but he didn't mention anything about even knowing Megan, never mind dating her."

Rose looked deflated. She stared out at the pool, where a middle-aged man was splashing about in the water with two girls aged about eight and twelve. Jessica wondered if they were in town to visit their mom at the prison, what the woman was inside for.

"There's someone else I want to ask you about, Rose."

"Who?"

"Clayton Manners."

All the color drained from Rose's face, like bathwater being sucked down a drain. She gripped the edge of the plastic table, as though she might keel over, and her chin began to tremble. There was no hiding the fact Clayton Manner's name was familiar to Rose Dalton.

When Rue had denied all knowledge of the man, Jessica had decided to quiz Rose. It was more than just a hunch or a gut feeling. You didn't have nightmares about a guy for three decades because you heard about him in the news. Manners *had* to be connected to the Hunters somehow. Jessica felt her pulse spike even though she wasn't completely surprised by Rose's reaction.

She waited for the woman to speak.

When she did, all Rose could manage was "What . . . ? How . . . ?"

Jessica said, "I know Clayton Manners's body was found on the site of Bruce Lucchese's casino. And I know, when he disappeared, his clothing was identical to what Rue claimed Lucas James was wearing at Devil's Drop. I also know from your reaction you know exactly who Clayton Manners was."

Rose blinked, and fat tears rolled down her cheeks. She didn't bother to wipe them away.

"I haven't heard anyone say his name out loud for forty years. But there's not a day that's gone by since when I haven't thought about him and what he did. What *we* did."

221

"If you want me to help you—if you want me to help Rue—you need to start telling me the truth."

Rose watched the two sisters fooling around in the pool for a few minutes. Their laughter bounced off the tiled surroundings as they flicked water at their daddy, who yelled, "Hey, two against one! Not fair!"

Then Rose turned to Jessica, leaned in closer, and spoke very quietly. "Rue *is* a killer," she said. "Just not in the way everyone thinks she is."

34
ROSE

1979

The screen door snapped shut with a sharp crack, jerking Rose awake.

Her heart hammered, and she sat up in bed. Nothing but impenetrable blackness lay beyond the thin gauze of the drapes on the bedroom window. It was late. She listened in the darkness.

There was a soft thud from the hallway, like a shoulder hitting the wall. Some giggles barely stifled by a hand over a mouth. A stage-whispered "Sssshhhhh." A low, guttural growl. More giggles. Then wet smacking and sucking sounds and soft moaning.

Rose lay back down in bed and pulled the bedsheet up to her chin. "Gross," she muttered.

She hoped Rue was still fast asleep and wasn't having to listen to their mom making out with whatever guy she'd picked up tonight. She knew the noises were about to get a whole lot worse. Footsteps padded along the hallway before stopping outside Barb's bedroom door. There was a creak of old springs as a heavy weight landed on the bed. More giggling and moaning. A male voice mumbled something, and Barb slurred, "Don't be long, lover."

Heavy footsteps headed back down the hallway, followed by the steady flow of water hitting water. He hadn't even bothered to close the bathroom door when taking a leak.

"Gross," Rose muttered again.

She heard the toilet being flushed, just as a loud, wet snore filled the house. Rose breathed a sigh of relief. Most of the time, Barb's snoring set her teeth on edge, made her want to scream. The exception was nights like this, when Barb had company. The snoring was a welcome alternative to the headboard banging against the wall and the heavy panting and moaning. Rose knew Barb was out cold until the morning, and she hoped the guy would do what the rest of them usually did and slip quietly out into the night, instead of sleeping over and then picking up where they'd both left off.

She held her breath as his footsteps echoed along the hallway again, in the opposite direction of the front door. He stopped, she guessed, in front of Barb's bedroom. Maybe he'd left his wallet or watch on the nightstand or had dropped his coat on the floor in the heat of passion and had to collect his things.

Rose breathed out slowly. Barb was now snoring so loudly she was in danger of waking the whole town. Over the rhythmic snorts and sighs, she heard the guy on the move again.

Please leave. Please leave. Please leave.

But the footsteps were heading in the wrong direction. Even farther away from the front door. Traveling toward her own bedroom. The heavy boots stopped right outside her door. She flipped over onto her side and faced the wall. Tried to slow her rapid breathing. There was a creak of hinges. Dull yellow light from the hallway spilled into the room.

The man's own heavy breathing was much louder than her own, as he stood there in the doorway. She could feel him watching her. Rose remained still and silent, but she was sure he must be able to hear the thundering of her heartbeat.

Boot soles shuffled across the wooden floor. There was another creak, and a soft click, as the room was plunged into darkness again.

Slow, deliberate footsteps carried him toward her bed. The mattress dipped under his weight as he sat down. She felt a hand on her shoulder.

"C'mon, sugar pie, we both know you're awake."

His voice was low, hoarse, gravelly.

When she didn't respond, didn't move, the hand tightened on her shoulder and pulled her roughly onto her back. She could see the outline of a figure looming over her. The shadow shifted, and in one clumsy movement, he was straddling her, her legs pinned beneath him.

"Why don't me and you have ourselves a little fun?"

"No," she said. "Get off me."

She heard a jangling sound, like a belt buckle being unfastened. The metallic scrape of a zipper being undone. Felt his hand fumbling around, his breathing coming fast and heavy now. Rose felt a scream build up in her throat, but before she could unleash it, a meaty hand was clamped over her mouth. She smelled stale cigarettes on his fingers. He leaned in close, and his breath stank of beer and whiskey and tobacco.

"Stop playing hard to get, you little slut," he whispered in her ear.

He licked her face, and she could feel his hardness pressing against her belly. The hand over her mouth was replaced by wet lips. Rough stubble scraped against her chin like sandpaper. His tongue slid into her mouth, thick and fat and wet and probing. She thrashed her head from side to side. Reached out and grabbed a handful of hair slick with grease and yanked as hard as she could. His head snapped back.

"You fucking bitch," he snarled.

Rose heard a flicking sound and felt something cold against the soft flesh of her neck.

"Are you going to be a good girl for Clayton, or do I have to cut your fucking throat open?"

Hot tears spilled down each temple and soaked into the pillow. The hand not holding the knife searched under her nightshirt and closed around a small breast. She felt the nipple harden involuntarily under his fingers, and he moaned loudly. The hand moved down and tore at her underpants.

"Open your legs," he gasped.

Rose shook her head. She squeezed her legs tightly together.

"Please stop," she pleaded.

She heard the clatter of the knife hitting the floor; then both of his hands were grabbing at the inside of her thighs, trying to pry them apart. Her hand was in his hair again, trying to pull him off her, but he was too strong.

Her thighs parted.

He adjusted his position on top of her.

The room suddenly seemed brighter.

She could see his face now, inches from her own.

Dark eyes filled with lust, teeth bared, white spit foaming in the corners of his mouth.

Then a dreadful scream tore through the air, like the howling of a wild animal. The man's eyes widened in shock. He slumped heavily on top of her, winding her. He jerked once, twice, three times. A sickly, wet wheeze escaped from his lips.

Then there was nothing.

Only stillness.

Rose lay there panting, trying to catch her breath, his weight suffocating on top of her, crushing her lungs. She turned her head and saw Rue standing next to the bed. Skinny, pale, shaking, teeth chattering. Ten years old. Her hands were covered in blood.

Rose pushed the man off her and slid out from under his bulk. Felt her legs collapse beneath her as her feet hit the wooden boards. She crawled toward Rue and pulled her sister into her arms. Hushed her and stroked her hair as Rue began screaming again.

The overhead light snapped on, and Rose blinked.

"What the hell is going on in here?"

She looked up to see her mom swaying in the doorway, her arms outstretched, hands grabbing for the doorframe to steady herself. Barb Hunter took in the room. Her glazed eyes fixed on the bed and rapidly became a whole lot clearer. Her jaw slackened, and her mouth dropped open. Rose turned and followed her mom's gaze.

The dead man was lying on his belly, his head twisted to the side. His eyes staring straight at them but seeing nothing. The back of his black-and-white plaid shirt was torn and soaked dark red. His jeans were around his knees, his bare ass exposed under the harsh glow of a hundred-watt light bulb. The knife was wedged in the side of his neck, the blade buried up to the hilt.

"What did you do?" Barb said quietly.

"He was trying to hurt Rose," Rue said.

Rose realized her sister had finally stopped screaming. Tears spilled down Rue's cheeks now.

Barb lurched toward them, pulled Rue from Rose's grasp, and shook her youngest daughter hard by the shoulders.

"What did you do?" she screamed into Rue's face. "What did you do?"

"I . . . didn't . . . mean . . . to," Rue gasped between sobs and hiccups.

"Fuck!"

Barb slapped Rue hard around the head. Then she hit the little girl again.

"Stop it!" Rose yelled. She jumped to her feet. Lunged at her mother and shoved her hard against the wall. Barb slid to the floor, her bony chest heaving under the clingy material of her green Lycra minidress.

"It was me, okay?" Rose said, pulling Rue close to her again. "I did it."

Barb glanced at the dead body, then back at Rose.

"What did you do?" she demanded. "Lure him in here? Try to seduce him?"

"He tried to rape me."

"You little whore," Barb spat.

"You're the only whore around here," Rose yelled. "The whole town knows it. I bet you don't even know his name."

The spiteful expression on Barb's face turned to shame, and she looked away.

"He tried to rape me, Mom," Rose whispered. "Why do you think he had a knife?"

Barb pulled her knees up to her chin, buried her face in her arms, and cried like a baby for what felt like a long time. Her slim frame rattled with the force of the sobs. Eventually, her bony shoulders stilled, and she fell silent.

Rose said, "We need to call 911."

Barb looked up. Her eyes were red and swollen. Her cheeks sooty with mascara. She looked a decade older all of a sudden.

"No," she said calmly, her voice raw. "No police."

"But I told you what happened. You do believe me, don't you?"

"I believe you, but the cops won't. All they'll see is a dead body in a house belonging to a drunken piece of trash. They'll pin this on me."

"I'll tell them what happened. I'll tell them what he tried to do to me."

Barb smiled sadly. "Did he beat you up? Cut you with the knife? Leave his seed inside you?"

Rose shook her head.

Barb went on, "Then they won't believe you. Even if he had done all those things, they still wouldn't believe you." She laughed bitterly. "Trust me; I know."

"So what do we do?"

"We get rid of him," Barb said. "That's what we do."

35

JESSICA

"What happened next?" Jessica asked.

They had relocated to the privacy of Rose's room, the woman understandably reluctant to share her story in a public area, within earshot of a father and his two young daughters. The room was basic but clean and tidy. Rose's clothing hung pressed and ready to wear in the closet; a dog-eared paperback and reading glasses were the only personal items on the nightstand. There was no mess and no clutter, but Jessica had spotted the two empty wine bottles in the trash can and wondered how well Rose was really coping.

There was no table, chairs, or even a bureau, so they both perched on the edge of two neatly made-up queen beds and faced each other across the small space between them.

Rose said, "We rolled him off the bed onto the floor. My mom dragged him by the arms along the hallway and outside into the front yard, where his pickup was parked. We removed his sale stock from the truck and stored it in the garage for several weeks before burning the lot along with his wallet and driver's license. The house on Perry Street was fairly isolated, but we didn't want to risk lighting a fire in the middle of the night. Between the three of us, we managed to bundle him into the space we'd cleared on his truck's flatbed. It was not an easy task, I can tell you. Took us around a half hour and a lot of sweat and energy.

"We drove out to some wasteland, and my mom spent another hour digging, while Rue and I kept watch for any headlights. We wrapped the body in plastic trash bags and rolled it into the hole in the ground. Covered it with dirt and prayed the grave wouldn't be disturbed by wild animals.

"Then we drove the pickup to Devil's Drop, wiped every inch of it with bleach, released the hand brake, and rolled the truck off the edge. The crash when it landed at the bottom of the canyon was so loud we were sure the whole of Southern California must have heard it."

"But no one ever found out?" Jessica asked.

Rose shook her head. "A few weeks later, my mom heard the cops had been asking about Manners in some local bars, but nothing ever came of it."

"Wasn't Barb worried someone might remember her leaving the bar with Manners the night he vanished?"

"They hadn't been drinking together," Rose explained. "They'd been in different bars. Manners picked her up by the side of the road when she tried to hitch a ride back to Hundred Acres. I guess they'd both struck out trying to get laid earlier in the evening and settled for each other. Or so Barb thought. I assume he'd asked if she had any kids and thought he'd hit the jackpot when she said yes."

Rose went on, "The next time I heard Clayton Manners's name was when those construction workers pulled him from the ground in late '87, and the cops eventually figured out who he was. By then, Rue was in prison, and my mom was dead. I sold the house on Perry Street and left for Arizona soon after the body was discovered."

"You never told Rue about him being found?"

"No. She had been through enough already."

"When I spoke to Rue on the telephone earlier today, she claimed she'd never heard of Clayton Manners. Didn't react at all until I mentioned the clothing he was wearing."

Rose said, "I think she repressed a lot of what happened the night he died. It would have been traumatic enough for anyone to deal with, let alone a ten-year-old kid. She was never the same after that night. For a long time, she was withdrawn, wouldn't speak to anyone. Then she started acting out and being disruptive. You already know how she went off the rails when she was a teenager, boozing and taking drugs, but she never once mentioned Clayton Manners or what she did to him. I started to believe she'd buried the memories a whole lot deeper than we were able to bury his body. So deep, she didn't know where to find them anymore. For her sake, I hoped that was the case anyway."

Jessica said, "You told her to put all her bad thoughts into a box, lock it, and throw away the key."

Rose was surprised. "Yes, I did. How did you know?"

"Rue spoke about it during her interview with Dr. Ted Blume, shortly after her arrest. What about you, Rose? Were you able to lock those memories in a box and throw away the key?"

"What do you mean?"

"I know about Jed Lockerman and his broken nose. I also know about the guy in Randy's who ended up with scalding coffee all over his baby-making parts."

"You're right," Rose said. "I was never able to forget, not like Rue was. For years, I couldn't stand the thought of anyone touching me. Was terrified of being alone with a man. Moving to Arizona and escaping the ghosts of Hundred Acres was the best thing I ever did." She smiled. "Bob was a coworker, and we became friends over time. He was the gentlest, kindest, and most patient man I'd ever met. Between the love and support of my husband, and the help of a very good therapist, I eventually got better—but it was a long and difficult journey."

"Does your husband know about Clayton Manners?"

"He knows about the attempted rape. That's all. The official story is, between the three of us, we managed to fight him off, he fled, and was never seen or heard of again."

"I need to ask you a difficult question now."

Rose smiled tightly. "And here was me thinking we'd just been shooting the breeze until now."

"When Rue confessed to the murders of Lucas and Megan, did you believe she was confusing the events at Devil's Drop with Clayton Manners's death?"

"To begin with, no. There was a lot of evidence against Rue after Devil's Drop—the murder weapon, the blood on her dress, the eyewitness placing her near the scene around the time of the murders. All things I still can't explain. At first, it didn't even occur to me that Devil's Drop and Clayton Manners could be connected. After a while, when Rue told me about the flashbacks and nightmares, it did seem possible she was confusing the two incidents."

"Those flashbacks and nightmares were a major contributory factor to Rue's confession," Jessica pointed out. "Don't you think you should have talked it over with her? Told the cops that her memories of Devil's Drop were not reliable and could have been related to something else entirely?"

"What was I supposed to say to the cops? 'Hey, you know those two murders you think my sister committed? Well, here's another one to add to the list.' I don't think so, Jessica. Please believe me when I tell you I agonized for weeks, months, years over the best thing to do. In the end, I truly believed telling the authorities the truth about Clayton Manners would only have made a very bad situation even worse."

"For yourself, you mean," Jessica said. "Things couldn't really have gotten much worse for Rue. She was already on death row."

Rose said, "I guess I always hoped something would turn up to prove she was innocent of the Devil's Drop murders. Clayton Manners, though? There would've been no way out of that one. It's like my mom said all those years ago—who would have believed us?"

"You really don't think Rue killed Lucas and Megan?" Jessica asked. "You said it yourself; the evidence against her is pretty damning."

"I can't explain the knife or the dress or how she managed to walk away from that place with barely a scratch on her. But I know my sister, and I know, in my heart, she wasn't capable of what they said she did. Especially not to Lucas and Megan. Sure, she was troubled and wild, but deep down, she was a good person. Still *is* a good person."

"Why ask me to take on this job, Rose? Pay me to dig into the past when you must have known there was a chance I'd find out about Clayton Manners."

"It's like I said when we spoke on Friday. I owe her."

Jessica nodded. "I guess I understand now what you meant."

"Exactly." Rose smiled sadly. "Rue saved my life, and it destroyed her own."

36

JESSICA

The digital numbers on the dash glowed bright green in the gloom of the truck's cab as Jessica parked in front of the trailer.

It was 10:08. Most of the four-hour journey back to Hundred Acres had been spent thinking about Rue Hunter. About how an act of bravery, born out of unconditional love for her big sister, had robbed a little girl of any chance of a normal life.

But did the tragic events of one night in 1979 mean that same little girl had grown up to be a cold-blooded killer eight years later?

Jessica didn't think so.

She no longer believed Rue Hunter was responsible for the murders of Lucas James and Megan Meeks. But if not her—then who? Rue would soon be put on a bus to San Quentin, where the death chamber awaited her. Time was fast running out to come up with answers.

Jessica turned off the engine and climbed out of the truck, her head still full of Rue Hunter and Lucas James and Megan Meeks. As she approached the trailer, a feeling of unease washed over her like unexpected summer rainfall. In the half light from the street, she could see the Airstream's door was not fully closed. Not quite ajar but not flush against the doorframe either, like it should be.

She pulled the Baby Glock from her bag and approached the trailer slowly, her sneakers silent on the packed dirt. The window shades were up, and the overhead light inside was off, but the thick darkness beyond the glass was pierced by a flickering brightness, like the frantic beam of a miniflashlight.

Jessica held her gun hand up in front of her face. It was steady, not even a hint of a tremor. Good. She huffed out a breath, quietly pulled opened the door, and slipped quickly into the room, leading with the weapon. She hit the light switch.

Dylan was sitting at the dinette table, his cell phone in his hand. He glanced up. The smile on his face froze when he found himself staring at the barrel of a gun.

"Jeez, Jessica," he said, his eyes widening. "Can you please not point that thing at me?"

"Dylan," she breathed, lowering the weapon. She dropped the Baby Glock into her bag. Dumped the bag on the seat. "What the hell are you doing in my trailer sitting in the dark?"

He held up the phone. "I was watching YouTube videos while waiting for you."

And drinking her beer, too, by the looks of it. A half-full bottle of Budweiser stood next to three empty ones on the table.

"You didn't think to ask before just letting yourself in?"

"Do I need permission to visit my girlfriend now?"

"When it involves breaking into my home, yes, you do. Especially so soon after someone else broke in."

"Ah, shit, Jessica. I didn't think. I'm sorry. I didn't mean to scare you."

"How did you get in? I had a new lock installed."

"Mrs. Sugarman let me in with the new key you left her. She thought it was romantic that I wanted to surprise you."

Jessica eyed the bottles of beer. *Her* beer.

"Yeah, real romantic."

He frowned. "Mrs. Sugarman didn't know anything about the break-in, though."

Jessica sighed. "You told her about that?"

235

"Sure, why wouldn't I? Why didn't you tell her?"

"She's an older lady who lives alone—that's why. I didn't want to worry her. Whoever was here, in this trailer, was after me or something belonging to me. It had nothing to do with Sylvia; I'm absolutely sure of it. Now the poor woman is going to be jumping at every little sound she hears."

Dylan's frown deepened. "If you truly believe someone is out to get you, Jessica, then I really think you ought to seriously consider what I said about moving in to my place."

"Not gonna happen."

"Why?"

"It's way too soon, for a start."

"Too soon?" Dylan threw his hands up in the air in exasperation, almost knocking over the half-full beer bottle. "We've been dating for six months."

"Exactly. Six months is nothing."

"When *is* going to be the right time? After a year together? Two years?"

"Never," Jessica said quietly.

Dylan pushed himself unsteadily out of the seat and stood swaying in front of her.

"What the hell does that mean?"

"It means I don't plan on sticking around in Hundred Acres any longer than I have to," Jessica said. "I never did. You and me getting together doesn't change anything."

"What are you saying?"

"I'm saying maybe we should call time on whatever this is. Maybe it's better to do it now rather than later."

"Why, Jessica? We've got a good thing going on."

He took a step toward her and reached out to stroke her cheek.

She turned her face away.

"No, Dylan, we don't. It's not working. At least, not for me anyway."

"Is this about him?" Anger flared in Dylan's eyes suddenly. "You're throwing me away like a piece of trash so you can be with him, huh?"

"What? Who?"

"Don't give me the 'Little Miss Innocent' act, Jessica. It really doesn't suit you."

Jessica was genuinely baffled. But one thing she did know was that she didn't like the sudden hard tone of his voice or the direction the conversation was headed. Not one little bit.

"I have no idea what—or who—you're talking about."

"'MC.'" He made bunny-ear fingers around the initials. "That's who I'm talking about."

MC?

Matt Connor?

Jessica hadn't seen Connor in months. Not since Eagle Rock. Not since moving to Hundred Acres and dating Dylan. Why was he bringing up Matt Connor now? Then she remembered. The text.

"You've been reading my messages?"

Dylan looked away, his jaw clenched, wouldn't answer her.

"I asked you a question." Jessica could feel white-hot anger building inside her. "Have you been going through my cell and reading my messages?"

"Not until you started cheating on me with another guy."

"And where did this ridiculous cheating theory come from?"

"I was with you when you got the text, remember? I saw the look on your face when you read it. Surprise and then, I don't know, happiness or delight or something. I don't think you heard a word I said to you for the rest of the evening. Your mind was clearly on whoever had sent that damn text. So, yes, when you went to the bathroom, I read it. Who is he, Jessica?"

She ignored the question. "How did you manage to access my messages? My cell phone has a security code."

"Oh, come on, Jessica. We've been dating for six months. You don't think I've seen you tap in that code a million times? It wouldn't have been too hard to figure out anyway. Your birthday? Seriously? You're as bad as my dad."

"Have you been following me?" she asked.

"What?"

"I thought I saw your car in LA a couple of days ago when I was meeting Pryce. Did you follow me?"

Dylan didn't answer, but the expression on his face told her everything she needed to know.

"Did you break into my trailer too? Snoop around in my things looking for proof of this so-called affair?"

"Of course I didn't break into your trailer."

"Let me rephrase the question—did you use a key to gain access to my home when I wasn't here? You knew where Sylvia kept the spare."

"The whole town knows where Sylvia keeps that key. It's not exactly an original hiding place."

Jessica didn't know whether to believe him or not. Wasn't sure she even cared anymore if he was telling her the truth.

She said, "Okay, I think we're done here. I have work to do. You should leave now."

"You're throwing me out?"

"I'm asking you politely to go home. Go sleep off your three and a half beers. We can talk tomorrow."

"Is he coming over?" Dylan demanded. "Is that it? You trying to get me out of the way so you can screw him?"

"Just go."

"You're nothing but a cheating whore."

Jessica felt like she'd been slapped. It was a side to Dylan she'd never seen before. But no way was she going to give him the satisfaction of seeing how rattled she was.

"Do you know what?" she said calmly. "Michelle deserved better, and so do I. Now get the fuck out of my trailer."

Dylan pushed past her roughly, and Jessica jumped as he slammed the door hard behind him. She snapped the lock in place and noticed her hands were shaking, but all she felt was relief. Relief that he was gone and relief that it was over.

She poured what was left of the opened beer down the sink and tossed the empty bottles in the trash. Opened the refrigerator door to grab a Bud for herself and saw that she was all out.

"Asshole," she muttered.

Jessica sloshed two fingers of Scotch into a tumbler instead, sat at the dinette table, and fired up the laptop. She pushed all thoughts of Dylan aside and turned her focus back to Devil's Drop.

Either Tom Lucchese was Megan's secret boyfriend, like Rue had said. Or the guy had simply been a Good Samaritan who'd gotten caught up in a very bad situation, as Lucchese himself had claimed.

One thing was for sure—someone was lying.

And, if she was as big a gambler as the folks who frequented his casino, Jessica would be placing all her chips on Tom Lucchese.

She spent the next half hour trying to find out all she could about the man. Nothing untoward stood out, although she was surprised to discover he lived in a relatively modest house in North Las Vegas with his family and drove a fairly average car. She would have expected, as the owner of a casino, even a small one, Lucchese would have enjoyed a far more extravagant lifestyle. Maybe he had simply grown out of the fast cars and designer labels he'd clearly coveted in his youth.

Jessica also found out the cash Tom Lucchese had used to buy the casino had been inherited following his father's death in 1997. She began a new search, this time on Bruce Lucchese. She read the results on the screen.

Then she sat back in the seat stunned.

Bruce hadn't died as a result of illness or an accident, like she'd expected. He'd put a shotgun in his mouth and blown a hole in the back of his skull. His suicide had resulted in a fair amount of coverage in the local Nevada press. She scrolled down the list of articles.

Gambling community shocked by businessman's sudden death
Casino boss found dead in own home in suspected suicide
How a Vegas shining light tragically burned out in the end

Jessica liked that last headline best. She clicked on the link for the story and read a brief history of the life and death of Bruce Lucchese. How he had demonstrated his entrepreneurial spirit as a young man by setting up a small bookmakers' business in his hometown of Hundred Acres, before moving to Vegas in his midtwenties, with his wife and baby son, to make his fortune. About the ill-fated casino and hotel development that apparently sparked his downward spiral into alcohol abuse and depression. The numerous expensive stints in rehab that followed. How he had finally succumbed to his demons on the Fourth of July 1997 when he went out to the garage attached to his home and shot himself dead.

Jessica read the sentence again. Fourth of July 1997. Exactly ten years to the day since the murders of Lucas and Megan.

Shit.

She returned to the search results and found another article that caught her eye.

Family and friends bid final farewell to Vegas magnate

This story was illustrated with a bunch of candid photos of mourners leaving the church after Bruce Lucchese's funeral service. The main image showed a younger Tom Lucchese comforting his mother, Cynthia. There were pictures of gray-haired men in sharp suits and skinny black ties who were identified as prominent movers and shakers in the gambling world. Other photos featured attractive women in their twenties dressed in black lace and huge hats with extravagant veils who were described as being the star turns in some of the big Vegas shows at the time.

Off to one side, away from the throng, was someone Jessica wasn't expecting to see.

Like the other mourners, the woman was dressed in a dark suit and wore a suitably somber expression. But, to Jessica, she seemed completely out of place at Bruce Lucchese's funeral—around ten years after he had quit Hundred Acres for good. Jessica leaned in closer to the laptop screen and squinted at the image. It was black and white and grainy, but there was definitely no mistake.

She was looking at the face of Patty Meeks.

37
JESSICA

Ed was already behind his desk when Jessica arrived at the detective agency early the next day. He was wearing a shirt adorned with palm trees and peaches that was way too pink for his ruddy complexion.

"Peaches," she said.

"Yup. Do you know why?"

"Because you're peachy keen today?"

Ed winked and pointed at her.

"Got it in one."

The rest of Jessica's morning was spent thinking and waiting.

She was thinking about Rue's revelation that Tom Lucchese was Megan's boyfriend. Why the cops would cover up his involvement. Why Patty Meeks was at Bruce Lucchese's funeral. What role the Luccheses had to play in the deaths of two teenagers on a summer's night more than three decades ago.

And while she was doing all this thinking, she was waiting for Ed to leave the office.

Finally, sometime after noon, he picked himself up and announced he was going to Randy's for lunch. He invited Jessica to join him.

"I'll pass if you don't mind," she said. "Dylan and I broke up last night. It might be awkward."

"That's a shame. You made a cute couple. Can I bring you something back?"

"Sure, thanks. There's no rush, though. I don't have much of an appetite."

Jessica followed Ed out of the front door and smoked a cigarette while she watched him stroll down the side of the highway. It was a hot day, and there was a smell of burning dust in the air, along with the usual roadside perfume of exhaust fumes. Once Ed disappeared inside the diner, she dropped the butt and returned to her desk. She found her picklock set in her bag and selected the tool best suited for the job. Jessica figured, when it came to affairs and family secrets in Hundred Acres, most of the sordid details could be found in one place—Ed's files.

His locked filing cabinets were labeled *A* to *Z*, and cases were filed by client surnames. Jessica glanced at the picture window. No sign of movement outside other than the traffic on the highway.

Settling on the cabinet most likely to yield results, she jimmied the tiny lock in the top right corner and pulled open one of the metal drawers. Flicked through the folders nestling in the swinging file tabbed *M*. There were a lot of *M*s, but none was labeled *Meeks*. Next, she tried the *L* file, and there it was—*Lucchese*.

Jessica had another look at the picture window. Consulted her watch. Reassured herself Ed would be at Randy's for at least another twenty minutes.

She removed the cardboard file from its swinging pocket, flipped open to the first page, and saw the client listed was Cynthia Lucchese. She skimmed the case overview. It was a classic infidelity job. Cynthia had suspected her husband of cheating and had hired Ed to carry out some surveillance on Bruce Lucchese. The case file was dated May 1987.

Cynthia believed Bruce had had a mistress in Hundred Acres in the late sixties, before the family left for Vegas. Now that they were back in town, she was convinced he was hiding something, had possibly rekindled an old romance. Jessica turned the page. Ed had documented Bruce Lucchese's movements over a number of weeks, including a couple of visits to the Meeks residence and a meeting with Patty in a coffee shop outside of town. Bruce had also been spotted parked outside Hundred Acres High School on a few occasions. Ed's typed account of the surveillance was backed up by some covert photography.

But, when Jessica turned to the copy of the report Ed had delivered to Cynthia, there was no mention of clandestine meetings with Patty, no incriminating photos. No suspicious behavior by Bruce Lucchese had been noted anywhere in Ed's findings at all.

"I don't think that belongs to you."

Jessica spun around, her heart pounding. Ed was standing in the doorway. She looked at the folder in her hand, and heat rushed to her cheeks.

"I didn't expect you back so soon."

"Clearly." Ed held up a brown paper bag. "A sandwich. For you."

"Shit," Jessica muttered. "Look, I'm sorry for breaking into your filing cabinet, but why didn't you tell me Cynthia Lucchese was one of your clients?"

"You know why, Jessica. Client confidentiality."

"Even when it's relevant to the case I'm working on?"

"I didn't think it was relevant. I still don't. Everyone has secrets. Some should stay in the past."

Jessica showed him the file. "I think what's in here *is* relevant to Devil's Drop. I think this is where it all began."

Ed sighed and sank into Jessica's visitor's chair. Dropped the brown paper bag on the desk. She sat in her own seat facing him and placed the Cynthia Lucchese file between them.

"Tell me what you know, Ed. It's important."

He nodded. "Cynthia first suspected Bruce was having an affair in February 1969 when she found a receipt for an expensive diamond-and-emerald bracelet in his wallet—a gift Cynthia never received. Her description of the bracelet seemed familiar to me somehow. I was sure I'd seen something just like it, but I couldn't remember where. Anyway, the Luccheses moved to Vegas a short while later. Cynthia was pretty sure more flings followed, but she turned a blind eye for the sake of Tom and keeping the family together.

"When they moved back to Hundred Acres in the 1980s, she was convinced Bruce was up to no good again, said he was definitely hiding something. By now, Tom was a young man, and Cynthia had had enough. She wanted a divorce, and she wanted me to find evidence of Bruce's affairs that she could take to a lawyer. I agreed to take on the job, and I began tailing him. I saw him visit Patty Meeks's house, meet with her out of town, and spend some time outside the high school, just watching the kids from his car. On senior prom night, he was parked on Patty's street, watching the house, while I watched him. Then Megan stepped outside the front door, and she was wearing a diamond-and-emerald bracelet."

Jessica thought of Patty Meeks's words to her.

In a place like Hundred Acres, everyone has secrets. And Ed's line of work means he knows most of them.

"Megan was Bruce Lucchese's daughter," she said.

Ed nodded. "I was friends with Patty, real fond of her. We'd even dated for a while between my first and second wives. I told her what I'd found out. Patty admitted Bruce was Megan's father and begged me not to tell Cynthia. I told her Cynthia was my client, and she had a right to know what I'd discovered about her husband."

"What changed?" Jessica asked. "The report you gave Cynthia claimed you had witnessed no suspicious behavior by Bruce Lucchese during your extensive surveillance. There's no mention of Patty or Megan Meeks. That's quite an omission."

Ed smiled sadly. "Megan died—that's what changed." He shrugged. "Why cause any more hurt?"

"His family never knew the truth? Cynthia and Tom never found out about Megan?"

"No."

"What about Megan? Did she know who her father was?"

"No."

"But Bruce knew?"

Ed nodded. "He figured it out after he returned to Hundred Acres and discovered Patty had a seventeen-year-old daughter. He confronted her, and she confirmed she had been pregnant with his baby when he'd left for Vegas with his wife and kid."

"Shit." Jessica rubbed her eyes. "What a fucking mess."

"Now do you see why Rue Hunter has to be lying, or at least mistaken, about Megan and Tom being a couple? Like I said, it's impossible."

"That's where you're wrong, Ed. It's unthinkable, but it's not impossible."

"What are you saying?"

Jessica's eyes locked on his.

"What if Rue was telling the truth? And what if someone had so much to lose they resorted to murder to keep their secrets?"

38
FOURTH OF JULY

1987

"Something on your mind, Bruce?"

Bruce Lucchese looked up from his double bourbon and saw his wife staring at him. He had no idea how long he had been gazing into the amber liquid, how long his fingers had been tracing the cut crystal of the tumbler, paying zero attention to the conversation going on around him.

"Rick was speaking to you," Cynthia said in her most disapproving tone. He'd been hearing it a lot lately. "You were lost in your own little world. *Again.*"

"Thinking of all that dough we're going to be making from the new development, huh?" Rick laughed.

Bruce smiled. "You got it, Rick."

Cynthia had come up with the idea of getting some friends together for a Fourth of July barbecue at the house. The only problem was the Luccheses didn't have any friends in Hundred Acres, so business associates from out of town had been drafted in instead. Rick Wakefield was one of the main investors in the Lucky by Lucchese project and had brought his wife, Linda, to the get-together. Lonnie Strickland, another financial backer, and his girlfriend, Kathleen, had yet to show.

It was a beautiful afternoon. The sun was warm but not too hot, and the rays glistened on the still water of the pool. The scent of roses filled the backyard, their fragrance soon to be replaced by the aroma of cooking meat once the other guests arrived. Burgers and sausages and chicken thighs were lined up next to the grill.

The house was small compared to the place they'd owned in Vegas, but Rick was right—once the new development was up and running, it would be like printing their own money. In the meantime, Cynthia had made the most of their new surroundings by hiring a gardener and a pool guy and having a patio area built, a state-of-the-art barbecue station installed, and fairy lights strung all over the place. To Bruce, it was all a little too much for Hundred Acres, just like Cynthia herself.

It was supposed to be an informal gathering on a holiday weekend, but his wife had had her blonde hair professionally curled and teased and back-combed at the salon. She was dressed in a gold silk blouse tucked into white tailored pants, which were belted around her tiny waist and matched her stiletto heels. She wore far too much makeup and perfume, both of which were getting heavier and more noticeable the older she got.

Cynthia consulted the Cartier watch on her slim wrist, and her perfectly plucked eyebrows bunched into a delicate frown.

"Lonnie and Kathleen should have been here thirty minutes ago."

"I'm sure they're on their way," Bruce said.

Rick patted his fat belly. "I sure hope so. I'm so hungry I could eat a whole cow all to myself."

"Why don't you give them a call, Bruce?" Cynthia said. "Make sure they haven't forgotten."

"Sure thing."

Bruce was glad of the excuse to escape for five minutes. He finished his drink, placed the tumbler on a coaster on the glass dining table, and headed through the open french doors into the kitchen. Lonnie's home and car phone numbers were both scribbled on a note stuck under a refrigerator magnet. Bruce lifted the receiver on the wall telephone and was just about to dial the car phone digits when he heard a voice on the line and realized his son was using the extension in the den. Tom was speaking in a soft voice and was calling the other person *baby*, and it was pretty clear he was talking to a girl. Bruce smiled and was about to hang up when he heard Tom say the girl's name.

Bruce's heart stopped.

He covered the mouthpiece with his hand so they wouldn't hear his heavy breathing and listened to the conversation with a growing sense of horror. They were planning a rendezvous at Devil's Drop that night at nine p.m. Bruce was familiar with the make-out spot from his own youth and knew the place meant one thing—sex. He heard them agree to arrive in separate cars so Megan's mom wouldn't suspect her daughter was going on a date.

There was a click as Tom ended the call, and Bruce quickly replaced his own handset. He just made it to the sink before throwing up. His son walked into the kitchen, helped himself to a beer from the refrigerator, then spotted Bruce hunched and retching.

Tom laughed. "Let me guess? You let mom take charge of the barbecue again?"

Bruce splashed cold water on his face and turned to face Tom as he dried off.

"I'm fine."

"Man, you really don't look too good. You sure you're okay?"

Bruce smiled weakly. "Nothing to worry about. Probably your mom's cooking, like you said. Or too much daytime drinking."

Tom snorted. "Yeah, right, like that's ever been a problem before." He popped the top on the bottle of Coors. "I'm going to my room to chill for a while before going out later. Take it easy, Pops."

"Uh, big night planned? Going to a party someplace?"

Bruce was trying to come across as nonchalant, but his voice sounded weird even to his own ears.

Tom grinned. "Yeah, but it's a private party, if you catch my drift?"

"New girlfriend?"

"Yup."

"Anyone I know?"

"Nope."

"You're not giving much away, are you?" Bruce laughed, and it was an odd, high-pitched sound. "You been seeing this girl for a while? Is it serious?"

"We've been dating for about a month. Nothing serious, just a bit of fun. And this evening is gonna be a whole lot more fun." Tom winked. "Let's just say they don't call me 'Lucky' for nothing. Tonight, Lucky is finally gonna get lucky with the lovely Megan."

Tom took a swallow of beer and walked out of the kitchen whistling a Bon Jovi song.

Bruce watched him leave, then purged the remaining contents of his stomach into the sink.

◆ ◆ ◆

Bruce forgot all about the phone call to Lonnie, his thoughts occupied by the one he'd just overheard between his son and Megan Meeks. He felt like he had just gone twelve rounds with Mike Tyson.

Lonnie and Kathleen turned up five minutes later, and the rest of the afternoon was spent pretending to listen to inane conversations and trying to stem the nausea that was being made worse by the smell of charred meat. Even his favorite liquor left a bad taste in his mouth. Bruce noticed Cynthia giving him "the look" a few times—the one that meant he'd have some explaining to do later—but he ignored her.

He was thinking.

He needed a plan.

It was what Bruce Lucchese did best.

So he laughed and nodded in all the right places as Rick and Lonnie droned on and on about the development, and he nursed his bourbon, and he ignored Cynthia's pointed looks, and he kept on thinking.

And a plan began to form in his mind.

◆ ◆ ◆

Later, once Rick and Linda and Lonnie and Kathleen had left, their bellies suitably stuffed full of bread and meat and booze, Bruce encouraged Cynthia to go take a nap, told her he'd clear up the mess.

"Why not?" Her words were thick with too much chardonnay. "It's not like you contributed anything else to the party."

After slipping out of her stilettos, she padded through to the den and closed the door behind her. Bruce knew the *Z*s would be hitting the ceiling in five minutes tops. Cynthia never could handle wine in the afternoon. He waited in the kitchen and watched the minute hand on the wall clock jerk forward five times; then he tiptoed to the den and peeked inside. Sure enough, Cynthia was sprawled on her back on the couch, eyes shut, mouth open, a trashy soap opera muted on the television. He pulled the door shut and returned to the kitchen.

Bruce picked up the telephone receiver and dialed the number for Ed Crozier's private detective agency. The office machine kicked in after one ring, the message advising callers the agency was closed for the holiday weekend and would reopen on Tuesday. Good. Far less chance of being followed by the private dick. Patty was confident she had convinced Crozier to drop Cynthia's case, but tonight's business was different. An audience was out of the question. He hung up.

Then Bruce set about collecting what he'd need: a medium-size knife from the kitchen drawer; a pair of latex gloves from the cardboard box in the garage; the Glock he'd purchased illegally in Vegas stored in the locked gun cabinet in the hallway closet; and an old windbreaker, jogging pants, tee, and sneakers from the bedroom closet. He slid the knife into his pocket and dumped everything else into a duffel bag. As he passed by Tom's bedroom, Bon Jovi's "Livin' on a Prayer" was playing on the stereo.

Bruce Lucchese didn't believe in prayers.

He believed in plans.

He made his way downstairs.

◆ ◆ ◆

At eight fifteen p.m., Bruce slipped silently into the den and left a note for his sleeping wife on the glass coffee table.

Emergency at the construction site. Back soon. B.

He walked out the front door with the duffel bag slung over his shoulder and the knife weighing down his pocket. He looked up and saw a lamp glowing softly in the window of Tom's bedroom. Dusk was beginning to claim the day. A streetlight hummed to life on the sidewalk. Bruce cut across the front yard to the driveway, where Tom's Toyota Supra was parked next to his own BMW.

He pulled the knife from his pocket, bent down on his haunches, and pushed the blade into the thick rubber of the Toyota's rear tire. Twisted it from side to side. Heard a soft hiss and removed the knife. After walking around the trunk to his own car, Bruce climbed inside and tossed the duffel bag and knife onto the passenger seat.

Then he set off for Devil's Drop.

◆ ◆ ◆

Bruce Lucchese had killed a man once.

It'd happened a long time ago in Vegas. Not with his own hands, but the guy was dead because of Bruce all the same. A onetime business associate who had made the fatal error of stealing a lot of money from

Bruce. Once the orders were given, the guy never stole from anyone else again.

Sweat dampened Bruce's brow now, and he cranked up the AC. A similar outcome wouldn't be necessary tonight, he told himself. The gun, the gloves, the change of clothing—they were all just part of a backup plan. All he wanted to do was talk to the girl. Make her see sense. Paint a picture of the life she could soon be enjoying—a college education, a job, an apartment, travel.

All Megan Meeks had to do was keep away from his son and keep her mouth shut.

He'd considered telling Patty what was going on with Megan and Tom but had decided against it. Patty was too emotional. She'd only panic, probably tell Megan the truth about her father, and that would increase the chances of Cynthia discovering he had an illegitimate child. No way was Bruce handing his wife that kind of ammunition. No, better he sort this mess out himself. Megan didn't need to know why she had to stay away from Tom—she just had to take the money.

Bruce flipped the blinker out of habit, even though the highway was deserted, and took the turn for Devil's Drop.

◆　◆　◆

Once he reached the clearing, Bruce kept going and found a smaller space farther along the hilly terrain, where his car would be concealed from the make-out spot by a cluster of Joshua trees and California juniper.

He swapped his chinos and Aquascutum polo shirt for the clothing he had packed in the duffel bag. After zipping the gun into the inside pocket of the jacket, he snapped on the latex gloves. The plan was for the weapon to remain inside the windbreaker and to keep his hands out of sight throughout the conversation with the girl.

But it was better to be prepared in case the plan had to change.

And Bruce Lucchese was always prepared.

After twenty minutes, he heard the growl of an engine and the crunch of tires on twigs and rocks and dried wildflowers; then he saw the twin sodium beams of headlights through the foliage.

She had arrived.

Bruce emerged into the clearing. It was full dark now, and he could just make out the dark silhouette of a car, its lights off, parked nose facing out toward the canyon. He shoved his gloved hands deep into the windbreaker's pockets, felt the cold steel of the Glock pressed against his chest.

He hoped Tom would blow off the date completely once he discovered the flat tire. He was counting on his son being too lazy to fit the spare, as well as a lack of taxicabs in town on a holiday weekend to take him to Devil's Drop. Cynthia didn't drive, and Bruce was pretty sure Tom, like his mom and dad, didn't have too many friends in Hundred Acres willing to drop their plans on a Saturday night and offer him a ride.

He should have plenty of time with the girl, but Bruce wanted the job completed quickly. He approached the car. As he reached the driver's side, the silence was shattered by a whistle and a crash and a bang. Fireworks from the town below lit up the black night, and Bruce Lucchese knew immediately he had made a mistake.

Megan Meeks wasn't alone.

A young guy of about eighteen sat behind the wheel. As the sky exploded in pinks and greens and yellows and reds, the driver turned his head, and his eyes met Bruce's. Shock registered on his face and quickly turned to confusion and then disgust. The teenager turned and spoke to Megan, who was beside him in the passenger seat; then he pushed open the door and got out of the car. The younger guy was tall, similar in height to Bruce, but far less muscular.

"What the fuck are you doing creeping around my car?" the kid shouted. "Trying to get your kicks from watching folks get it on or something?"

"I was looking for someone." Bruce held up his hands in surrender and began to back away. "I clearly got the wrong car. I'm sorry."

The kid stared at the hands wrapped in the latex gloves.

"What the fuck?" He reached into the pocket of his shorts, and Bruce heard a flick and saw the glint of a blade. "You fucking pervert."

Bruce took another step back as the younger guy moved toward him with the knife.

"It really was a genuine mistake. I'll get out of here, leave you kids to enjoy your night."

Then the inky sky turned pink and green and yellow and red again, and the kid said something that changed everything.

"Wait a minute; I know you. You're that casino dude."

Bruce said nothing.

The kid called over his shoulder. "Hey, Megan, is this your boyfriend's dad?"

Megan leaned across the driver's seat and peeked out of the car. Her face was pale, and her eyes were wide.

"Uh, I don't know. I've never met Lucky's dad." Then she frowned. "I do recognize this guy, though. He's the one who was hanging around outside school a couple of times."

"You sick fuck," the young guy said.

Then he lunged forward, waving the knife back and forth, and Bruce charged at the kid and made a grab for the weapon. They grappled with each other, and then they were on the ground, rolling in the dirt. Nature's potpourri of burnt earth and dried leaves and wildflowers filled Bruce's nostrils, along with the kid's sweat. He clamped his fist around the knife hand. He was a lot stronger than the kid, and he pushed down, away from his own chest. Didn't even realize the blade had pierced flesh until the kid's eyes widened, inches from his own, and he gasped.

Bruce fell back and saw a dark stain spreading at the top of the guy's shorts. The knife was lying beside him on the ground. The kid was breathing heavily, and his face was gray and coated with a sickly sheen. With some considerable effort, the kid pulled himself to his feet, clamped a hand over the wound to stem the blood, and staggered toward the vehicle's rear door.

"Megan," he called, his voice hoarse. "Start the car."

Panic flooded through Bruce and made him feel light headed. He had crossed a line. He knew there was no way back now. He grabbed the knife and threw himself at the kid. As the young guy tried to climb into the back seat, Bruce plunged the blade between his shoulder blades once, twice, three times. The kid slumped forward into the car and stopped moving.

Megan started screaming. Bruce's eyes went to the knife in his hand, the blood dripping onto the dirt. He looked at Megan. She was screaming the kid's name. Lucas. Over and over again. Her eyes met Bruce's, and she stopped screaming. She slid into the driver's seat and reached for the keys in the ignition to start the engine, but her fingers were trembling so badly she knocked them into the dark floorboard. Bruce's head cleared suddenly, and he knew what he had to do. He swallowed the bile rising in his throat and threw himself at the open driver's door before she could close it and lock it. Megan scrabbled backward into the passenger seat, her face streaked with tears and mascara.

"Please don't hurt me," she whispered.

She reached behind and opened the passenger door, and Bruce could see her weighing the options. Make a run for it or stay and fight. Neither of them was good. Before she had even reached a decision, Bruce had slid across the hood and was on top of her.

"I'm so sorry, sweetheart."

He'd come here thinking he'd be able to shoot Megan if she refused the hush money. A last resort. Clean and quick. He didn't know the girl, wouldn't feel any more for her than he did the guy who had crossed him in Vegas. It wouldn't come to that anyway, he had reassured himself; she would take the money. But his plan was shot to shit. Another kid was already dead. The girl had to die, too, and that knowledge broke a part of Bruce's heart. He'd been wrong when he thought he'd feel nothing. He knew now, had things turned out differently, he wouldn't have pulled the gun on her. Wouldn't have taken her life. Now, he had no choice.

Bruce reached out a hand to wipe away a sooty tear, and with the other he drove the knife deep into Megan's heart. Blood spurted from her mouth onto his shoulder, like a just-burped baby throwing up milk. He held his daughter in his arms for the first time and cradled her gently as the life drained from her, and he bellowed until his lungs burned as fireworks continued to explode across Hundred Acres.

Then Bruce Lucchese noticed the diamond-and-emerald bracelet wrapped around Megan's wrist, and he knew he needed one more plan.

This one was simple.

Two kids fooling around in the back seat of a car.

A robbery that went horribly wrong.

39
FOURTH OF JULY

1987

Rue Hunter pushed her way through the crowd to the window and wiped the condensation steaming the glass.

Through the damp smear, she could see the parking lot and the street beyond. There was no car, fancy or otherwise, parked at the curb with its engine gunning. She grabbed the wrist of the guy closest to her and twisted it until she could see the display on his digital watch: 9:14.

"Shit," she cursed, the word swallowed up by the thundering beat of the music. Rue beckoned the guy toward her and shouted in his ear. "You got a couple of quarters for the phone?"

His mouth formed the word *sure*, and he plunged a hand into his front jeans pocket and came up with the coins. She drained her beer, took the money, and handed him the empty bottle. After weaving through a sea of hot, sweaty bodies, she burst through the front door. It was cooler outside than it was in the bar, but the evening was still sultry.

Rue tottered unsteadily in her heeled sandals over to the phone booth, dropped a quarter into the slot, and dialed Megan's private line at home. It rang and rang and rang, and eventually someone picked up, but the voice on the other end belonged to Patty, not Megan. Rue slammed the receiver hard into the cradle.

"Shit!" she yelled, and this time, the word seemed too loud in the empty street.

She paced in front of the phone booth, listened for the roar of a car engine, and squinted at the corner up ahead. Everything was blurry around the edges now, just the way she liked it. Behind her, there was the scrape and hiss of a match being struck, and she spun around too fast and almost lost her balance. The ugly bartender, the one who'd once tried to feel up Rose, was staring at her.

"What the fuck are you looking at?" she shouted.

He took a long drag of his cigarette and turned his head away.

A heavy bass line continued to pound through the walls of Cooper's over the muted whoops and cheers and chatter of folks having a good time inside. Rue was just about to head back into the bar when a cherry-red Toyota Supra screeched to a halt in front of her. Lucky Lucchese wound down the window, leaned an elbow on the sill, and grinned at her.

"Need a ride?"

Rue marched over to the car, her cheap heels clacking on asphalt.

"You're late, asshole. Where the hell have you been? I swear to God, you better not have ruined the plan. You're such an asshole, d'you know that?"

Lucky's grin widened. "Yeah, you told me already. I'm sorry I'm late, but I had car trouble."

"Yeah, whatever." Rue folded her arms across her chest and pouted. "We're probably too late to meet Megan and Lucas now. They probably left already. I might as well go back into Cooper's and get myself another drink."

Lucky jerked his thumb in the direction of a six-pack sitting on the back seat.

"I have booze right here." Then he pulled a joint from where it had been tucked behind his ear. Held it up for Rue to see. "And a little something else you won't find in that dump."

Rue could feel her pout turn into a smile despite her best efforts to stay mad at him.

"Still plenty of time to party," he said. "You want a ride or not?"

Rue paused a beat, then walked around the car and climbed in the passenger side. A key chain shaped like a four-leaf clover hanging from the rearview mirror bobbed and swirled in the cool air blasting from the vents.

In the mirror's reflection, she saw the ugly bartender watching them as the Toyota burned rubber and headed in the direction of Devil's Drop.

Rue told herself Lucas and Megan would still be waiting for her and Lucky. They'd be a half hour late tops. She didn't know Lucky at all, hadn't even met him before tonight, so she had no idea if he was the reliable type. But she knew she couldn't always be depended on herself, especially where booze was involved. Lucas and Megan knew it too. But they would still be at Devil's Drop—wouldn't they?

Why hadn't she just agreed to the ride with her best friends? Rue knew the answer. Because she'd wanted to start the party early by getting lit with a bunch of strangers in Cooper's. Lucky's place was on the same side of town as the bar, so it was agreed he would pick her up. But Rue knew she should have stuck with her friends. It'd be her own damn fault if Lucas and Megan *had* ditched her and Lucky. The whole evening was in danger of being ruined, and to make matters worse, her feet were in agony, the straps of the sandals biting into the skin. She pulled off the shoes and threw them on the floorboard. Then she reached into the back and helped herself to a beer from the six-pack.

"You want one?" she asked.

Lucky sucked hard on the joint and nodded.

"Sure. There should be a bottle opener in the glove box."

Rue popped the tops off both bottles, handed him one, and greedily drank half of her own in one go. Felt herself begin to relax a little. She leaned back and put her feet up on the dash and took another long pull of beer. Lucky passed her the joint. The radio was tuned to a station playing chart hits, and the orchestral intro of a recent power ballad streamed through the speakers.

"Oh my God, I love this song!"

Rue twisted the volume knob up a notch and tapped her feet in time with the music. Joined in loudly and tunelessly with the chorus, and they both laughed at her bad singing.

"You do know what that song's about, don't you?" Lucky wiggled his eyebrows in what looked to be a suggestive manner.

"Yeah, it's about being so much in love with someone that you feel like you might die of happiness when you're in their arms."

Lucky smirked. "Yeah, if you say so."

"What's it about then, smart-ass?"

"You never heard the phrase *la petite mort*?"

"I don't think so. Sounds French or something."

"It is. Maybe I'll tell you what the song's about later. Better still, maybe I'll show you."

His eyes flicked to her bare thighs for a long moment before returning to the road.

Rue frowned, decided to change the subject, which was getting too fucking weird for her liking.

"You and Megan, it's the real deal? You like her, huh?"

Lucky shrugged. "Sure, she's a nice girl."

Nice.

Rue hated the word. No one wanted to be described as *nice*, especially by a guy you liked. Sexy, beautiful, fun, hot, amazing—yes. But not nice. Nice sucked.

She smiled sweetly at Lucky. "Yeah, well, you better not hurt her, or I'll hunt you down and rip your fucking throat open."

Lucky laughed. "Feisty. I like that in a woman."

Rue opened another bottle of beer as they reached the turn for Devil's Drop.

◆ ◆ ◆

The Supra wasn't designed for off-road driving, and it lurched and bounced wildly over the rough terrain as they slowly ascended the dirt trail. With the highway lights now far behind them, the darkness was thick and heavy and suffocating, like a blanket thrown over a birdcage. The branches of the Joshua trees on either side reached out like gnarly monster fingers.

Rue shivered. Maybe Devil's Drop hadn't been such a good idea after all.

There had been rumors of perverts creeping around, peering through car windows, and jerking off at the sight of teenagers getting it on. Most folks in town had stopped using the make-out spot in recent months. No one wanted to put on a show for dirty old men. When they had come up with the plan for the four of them to meet at Devil's Drop, though, the anticipated absence of other kids had been seen as a bonus. Now Rue wasn't so sure. The place felt eerie tonight.

They reached the clearing, and the car's headlights swept over Lucas's Toyota Cressida, and she could see the shadowy silhouette of two people sitting in the back seat. Rue breathed out a sigh of relief and finished her beer.

Lucas and Megan had waited for them.

◆ ◆ ◆

Rue hooked her fingers through the straps of the sandals, opened the door, and placed her bare feet on the warm dirt. It was time for the swap. If she was being honest, she was glad to put some distance between herself and Lucky. The guy might be hot and rich, but he was also a grade A jerk. As far as Rue was concerned, Megan could do better for herself. Her friend lacked confidence; that was her problem. She had no idea just how much of a catch she was. Megan hadn't even told Rue and Lucas about Lucky for two whole weeks because she was convinced his interest in her was some kind of elaborate prank.

"Maybe catch you later," she said.

"Hey, tell Megan to give me a few minutes, okay? I need to go take a leak. That beer has gone right through me. Feels like my bladder is about to explode."

Rue shook her head. "Too much information."

Lucky jogged back toward the trail in search of a thick-enough cluster of trees and foliage to provide some cover, while Rue made her way to Lucas's car. Neither Megan nor Lucas got out to greet her as she approached. They were probably pissed at her for being late, for letting them down as usual.

She gripped the handle of the rear passenger door, and it felt wet to the touch as she yanked it open. The dome light above the dash blinked on, weak and yellow. She immediately noticed a red stain on Megan's white jeans, and the first thought that flashed through her mind was, *Man, what a time to get your period, and a really heavy one at that.* Rue's eyes traveled up to where the wooden hilt of a knife protruded from Megan's chest. She looked at her friend's face. Her eyes were wide open and unblinking, her mouth and chin streaked scarlet. Megan wasn't moving, didn't seem to be breathing.

Rue's insides turned to ice. She dragged her gaze to Lucas, who was in the back seat next to Megan. Same story. Unseeing eyes staring straight ahead, his complexion the color of wet newspaper. His tan shorts were soaked dark red. He was as still as a statue and every bit as lifeless.

No.

This wasn't real.

It was a joke—that's all.

Lucas and Megan's way of getting back at Rue and Lucky for being late.

A fake knife. Fake blood. Fake death.

"Come on, guys, this isn't funny."

Her voice, thick with fear, didn't sound like her own.

Rue pushed Megan hard, and she flopped to one side.

"Quite acting. You got me, okay? Now stop it. This isn't funny."

Fireworks exploded somewhere in the town below, and she jumped, but Lucas and Megan didn't even flinch at the sudden crash of noise and color. Rue dropped the sandals on the dirt. The warm, pleasant booze haze was long gone, replaced by a cold numbness. Her fingers tingled. She crawled over Megan to reach Lucas and grabbed his shoulders and shook him.

"I mean it, Lucas, stop playing stupid fucking games."

She pulled up his T-shirt, and her fingers found sticky, gaping flesh above the hip.

"No."

The word was strangled. It hurt to breathe.

Rue scrabbled backward violently and fell out of the car, pulling Megan part of the way with her, the girl's long dark hair brushing the dirt. Music was playing somewhere, and she remembered Lucky was waiting in his own car.

This wasn't real; it was a hallucination, a bad trip. She'd had a lot to drink, been smoking pot. Maybe she'd dropped a tab of acid and forgotten all about it, or someone had popped a pill in her drink.

Rue squeezed her eyes shut tight.

Saw the wicked glint of a knife.

A black-and-white plaid shirt being ripped apart.

Dirt falling on a stranger's face and filling his open mouth.

She opened her eyes.

Lucas and Megan were dead. The realization hit her like a runaway freight train. She reached over and pulled the knife from Megan's chest and stared at it. Somewhere in the fog of her brain, she registered it was the gift she'd bought for Lucas for their one-year anniversary. Something raw and primal stirred in the pit of her belly and grew inside her until, like a cork bursting from a champagne bottle, it exploded from her lips in the form of a terrible animal howl. She fell to her knees and screamed and wailed and moaned and whimpered until she heard footsteps running toward her.

"What the fuck did you do?"

Lucky was standing about fifteen feet away, his eyes wild and terrified.

"They're both dead," she said in a stranger's voice.

"Oh Jesus," he whispered. "No. No way. This can't be happening. Fuck."

Lucky backed away, and then he was running back to his car. There was the dull thunk of a door shutting, the roar of an engine, a flash of headlights. Then there was nothing but a dust cloud left in his wake.

Rue watched in a daze. Then, as though in a dream, she pushed herself to her feet and stumbled through the dust cloud and followed where the glowing red dots of the taillights had disappeared through the trees.

She was still clutching Lucas's knife tight to her chest.

40

JESSICA

"What are you saying, Jessica?" Ed asked.

"I think Megan was killed because she was Bruce's daughter. Either by Tom Lucchese or Bruce himself."

Ed whistled through his teeth. "That's quite a claim. What about Rue Hunter?"

"I never really bought the double motive," Jessica said. "The idea she killed Lucas and Megan in a jealous rage and then robbed them of their possessions? It doesn't sit right with me. One is an act of passion; the other is cold and calculated. It should be one or the other. Then there's Megan's relationship with Tom Lucchese, which makes the jealous rage theory seem far less likely."

"If there *was* something going on between Megan and Tom. I find that harder to buy than the prosecution's double motive claim."

"Jed Lockerman told me he saw Tom Lucchese pick up Rue outside Cooper's the night of the murders. From what Lockerman said, it sounded to me like the ride had been planned in advance. Not the random, impromptu favor Tom claimed it was."

"You like Tom Lucchese for the murders?"

"No, I think Bruce is the more likely suspect."

"Why? At least we know Tom Lucchese was at Devil's Drop that night. There's nothing to suggest Bruce was there too."

"It all comes back to motive," Jessica said. "If Tom had discovered he was dating his half sister, his anger would have been directed at his father, not Megan. However, if Bruce had somehow found out his son was romantically involved with Megan, a bad situation had just gotten a million times worse for him. His wife was paying a PI to tail him; he was already facing the possibility of a very expensive and public divorce."

"Bruce wouldn't have known about me or the divorce plans," Ed countered.

"You told Patty, though. Right?"

"Right."

"And you don't think she would've passed on that information to Bruce?"

Ed's face colored an even deeper shade of red than usual.

"I guess she might have."

"If the truth came out about Megan, it wasn't just his wife he was going to lose; it would have been his son too."

"Okay, let's say you're right—how do we prove it?"

"That's what I'm still trying to figure out."

Jessica's cell phone chirped. She read the caller ID. Polly Perez. The wannabe actress she'd tracked down to a strip club in Vegas while working a previous missing persons case. After her visit with Tom Lucchese, Jessica had asked the dancer to do some digging for her.

She swiped to answer.

"Hey, Polly. You got something for me?"

"Yes, I do," Polly said. "But you need to be in Vegas by this evening. You'll see why."

They arranged a time and place to meet, and Jessica ended the call. She began gathering up her stuff.

"Sorry, Ed, I gotta go."

"Where?"

"Vegas."

"Tom Lucchese?"

"Let's just say I ain't going all the way out there to play the slots."

Jessica turned into the lot of Buddy's Truck Stop & Café on North Las Vegas Boulevard.

The place had big front windows and was busy with the dinner crowd. She figured Polly wouldn't appreciate an audience, so Jessica found a space in the farthest corner of the parking lot out of sight of diners.

She was early, for once, so she lifted her cell phone from the charger on the dash and googled the number for Lucky's Casino. Jessica asked to speak to the owner, told the front desk attendant she was a friend of Mr. Lucchese's and the call was urgent. After a blast of "Viva Las Vegas" down the line, Elvis's dulcet tones were replaced by a pissed-sounding Tom Lucchese.

"Miss Shaw," he said impatiently, "I thought we agreed I wouldn't hear from you again."

"I guess I lied. I have a few more questions."

Jessica was met by the sound of dead air. She would have preferred to say what she had to say to Lucchese face to face, see his reaction. But that would tip him off that she was in Vegas ahead of her meeting with Polly. So it had to be now.

"Were you and Megan Meeks dating at the time of the murders?" she asked.

"Don't be ridiculous. I didn't even know the girl."

"Did you know Megan was your half sister?"

There was a sharp intake of breath, but Lucchese said nothing.

"Did your father kill Megan to cover up the truth?"

Silence.

Then there was a click and a series of beeps as Lucchese ended the call.

Jessica shoved the cell phone back into the charger and saw Polly Perez walking across the lot, head moving from side to side searching for the Silverado. Jessica flashed her lights.

Even dressed casually in jeans, a light sweater, and sneakers, Polly was a knockout. Her glossy black hair was pulled back in a ponytail, and her dark eyes were warm and intelligent. She was petite with the kind of killer curves that brought to mind a younger Salma Hayek. Polly might not have been deemed beautiful or unique or talented enough by Hollywood's top casting directors, but Jessica was pretty sure she was a big hit with the regulars at the Midnight Lounge, where she performed every weeknight.

The woman climbed into the passenger seat, and they exchanged greetings.

"You got some information for me?" Jessica asked.

Polly nodded. "You got the money?"

"In the glove box."

Polly popped open the compartment in front of her and found the slim brown envelope and slipped it into the back pocket of her jeans. It contained $200 in crisp twenties fresh from the ATM. Jessica hoped the information would be worth the payout.

"What have you got for me?" she asked.

Polly said, "When I first started working at the Lounge, Tom Lucchese came in one night and paid for a couple of dances. Then he offered more cash for some 'extras' off premises. I declined. It's not my style. Later, when I found out he had a reputation for hitting on the dancers, it came as no real surprise. His whole family-guy image is a farce, and all the girls in the clubs know it. When you told me you wanted information on him, I asked around and discovered one of the girls at the Lounge had a thing going with Tom Lucchese a while back. It lasted about six months or so and finished the night he raised his hand to her and gave her a black eye and a burst lip. Jenna couldn't work for a week after the beating."

Jessica wasn't surprised to learn Tom Lucchese had turned out to be a cheat and a bully, just like his father. But she needed more.

"Anything else?"

"Yes, I spoke to Jenna myself. She says Lucchese had money problems. He'd had a little too much liquor one night and was boasting about how smart he was and how rich he'd be if he didn't have to hand over 30 percent of his takings every month. Unsurprisingly, he seemed real pissed about it."

Jessica sat up straighter. "A protection racket?"

"Maybe," Polly said. "Jenna didn't know who was picking up the cash, but she was with Lucchese at the handover one time. His wife and kids were visiting the wife's parents out of town, so he and Jenna were planning on spending the night together at a fancy hotel in LA. Lucchese made the drop while Jenna waited in the car."

"So she knows where and when these meets take place?"

Polly nodded. "A rest area just off the Mojave Freeway. On the last Thursday of every month." She stared at Jessica in the gloom of the truck's cab. "Do you see now why I had to give you this information this evening?"

"Yes, I do," Jessica said.

Tonight was the last Thursday of the month.

◆ ◆ ◆

Polly Perez left to get ready for her shift at the Midnight Lounge, while Jessica ate a burger and fries at Buddy's Truck Stop & Cafe. Then she took up position across the street from Lucky's Casino and waited.

Forty minutes later, Tom Lucchese emerged wearing a messenger bag slung over his shoulder. He climbed into a Chevy Malibu that looked a few years old and was parked right outside the front door.

The relatively modest wheels suddenly made sense. He turned onto North Las Vegas Boulevard. Jessica put the Silverado into drive and pulled into the traffic behind him. She hung three cars back as Lucchese cruised along the main thoroughfare before taking East Lake Mead North Boulevard heading west and joined I-15 southbound. Jessica stayed with him on the freeway.

The sun dropped into the horizon, and the sky turned a darker shade of blue, and the bright lights of the Strip blinked on to the east. The blazing white of the Mirage; the purples, pinks, and greens of the High Roller; the glittering black pyramid of the Luxor. Soon, the shiny, towering megaresorts were replaced by the long, low buildings of business parks that housed furniture showrooms and car rental firms and tour companies. After a while, there was only vast, empty desert on either side to keep Jessica company as the dark sky turned from navy to eggplant.

She followed Lucchese's Chevy for 125 long miles, keeping her eyes fixed on the twin red dots of his taillights. Eventually, around halfway between Vegas and LA, his blinker flashed, and he guided the car onto the next off-ramp. Then he took two quick left turns and merged onto I-15 heading north back in the direction of Vegas.

Jessica was confused. Had he spotted the tail? Gotten spooked and decided to turn back without making the drop? She banged her hands against the steering wheel in frustration.

"Shit!"

She stayed with him and was trying to decide her next move when Lucchese signaled for an exit signposted for the Clyde V. Kane Rest Area. She breathed a sigh of relief. The place was in the middle of the Mojave Desert, but it was well lit and had modern restrooms and covered picnic tables and plenty of bays filled with RVs and eighteen-wheelers and regular pickups. Lucchese found a spot, and Jessica drove past before parking behind a Winnebago farther along the rest area. Lucchese didn't know what kind of vehicle she owned, wouldn't have been suspicious of the black Silverado, but Jessica figured it was a good idea to keep herself and her wheels out of sight anyway.

She fitted a zoom lens to the Nikon she used for surveillance jobs, got out of the truck, and crouched behind one of the rear wheels of the Winnebago. She looked through the camera's viewfinder and adjusted the lens until Lucchese's car was in sharp focus.

Then she waited.

Fifteen minutes later, a familiar vehicle drove into the rest area. Part of her wasn't completely surprised to see the sleek silver Dodge Ram, but her heart still thumped against her rib cage. The lavish home, the cash used to set his son up in business. It all made sense to her now.

"Shit," she whispered.

The Dodge backed into the bay right next to Lucchese's Chevy.

Jessica pressed her finger down on the shutter-release button and began clicking.

41

PRYCE

Twenty-four hours after going through Charlie Holten's cell phone records, the explanation for the call to Hundred Acres still bothered Pryce.

Or the lack of explanation.

Following his short conversation with the woman who'd answered yesterday, and establishing who the number belonged to, Pryce had mulled over what to do next.

He understood why the call hadn't thrown up any red flags for Hunt and Adams when they'd gone through the phone records more than two decades earlier. A cop phoning another cop. Why would it? But they didn't know Charlie the way Pryce had known him. Didn't know he'd never kept in touch with the man who had replaced him as sheriff, hadn't spoken to him in years. Pryce also knew the cases he and Charlie had been working at the time, and none of them had any connection to Hundred Acres.

So if the call hadn't been social or work related, what was the reason for Holten reaching out to someone from his past?

Eventually, after a lot of thinking, Pryce had decided the direct approach would be best. He would hit redial and ask why Holten had placed a call to the Hundred Acres Sheriff's Department the night he was murdered.

This time, the sheriff himself had picked up.

Pryce had met Pat McDonagh at Holten's funeral, just as he had Ed Crozier. Unlike with Crozier, Pryce hadn't kept in touch with McDonagh. There was something about the guy he didn't like, something he couldn't put his finger on.

Yesterday, when he'd spoken to McDonagh, Pryce had come right out and asked about Holten's phone call to the sheriff's department, like he'd planned. McDonagh had gone silent, as though thinking; then he'd said he hadn't spoken to Holten in the days before his death. Claimed he hadn't heard from his old boss in years, well before the shooting had happened. Maybe Charlie had wanted to shoot the breeze awhile with Sandy on the front desk? Or one of the other deputies who'd been on duty that night? But definitely not McDonagh, who said he would've remembered the conversation for sure.

McDonagh had asked if Holten's case had been reopened, and Pryce told him it had never closed. Then he had thanked the sheriff for his time and hung up.

Now, Pryce stared at the telephone number, circled on the sheet of paper on the desk in front of him. Tried to figure out what was niggling at him. Then he realized what it was. Two things.

One: The duration of the call made by Holten was two minutes and eight seconds. Not long enough for a proper stroll down memory lane with a former coworker. But long enough to arrange a meet at a bunch of deserted warehouses at Echo Park.

Two: Why had McDonagh answered the phone, instead of the receptionist, when Pryce had phoned a second time? Maybe the front desk had been unattended when McDonagh had passed by, and he'd decided to pick up. Or maybe front desk calls rang through to the squad room if they weren't answered by Sandy.

Or maybe Holten hadn't phoned the Hundred Acres Sheriff's Department main number at all.

Pryce shook the mouse to wake up his computer and opened a Google search page. He typed "Hundred Acres Sheriff's Department" and hit "Enter." On the right side of the screen appeared a listing with photos, a map, an address, and a contact telephone number—which he assumed was the main number. Pryce compared it to the one on Charlie Holten's phone records. The last four digits were different, suggesting he had called another extension within the station, rather than the front desk. Pryce lifted his phone and tapped in the number from the computer screen. Waited for the call to connect, listened as the same female voice as yesterday answered with the same greeting.

"Hello, my name is Detective Pryce from the LAPD. I'm working on a case that's connected to Hundred Acres, and Sheriff McDonagh asked me to share some information with him later. Can I check I have the correct direct line for the sheriff?"

Pryce read out the number circled on the call records. The number Holten had called the night he was shot.

"That's the one," the woman said cheerfully. "Although Sheriff McDonagh won't be back on duty until tomorrow. Thursdays are his day off."

"I'll bear that in mind. Many thanks for your help." A thought occurred to Pryce. "Is it Sandy I'm speaking to?"

"Yes, it is." She sounded surprised. "How did you know?"

"I believe you worked with my former partner, Charlie Holten? He mentioned you a couple of times."

"That's right," Sandy said. "Sheriff Holten was a lovely man, a very dedicated sheriff."

"Did you keep in touch after Charlie left Hundred Acres?"

"We swapped Christmas cards and the occasional email."

"Did Charlie ever call you at work for a catch-up?"

"Not that I recall," Sandy said. "I was friendly with his wife, Maggie, but my relationship with Sheriff Holten was more professional. I was sad when I heard what happened to him, though. Did the LAPD ever find out who shot him?"

"No. But we're working on it."

Pryce placed the receiver back in the cradle.

Holten had called the Hundred Acres sheriff's direct line. A number that had belonged to himself for a number of years. He hadn't been looking for a catch-up with Sandy or one of the deputies or anyone else. His intention had been to speak to the sheriff.

Pat McDonagh.

Pryce tapped his pen on the desk. Then he picked up the receiver again. A couple calls later, he had a list of every vehicle ever registered to Pat McDonagh. The sheriff's current civilian ride was a silver Dodge Ram, less than a year old. *Nice,* Pryce thought. He found the entry for the summer of 1997. A 1976 Chevrolet C30. Dark-gold metallic with frost-white side panels. The model had been known as "Big Doolie" on account of its dual rear wheels.

Pryce thought back to the visit with DaMarcus Jones, what the former gangbanger told him about the truck his boys had witnessed at the Echo Park warehouses.

A dark-colored dually covered in mud. Definitely not a sleek city ride like those favored by the crews at the time.

Pain flared behind Pryce's eyeballs, and he closed his eyes and rubbed them gently. After more than twenty years, he finally knew who had put a bullet between his partner's eyes.

What he still didn't know was why.

42

HOLTEN

1997

Holten lifted the pint bottle of Jim Beam Black to his lips and sucked down a generous swallow of bourbon.

He didn't even wince at the burn. He'd had his first drink of the night placed on the bar in front of him twenty minutes after his shift had ended. A bid to cure the hangover he'd endured all day following last night's binge, as well as an attempt to numb real life.

It was now almost midnight. The hangover was gone, but he couldn't escape the reality of his situation, no matter how much liquor he threw down his throat.

Holten shouldn't have been behind the wheel in his state, was well aware that a DUI could cost him his badge. He laughed bitterly to himself in the darkness of the still car. What did it matter now? His career would soon be over anyway.

He took another pull from the bottle, scratched the rough stubble on his chin, and stared out of the window while he waited. Deserted warehouses lay in the shadows, just beyond the reach of the nearest streetlamp, a darker shade of black against the starless night sky. The abandoned buildings were just like Holten—empty, soulless, no use to anyone. On previous meets at this location, adrenaline would have been flowing through his veins, excitement bubbling at the knowledge a snitch could be about to give him a nugget of information that could crack open a case. Not tonight. This time, Holten already knew how the story would end.

He had made a mistake. Lives had been ruined. Now he had to put things right, regardless of the consequences. Holten was willing to take the hit for what he'd done, but he wasn't prepared to take the fall on his own. He was blinded suddenly by bright headlights and raised a hand to shield his bloodshot eyes. He heard, rather than saw, McDonagh's rust-bucket truck pull up beside his own car.

Holten got out, a small parcel wrapped in an evidence bag clutched tightly in his hand. He walked around behind the Chevy's big flatbed and pulled himself up into the truck's cab on the passenger side.

"Jesus, Charlie," McDonagh said. "You look and smell like an old tramp." He sniffed the air. "Have you been drinking?"

Holten shrugged and said nothing.

"You know, I should take your car keys off you right now."

"We both know that's not going to happen, Pat. If I wind up with a DUI or dead in a ditch tonight, you wouldn't give a damn. You don't care about what's right or wrong. All you care about is yourself."

"What's going on, Charlie? If you dragged me out here, in the middle of nowhere at this time of night, just to hurl abuse at me, I'm outa here."

"We screwed up." Holten pushed a finger into McDonagh's shoulder. "*You* screwed up, and I stood back and let it happen. Now we have to pay for what we did."

"You're drunk. Go home and sleep it off, and we can talk some other time. Okay?"

McDonagh moved to put the gear into drive, signaling the conversation was over. Holten handed over the evidence bag.

"What is it?"

"Take a look inside. But put these on first."

Holten took a pair of latex gloves from his pocket and passed them to McDonagh, who frowned but snapped them on.

"You're not gloved up," he noted.

Holten said, "My prints are already on the envelope and its contents from when I opened the package. It was mailed to me at Hollywood Division. It's been in the evidence bag since."

McDonagh unsealed the evidence bag and removed the package. He tilted the padded envelope upside down, and a clear ziplock freezer bag dropped onto his lap. Inside was a gold watch, a diamond-and-emerald bracelet, and a neatly folded stack of dollar bills. All spattered with dried blood. McDonagh recoiled as though a snake had landed on his lap instead.

"What the fuck?" He stared at Holten, his eyes wide and his jaw slack. "How the hell did you get hold of this stuff?"

Holten said, "Read the letter."

McDonagh reached inside the envelope and withdrew a folded sheet of paper. He unfolded it and began to read. In his hand was Bruce Lucchese's suicide note and full confession to the murders of Megan Meeks and Lucas James.

The handwritten letter recounted Bruce's affair with Patty Meeks, how he'd found out he had a daughter upon his return to Hundred Acres, the devastating discovery that Megan Meeks was dating his son. Lucchese went on to claim his intention had been to buy Megan's silence, but an altercation at Devil's Drop had gotten out of hand, and two teenagers had ended up dead. He had then fixed the murder scene to look like a robbery gone bad, unaware that another life was about to be destroyed—that of Rue Hunter. Ten years after the murders, Bruce Lucchese could no longer live with the lies and the guilt. Prison wasn't an option, he wrote, so he was delivering his own punishment and trusting Holten to put things right. The letter was signed and dated. Fourth of July 1997.

"This . . . can't be real. It's not possible."

"It is," Holten said. "Lucchese killed himself on Friday. Blew his brains out with a shotgun in his garage. This package was waiting for me in my work mailbox on Monday."

McDonagh turned in his seat and faced Holten.

"You've had this letter and the personal effects of two murder victims since Monday? Two whole days? Why the hell haven't you gotten rid of them already?"

"Get rid of them?" Holten was stunned. "You read the letter, right? A girl has been in prison—on death row—for ten years for a crime she didn't commit. A case we brought against her. She's twenty-eight years old now. If she gets out now, Rue Hunter could still have a shot at a normal life. Get married, have kids. I don't have any option, Pat. I have to take Bruce Lucchese's confession to the county's top brass and tell them what he did. What *we* did."

"Are you out of your fucking mind?" McDonagh snapped. "How much booze have you had tonight exactly? We did nothing wrong."

"We withheld key information, we covered up a key witness at the murder scene, we didn't question why Tom Lucchese was at Devil's Drop or carry out anything close to a proper investigation. If we had done our jobs properly, maybe Bruce Lucchese would be rotting in a jail cell right now instead of an innocent girl."

"Okay, I get that we need to do the right thing by the girl, but why do we have to take the fall too? We go to the top brass with the confession and stolen goods, like you said, but no one needs to know about our meeting with Bruce and Tom Lucchese." McDonagh was talking fast, his words thick with panic and desperation. "Bruce is dead. The Hunter girl gets released from prison with a nice compensation payoff, and we get to carry on with our lives. Everybody wins."

Holten shook his head. "I'm done lying. Just like Bruce Lucchese was in the end. I'm sorry, Pat, but it's time the truth came out."

"It'll finish both of our careers," McDonagh said quietly. "I have a wife and a kid to support. Please, think about them before doing anything stupid."

"Ten years ago, I told you when the shit hit the fan, it'd all be on you. Well, the shit has well and truly hit the fan. I'm sorry, but we both have to take what's coming to us. It's the only way to put things right."

Holten reached out a hand for the package. McDonagh returned the freezer bag holding the jewelry and cash to the envelope, along with the letter, and resealed everything inside the evidence bag. He handed the bundle over without a word. Didn't look at Holten as he got out of the truck.

Back in his own car, Holten dropped the package onto the passenger seat and picked up the bottle of bourbon. He drank long and hard. The meet with McDonagh had killed his earlier buzz, that was for sure. He started the car and headed for home. It was late, and all he wanted was to feel Maggie's arms around him, for his wife to tell him everything would be okay.

As he approached a stoplight, Holten saw McDonagh's old Chevy in his rearview. The truck pulled up alongside Holten's car on the empty street. It was almost midnight, but there was still a heavy heat in the air, and Holten had both front windows rolled down. He heard McDonagh say something and turned to face the man he had once worked alongside, who had replaced him as sheriff.

He found himself staring at the barrel of a gun.

"I'm sorry, Charlie," McDonagh said. "But my family comes first."

There was a deafening bang and a flash of light.

Then there was nothing.

43

JESSICA

Jessica scrolled through the camera's preview mode and saw an image-by-image account of Tom Lucchese's handover to Pat McDonagh.

After the exchange had taken place, both men left the rest area in their respective vehicles before, presumably, heading in opposite directions once back on the freeway. Jessica waited fifteen minutes before following the route McDonagh would've taken to Hundred Acres. The remaining two hours of the journey gave her plenty of time to think.

There was no protection racket. The sheriff was blackmailing Lucchese—that much was clear. But how? What did he have that was so valuable as to merit the Vegas businessman handing over a substantial chunk of his takings each month? Whatever it was, it was something Lucchese didn't want in the public domain at any cost. Information likely stored somewhere secure by McDonagh. Such as in the personal safe in his study at home.

After crossing back into the city limits, Jessica rolled past the McDonagh residence. The best house on the best street in Hundred Acres. Partly paid for by Tom Lucchese's secret rest area payments. Ditto Dylan's diner. She wondered if her ex knew the breakfasts and burgers being served up to his customers each day were the result of dirty cash.

It was almost midnight. McDonagh's Dodge Ram was parked next to his cruiser. The windows of Dylan's studio apartment above the garage were dark, as were the upstairs windows of the house. Downstairs, a light glowed softly behind the curtains in the front room. Dylan's mom was an early sleeper and an early riser. His dad was the opposite. Jessica knew Pat would be in the den watching a late-night movie or playing online poker in his study.

She needed him out of the house fast.

At the end of the street, Jessica automatically turned in the direction of home, thinking about what to do next. As she passed a playground, she spotted three teenagers by the swings smoking cigarettes. They were about sixteen or seventeen years old. She stopped the truck, rolled down the window, and beckoned them over.

One of the kids said, "Hey, lady, you lost?"

Lady. Way to make her feel ancient. Jessica wasn't much more than a decade older than they were.

"No, I'm not lost. I need a favor."

"Hold up a minute," said one of the other kids. "Ain't you that lady PI who got Michelle Foster fired? The one who cut off our booze supply."

"Your liver will thank me for it one day," she said. "You're too young for alcohol anyway."

"Yeah, whatever," said the kid who had spoken first. "We don't do favors for snitches."

They turned to walk away.

Jessica said, "Not even when there's cash in it for you?"

They stopped walking. The first kid, who seemed to be the leader of the group, said, "How much?"

"Twenty bucks."

"Each?"

"No, not each, you greedy little shit."

"Not interested."

They began walking away again.

"Okay, okay. Twenty bucks each."

"What do you want us to do?" the group's leader asked.

"First of all, this stays strictly between us. Agreed?" Three nods. Jessica went on. "I need one of you to make an anonymous call to the sheriff's department. Tell the deputy on duty there's some kind of emergency. Something serious enough for him to call the sheriff at home for backup."

The mouthy kid frowned. "What do we say happened?"

Jessica sighed. "Use your imagination. Say you witnessed a home intrusion or a serious assault. I don't care. Just make it bad enough that McDonagh has to leave his house and get involved."

"Why can't you do it yourself?"

"I'm from New York—the deputy will recognize my voice."

"What if he recognizes my voice?"

"Do you know any of the sheriff's deputies?"

"Nope."

"He won't recognize your voice then, will he?"

"What if he traces the call to my cell phone? Like the cops do on TV."

"Withhold your number. Or find a pay phone. Jesus, it's not rocket science. Don't they teach you kids anything at school these days?"

The kid looked at his friends, and they both nodded.

"Okay, we'll do it."

He held out a hand, palm facing up. Jessica opened her wallet and pulled out three twenties.

"Don't screw up," she said. "This is important."

Then she made a wide U-turn on the street and headed back the way she had come.

◆ ◆ ◆

Jessica found a spot across the street and three houses down from McDonagh's place. She cut the engine and lights and waited. Fifteen minutes later, just as she was about to give up hope, the front door opened, and McDonagh emerged. He climbed into the cruiser. Jessica smiled. Those little jerks had pulled it off.

Once the cruiser was out of sight, Jessica jogged across the street and slipped round the back of the house. She gloved up and used the picklock set to gain access through the kitchen, silently praying Dylan's mom wouldn't choose this moment to fetch herself a glass of water. As she moved toward the hallway, Jessica's knee nudged a dining chair, and the scrape of wood on ceramic tile seemed to her as loud as the report of a shotgun in the silence of the house.

Jessica froze. She listened for the sound of footsteps upstairs. Her pulse thundered in her ears. She stood there in the gloom of the kitchen for a whole minute. When there was no sign of movement above her, she carried on. The door to the den was ajar, spilling faint lamplight into the hallway. Next door, the study was in almost darkness. Inside, she saw McDonagh's laptop open on the desk, the website for an online casino on the screen.

After finding the Mini Maglite at the bottom of her bag, she swept the beam around the room. She knew the home safe was located in the study, but she didn't know where. Her eyes fell upon a family portrait of the McDonaghs hanging on the wall, a teenage Dylan looking awkward and gawky. She pushed a corner of the picture to one side with a fingertip to reveal the safe built into the plasterboard behind. Jessica carefully lifted the frame off the hook and set it against the desk.

She shined the flashlight on the safe. It was modern and compact, with a digital keypad and a small LCD display. Like the ones found in hotel rooms. In her head, Jessica heard Dylan's mocking words during their argument.

Your birthday? Seriously? You're as bad as my dad.

"Is that so?" she muttered.

She keyed the day and month Dylan was born, wincing at each loud digital beep. No joy. Then she tried the month followed by the day. Still no luck. Shit. Perhaps McDonagh had used his own date of birth when setting the combination. She had no idea when his birthday was, couldn't recall it being celebrated while she'd been in town. Jessica chewed her bottom lip and racked her brain. Then she tapped the four digits of the year Dylan was born, and the safe's door popped open.

She peered inside. The flashlight's beam revealed bundles of cash. Thousands of dollars neatly stacked and bound by rubber bands. There was also a bunch of statements for a savings account in Pat McDonagh's name. The deposits were all for small amounts—a few thousand here, a couple of grand there. No huge sums that would arouse suspicion. Just a regular guy with a regular savings account. It was a smart move.

At the back of the safe was a package wrapped in a clear evidence bag.

Jessica lifted it out and turned it over in her latex-covered hands. She unsealed the bag and removed the contents from the envelope.

"Fuck," she whispered.

After carefully setting down the blood-spattered watch and bracelet and cash on the desk, she read the letter. Then she looked at the name on the front of the envelope. The parcel had been addressed to Charlie Holten.

"Find what you were looking for?"

Jessica turned around slowly. Her stomach gripped, and her blood ran cold. McDonagh was standing in the doorway holding a Sig Sauer semiautomatic pistol. It was pointing straight at her.

"Let's go," McDonagh said.

"Where?"

"You'll see."

◆　◆　◆

They took Jessica's truck, after he'd frisked her and confiscated her bag with the Glock inside.

She drove, while McDonagh sat in the passenger seat with the gun aimed at her. On the surface, she appeared calm. No crying, no screaming, no begging for her life. Her hands rested lightly on the wheel. She wouldn't give McDonagh the satisfaction of seeing her fear. But, underneath the cool exterior, her mind and her heart were in competition with each other to see which could race the fastest.

"What do you think Dylan would say if he could see you now?" Jessica asked. "You think he would approve of this kind of behavior by his father? The town's goddamn sheriff?"

"Shut your mouth. You don't get to talk about my boy. Not after the way you treated him."

"I did nothing wrong where Dylan was concerned."

"You lied and you cheated and you made it clear right from the get-go that you didn't think he was good enough for you. You think you're something special with your fancy New York ways? That you're smarter than us dumb townsfolk? Not so smart now, are you?"

"I never cheated on him, and I never lied to him. But you? I bet you've been lying to him most of his life. The poor guy probably has no clue about the things you've done, what you're really like."

McDonagh pushed the pistol hard against Jessica's right temple.

"Shut your mouth and drive."

The silence was broken only by the occasional barked instruction to take the next right or hook a left at the end of the street. Once on the main highway, Jessica spotted headlights in her rearview, but she knew the side window would be decorated with her gray matter faster than she could alert the other driver that she needed help.

"Take the next turn," McDonagh said, and Jessica knew where they were going. Realized she had known all along.

Devil's Drop.

◆ ◆ ◆

The truck rolled to a stop roughly where Jessica had parked two days earlier. The same spot where she'd come across McDonagh with his strange tales of finding solitude at a former crime scene and using the place as a makeshift shooting range. Only this time, Jessica was the target.

McDonagh reached behind him and pushed open the door. An aroma of dried earth mixed with the sickly sweet scent of grape soda lupine flooded into the cab. He kept the gun tight against the side of her head and snaked the free arm around her neck. Then he pulled Jessica roughly across the seat and out through the passenger side. McDonagh pushed her in the direction of the hundred-foot drop, the Sig Sauer now pressed against a kidney.

"Start walking," he said.

She took baby steps toward the canyon. Above her, a million stars and a big, fat moon illuminated the way. Somewhere in the distance was the mournful yip of a coyote.

"Did you follow me up here on Tuesday?" she asked.

"No. I already told you—I come up here to think sometimes. And you've given me a lot to think on this past week after poking your nose around in stuff that doesn't concern you."

"But you *did* break into my home?"

"If you mean did I use a so-called hidden key to gain access to Sylvia Sugarman's trailer, then yes, I did."

"Why?"

"To find the Hundred Acres County police file you had in your possession and confirm my suspicions that it was the Meeks/James murder book. The same murder book that mysteriously disappeared from Archives before turning up again a day later. How did you get hold of it?"

"I have no idea what you're talking about."

"Uh-huh. It's like that, huh? Keep walking."

McDonagh prodded her with the gun, his breath hot on the back of her neck. Jessica shuffled forward.

"I know you've been blackmailing Tom Lucchese," she said. "I saw you both at the rest area." She couldn't see his face, but Jessica could sense McDonagh's surprise. "What I don't get is why he ever agreed to pay you any cash?"

"You read Bruce Lucchese's letter. You really think Tom Lucchese wants the world to know his father was a murderer and he, himself, once dated his own sister? Believe me, that kind of information would be a lot more damaging to his business than a small cut of his takings each month."

"You covered up Tom Lucchese's involvement back in '87. Didn't he realize the truth coming out would have been pretty bad for you too?"

"That's where you're wrong, Jessica. Don't forget, I was a mere sheriff's deputy back then. Just a guy trying to take care of his wife and kid. Holten was calling the shots. I had to go along with the wishes of a dirty senior cop or face losing my job. What's a guy to do?"

"We both know you're the dirty cop, not Holten."

McDonagh chuckled. "Yeah? Says who? You? You're not going to be saying anything after tonight."

There was another prod with the gun, another baby step toward a wall of blackness, her sneakers kicking up a tiny dust cloud.

"You going to kill me like you killed Holten?"

Jessica didn't know for sure that McDonagh was the one who had pulled the trigger on his onetime boss. But, given that he had in his possession Bruce Lucchese's confession letter—which had been sent to Holten shortly before his death—and he was pointing a gun at her right now, she figured it was a safe bet.

McDonagh hesitated, just for a second, then said, "Holten gave me no choice."

"Bullshit," she said. "There's always a choice, and it usually involves not shooting someone. You're not just dirty—you're a killer. And a cop killer, at that."

"If Holten had been willing to see sense, he would still be alive today. Don't you think if I'd gone there with the intention of killing him, I'd have done it at the meeting point? A deserted wasteland, with no witnesses, rather than the middle of the street? When Holten drove off, determined to do the so-called right thing and come clean about the Luccheses, that's when he left me no choice. I had to think of my wife and son."

"And now? You going to shoot me too?"

"If I have to, I will. But you *do* have a choice."

"What's the alternative to a bullet in the brain? I'm guessing it ain't going to be much fun either."

They were now around ten feet from the cliff edge.

"It's simple," McDonagh said. "You just keep on walking."

Jessica spun around, catching McDonagh off guard. He took a step back but kept the weapon trained on her.

"In that case, I guess you're going to have to shoot me. But you can look me in the eye when you do it, you fucking coward."

"Like I said, your choice, Jessica."

He raised the gun so that it was level with the center of her forehead.

The moon seemed brighter now, and she looked into his eyes and thought she saw fear or regret. Something. Then, like the flick of a switch, there was nothing. His eyes went cold and dead. His jaw set, and his finger tensed on the trigger, and Jessica knew it was over. She would die here tonight, just like Megan Meeks and Lucas James had more than thirty years earlier.

Then a noise broke the silence.

It sounded like a boot sole crushing a dry, dead twig or piece of branch. Not loud, but loud enough for McDonagh to flinch, incline his head ever so slightly, and take his eyes off her for a split second. Jessica lunged. Hard and fast and low, the top of her skull connecting solidly with McDonagh's groin. He sucked in a breath and let out a strangled moan, and they both fell to the ground, Jessica sprawled on top of him. The gun flew from McDonagh's hand and landed somewhere in the shadows. She crawled after it, felt her fingertips brush cold steel; then she was yanked back by a hand wrapped tightly around her ankle.

Jessica twisted around and lashed out with feet and fists as they both rolled in the dirt like a pair of mismatched street brawlers. She could feel the heat of his body and smell his warm, sour breath too close to her face. Despite his age, McDonagh was strong. Too strong for Jessica. She squirmed her arms free from under him and clawed at his face, her fingers grabbing for his eyes.

"You little bitch," he snarled, spraying her face with spittle.

McDonagh climbed off her. Hauled Jessica up by the T-shirt and threw her toward the canyon. She lay in a heap a couple feet from the edge and tried to catch her breath. But McDonagh gave her no time to recover. He stuck out a boot and connected hard with her belly, and Jessica rolled backward and felt herself slip over the lip of the cliff. Gravity pulled at the lower half of her body, and her legs bicycled thin air as her fingers clung to dirt and dried brush.

Jessica's arms ached, and her muscles burned, and sweat rolled down her spine as she tried to pull herself up and over the ledge. She sucked in big, deep breaths and screamed at the sheer effort. She got one elbow onto the dirt, then the other, then her upper torso. She saw McDonagh push himself to his feet and walk toward her. He stood over her, grinning, and raised a boot and rested it against her shoulder.

"You don't have to do this, Pat," Jessica gasped.

"I think I do."

He pushed the boot harder into her shoulder, and she felt herself slip farther over the edge, her fingers unable to gain purchase on the dirt. She blinked sweat out of her eyes.

Jessica had never really thought of herself as particularly religious, but now she found herself sending up a silent prayer to God anyway.

McDonagh applied more pressure with the boot. She couldn't hold on any longer. One swift, brutal kick from the sheriff was all it would take to end it for her. She knew she couldn't beat him.

Jessica thought of her dad and the mother she never knew. She thought of Pryce and Angie and Dionne and how close she'd come to having a second shot at a family.

Then she closed her eyes and waited for the long drop into nothingness.

Instead, she heard the deafening crack of a gun being discharged and felt something wet and warm hit her face. She opened her eyes and saw McDonagh fall to his knees and then crumple to the ground. Blood spurted between fingers pressed against the hole left by a bullet that had ripped through the flesh and tissue of his right shoulder.

Jessica looked up to see a figure standing in the darkness holding a rifle.

It was Michelle Foster.

44
RUE

Rue Hunter had never felt special.

As a kid, she would sit cross-legged in front of the TV, watching *The Price Is Right*, and wishing she was an audience member and that her name would be the one called by the announcer.

"Rue Hunter, come on down!"

She wasn't interested in the prizes, couldn't care less about a new car or fancy furniture. Rue just wanted to be special enough to win a place on Contestants' Row and chat with Bob Barker, with his neatly combed black hair and white smile and year-round tan.

Instead, Rue had wound up on a very different kind of row. No Bob Barker, no Barker's Beauties, no Showcase Showdown. A different kind of notoriety.

Now, she was about to become the first inmate in California to be put to death since Clarence Ray Allen met his end in the death chamber in 2006. A number of legal challenges had meant a hiatus in executions; then, in 2016, voters had been given the choice to abolish the death penalty or speed up the appeals process. They had chosen, via Prop 66, to expedite executions. Rue remembered the look on Rose's face when her sister had told her the result of the ballot.

"It won't come to anything," Rose had said, trying to sound optimistic despite the tears flowing down her cheeks. "There are still so many legal obstacles; there's no way they'll be able to resume executions anytime soon."

But they had.

"There are more than seven hundred inmates on death row in California," Rose had pointed out. "More than double any other state in the country. Why would they come for you?"

But they had.

There were around twenty condemned prisoners who had exhausted their appeals, and there was Rue, who had rejected the appeals process altogether. Her name was first on the list.

"Rue Hunter, come on down!"

Finally, Rue Hunter was special.

She had spent two hours traveling from Chowchilla to San Quentin on Wednesday. When she'd emerged from the prison bus, the air had smelled different and had felt cooler on her skin, a light wind blowing in from the bay. Gray clouds had gathered overhead, blocking out the sun, as Rue had gazed at the sprawling facility built more than a hundred years ago by the hands of prisoners. Nothing about the place was new—apart from the renovated death chamber. A one-story addition near the prison's East Block, the new chamber had been completed in 2009 at a cost of thousands of dollars to the taxpayer.

It had never been used.

That was about to change.

Rue had refused a last meal. She had briefly considered ordering steak and fries and slaw and onion rings, but she'd never eaten steak before, had no idea whether she'd want it cooked rare or medium rare or well done. She figured she wouldn't have much of an appetite anyway. All she had requested was some tap water.

At 11:30, she had been given a new pair of denim jeans and a new shirt to wear. As she'd dressed, she'd known the witnesses would have been waiting to be led into their respective viewing rooms—one for the victims' families, one for the family of the condemned, and, finally, a gallery for public witnesses and the media. A grotesque fishbowl. She had no idea if Patty Meeks and Heather and Steve James would take their places behind the glass, but she hoped Rose would be there, sitting alone, in the space reserved for the inmate's family. Rue's last day should have been spent in the visiting room with her sister, before being taken to the deathwatch cell, but Rose hadn't shown. Maybe she'd been delayed on the journey to Marin County, but she was supposed to be staying overnight in a motel with Bob and the boys in San Francisco, less than twenty miles from the prison.

If Rose wasn't here tonight for the execution, Rue didn't know how she'd be able to go through with it. She laughed quietly to herself at the thought. Like she had a choice. It was an execution. It wasn't her wedding day or graduation ceremony, or any other milestone moment she would never experience, where an encouraging smile from her big sister could make all the difference.

If Rue had to face death alone, so be it. She was ready to die. She wouldn't be scared.

Right now, prison officials were probably making the midnight call to the state Department of Justice and Department of Corrections headquarters to establish if any last-minute stays had been issued. There would be none. The PI Rose had hired had only succeeded in coming up with more questions than answers. The confusion over Lucas's clothing. The man whose name had been unfamiliar yet had left a bad feeling Rue couldn't explain in the pit of her belly.

Rue heard footsteps on the concrete floor of the corridor outside the cell. The footsteps got louder. They were coming for her.

It was time.

"Don't be scared, Rue," she whispered to herself.

She had three final wishes.

One: For her legs to be strong enough to take her the short distance to the chamber without the indignity of being carried there by prison staff.

Two: For Rose to be waiting behind the glass of the viewing area.

Three: For it all to be over quickly.

The cell door opened, and she saw a pale face peer inside.

"There's been a development," the man said.

Rue's heart had begun to pound hard the moment she'd heard the footsteps. Now it felt like it might burst right out of her chest. She didn't know if it was hope or fear. She reached out a hand to the cell wall to steady herself.

"What kind of development?" she whispered.

The man paused a beat, his expression unreadable.

Then he said, "The execution is off."

45
JESSICA

Pryce was sitting at the same table outside Bru Coffeebar, two black coffees in front of him, steam rising from the mugs.

"Sorry I'm late," Jessica said, dropping into the chair facing him. "I spent all day packing up my things. Then there was the emotional farewell with Sylvia."

Pryce smiled. "I ordered for you. Hope you don't mind. It's the Ethiopian stuff again."

"Great, thanks." Jessica gulped down a mouthful of coffee and sat back and sighed. "Just what I needed. I'm totally beat."

"What's the latest with Rue Hunter?" Pryce asked, taking a sip from his own drink.

"After the execution was canceled, she was taken back to Chowchilla. A full review is underway, and a team of lawyers are working the case. Hopefully, she'll be released soon—weeks if not days—and be able to file a compensation claim. We're talking millions of dollars if she succeeds."

"I hope she does, although all the money in the world can't give her back all those years she's lost."

"I guess," Jessica said. "Rose wants Rue to move to Arizona and live with her and her family. It'll be a huge adjustment, and Rue will probably need one hell of a therapist to help her through it all, but I really hope she makes it." She met Pryce's gaze. "What about McDonagh?"

"He'll live. He's still in the hospital under armed guard. He'll be charged with Charlie Holten's murder. We're still working on Tom Lucchese with regards to extortion charges, but he's reluctant. He's worried the press will get hold of the details."

"Is McDonagh likely to end up on death row for killing another cop?" Jessica asked.

"It's possible," Pryce said.

Despite the late afternoon sun warming her skin, Jessica shivered when she thought about how close she'd come to being McDonagh's next victim.

She'd found out later how the kids she'd paid to make the fake emergency call to the sheriff's department had also called Michelle to fill her in on Jessica's shady plan. The teenagers had been more pissed than Jessica had realized about her ending the illicit booze scam. Plus, they knew there was some serious bad blood between the two women and probably hoped to earn a few extra bucks by letting Michelle know Jessica was clearly up to no good.

Knowing Jessica had been determined to get McDonagh out of his house, Michelle had then alerted the sheriff to what was going on, thinking she finally had some dirt on the woman she blamed for her losing her boyfriend and her job. Possibly a break-in. Definitely something dodgy. Michelle had taken up position across the street from McDonagh's place, all set to revel in Jessica's humiliating arrest, cell phone in hand to capture the moment.

Instead, she'd witnessed McDonagh march Jessica out of his front door at gunpoint.

Confused, Michelle had followed them to Devil's Drop, ditching her daddy's truck partway along the trail so her approach wouldn't be heard. She'd covered the remaining distance on foot, the hunting rifle that her daddy kept in the back seat gun rack clutched in sweaty hands. The same weapon she'd warned Jessica about during their altercation outside the trailer.

When she'd reached the clearing, Michelle had overheard McDonagh confessing to Charlie Holten's murder. The sheriff had his gun pointing at Jessica, who was standing precariously close to the drop. Michelle had stepped on a twig and instinctively ducked behind some California juniper for cover. When she'd emerged from the brush and chanced another look, McDonagh and Jessica were both rolling in the dirt. Michelle had raised the rifle but couldn't get a clear sight of McDonagh in her crosshairs. Then Jessica was hanging from the ledge, and Michelle knew she had to get closer to the sheriff. She had shot McDonagh just as he was about to send Jessica hurtling a hundred feet to her death.

Michelle Foster had saved her life.

"What will happen to Michelle?" Jessica asked Pryce now.

"She won't face any charges, not with your statement and the evidence we have against McDonagh."

Pryce had taken what he'd discovered about the Hundred Acres sheriff to his bosses, unaware that Jessica was also onto McDonagh and had been in danger.

"I'm just glad you're okay, Jessica," he said. "You mentioned packing. No chance of staying in Hundred Acres?"

Jessica shook her head. "Ed asked me to stick around, but I can't. Not after everything that's happened. I was already dreading the thought of seeing Dylan every day after we broke up. Now, a potentially awkward situation just got a whole lot more difficult. Dylan was so close to his dad. He's going to have a lot to deal with, and I think it's best if I'm not around while he does it. In any case, I don't think Hundred Acres was ever the place for me."

"Will you go back to New York?"

Jessica thought of the two photos she kept in her wallet. One of her and Tony, with Manhattan stretching out behind them. The other of Eleanor and a three-year-old Jessica in Los Angeles on a day she had no memory of. The picture had been printed from an old newspaper article found in Eagle Rock.

"I thought about it," she said. "But I'm not ready. Not just yet."

Pryce nodded. "I hope you won't go far. I kind of like having you around."

"I have a plan. If it works out, I'll be around for a while yet. You won't get rid of me that easily."

"Good. I'm glad."

Jessica gestured to the flowers on the table. A sunshine mix of roses and chrysanthemums. The bouquet looked expensive, like it'd been bought from a proper florist. Definitely not the cheap crap you'd pick up at the grocery store.

"Have you had an argument with Angie?"

Pryce shook his head. "They're for someone else. I made a promise, and I figure I should keep it."

The sun was beginning to set as Jessica strolled along Ocean Front Walk. The salty sea breeze blowing in from the beach carried the faint scent of burgers and surf wax. Venice was already buzzing with the early-evening crowd, a mix of bohemian, creative types and ripped guys in tight tees and tourists. She carried on past the markets and tattoo parlors and pizza places until she reached a bar called Larry's that looked casual and unpretentious.

Jessica found him inside, sitting at the bar, a Scotch on the rocks on the counter in front of him, watching ESPN on one of the big screens.

"Is this seat taken?" she asked.

Matt Connor turned around and grinned at Jessica in a way that made her insides melt faster than the ice in his whiskey. She climbed on the stool next to him, and he signaled to the bartender for another drink.

"I'd given up hope of ever seeing you again," he said. "When did you get back to California?"

"I never left. Well, not really."

"You never thought to look me up?"

"Every single day."

"But you didn't."

"Nope."

"Until now. What's changed?"

"I need a job."

"And you want to work with me?"

"I need a California PI license, so it was either you or give up being an investigator and wait tables for a living. It was a close call."

Connor smiled. "You always did know how to make a guy feel special."

"So what do you say?"

"When can you start?"

"Just as soon as I finish this drink."

"Good, because I took on a new client today, and the job is perfect for you."

"Oh yeah? How so?"

"It's a missing persons case."

Jessica smiled. "I guess you'd better tell me all about it."

AUTHOR'S NOTE

Some readers will be aware of recent developments affecting the death penalty in California.

While capital punishment remains a legal penalty in the state, further executions were temporarily halted by an official moratorium ordered by Governor Gavin Newsom in March 2019.

For clarification, the fictional events in this book take place prior to the moratorium.

California has the largest death row population in the United States of America. The last execution to take place in the state was in 2006.

ACKNOWLEDGMENTS

A bunch of people played a big part in helping me get this book into the hands of readers.

Thank you to my fantastic agent, Phil Patterson, and the rest of the team at Marjacq. You took a chance on me, and I'll always be grateful.

To my editor, Jack Butler, and the team at Thomas & Mercer—thanks for believing in Jessica Shaw and showing so much enthusiasm for the series. I'm lucky to have such a great publisher. A special mention for developmental editor Charlotte Herscher, whose insight and suggestions made this book so much better.

A few people helped with factual elements, so thanks to Ian Patrick for police procedure advice and to Kirsty Fowler for answering my Los Angeles–related questions. Scott Gray and Giles Blair were also a big help with car stuff, which I know nothing about. Any errors are entirely my own.

Some fellow authors took time out of their busy schedules to read my work and say nice things. So a big thanks to Robert Dugoni, T. R. Ragan, Susi Holliday, Steph Broadribb, Craig Robertson, Douglas Skelton, and Victoria Selman.

A big shout-out to blogger extraordinaire Sharon Bairden, who gave me my first-ever review at her fab Chapter in My Life blog.

I'm lucky to work with great colleagues in my day job. Thanks to Katrina Tweedie, Jackie McGuigan, Heather Suttie, Alice Hinds, Nicola Smith, Lorraine Howard, and Johnnie Blue for patiently listening to me talk endlessly about my books and for providing loads of encouragement.

My family means the world to me, so thanks to my mum and to Scott, Alison, Ben, Sam, and Cody for your unending love and support. This book is dedicated to my dad, whom I miss every single day.

Finally, a *huge* thanks to my readers for taking the time to read my stories. I hope you enjoyed this book. Please keep in touch at www.lisagraywriter.com or on social media @lisagraywriter.

ABOUT THE AUTHOR

Lisa Gray has been writing professionally for years, serving as the chief Scottish soccer writer at the Press Association and the books editor at the *Daily Record Saturday Magazine*. Lisa currently works as a journalist for the *Daily Record* and *Sunday Mail*. She is also the author of *Thin Air*. Learn more at www.lisagraywriter.com.